Praise for
Jaci Burton's
Demon Hunter Series

THE DARKEST TOUCH

"Strong characters and gripping suspense make *The Darkest Touch* a book you won't want to miss."
—*Romance Reviews Today*

"Gifted Burton adds more dark thrills and sexy danger to her well-paced story." —*Romantic Times*

SURVIVING DEMON'S ISLAND

"Creative, scary, sexy and fast-paced. Jaci Burton delivers." —CHERRY ADAIR, *New York Times* bestselling author

"Burton has an uncanny aptitude for intertwining the human and the paranormal so seamlessly that sudden demon attacks and labyrinthine underworlds are perfectly believable. Realistic dialogue, spicy bedroom scenes and a spitfire heroine make this one to pick up and savor." —*Publishers Weekly*

"Big applause to Burton for successfully setting up a rousing and timely premise that's a real roller-coaster ride. Not only does this book set the stage for further exciting adventures, it also delivers a great group of characters that have plenty of room for growth. Burton doesn't skimp on the sizzling sex or romance either. This book has it all!" —*Romantic Times*

"Exciting, intense. A ride you don't want to miss. Burton has written a reality blast that will leave you breathless." —LORA LEIGH, *USA Today* bestselling author

HUNTING THE DEMON

"Burton brings the heat.... Hot sex, fierce battles and an impending sequel make this title worth hunting down." —*Publishers Weekly*

"Burton is back with another intensely sexy and action-packed adventure.... Sassy, sexy, supernatural thrills!" —*Romantic Times*

"Aussies, heat waves, sex scenes, and demons galore." —The Romance Reader

"[Jaci Burton] spins an intriguingly sexy story with the most incredible characters.... If you haven't read anything of hers yet, I strongly suggest doing so now." —Fresh Fiction

TAKEN
BY
SIN

Jaci Burton

A DELL BOOK

Taken by Sin is a work of fiction. Names, characters, places, and
incidents are the products of the author's imagination or are used
fictitiously. Any resemblance to actual events, locales, or persons,
living or dead, is entirely coincidental.

A Dell Mass Market Original

Copyright © 2009 by Jaci Burton

Published in the United States by Dell, an imprint of The Random
House Publishing Group, a division of Random House, Inc., New York.

DELL is a registered trademark of Random House, Inc., and the
colophon is a trademark of Random House, Inc.

ISBN 978-0-440-24455-4

Cover illustration: Alan Ayers

Printed in the United States of America

www.bantamdell.com

2 4 6 8 9 7 5 3 1

To the readers who love the Demon Huner series and always await the next book in the series so eagerly—thank you so much for that. I hope this one meets your expectations.

And as always, to Charlie, for his love and patience.

Acknowledgments

To my agent, Kimberly Whalen, for her patient assistance with this book and my general hysteria.

To my editor, Shauna Summers, and to Jessica Sebor, for editorial guidance. I appreciate all you've done for this series.

To the Writeminded Readers Group, for my daily dose of fun and where everybody knows my name. Heh. You guys rock.

To all those who put up with me, who've shared my love and angst about the demon world and the writing world in general—Lara Adrian, Steph Tyler, Larissa Ione, Maya Banks, Jackie Kessler, Lauren Dane and, as always, to Angie, Mel, Shan, and Mandy.

Prologue

SICILY, ITALY

Hell was chasing them.

Dalton should stay and fight—there was only one mission occupying his world right now—save Isabelle. The only way he could do that was to get her out of here, away from the demons.

Away from hell.

As he jammed the accelerator and steered the SUV full-speed away from the cemetery, he caught sight of the blue lines of laser fire in his rearview mirror. They wanted to kill her. His own people. He couldn't let that happen.

His gut clenched. He was part of the Realm of Light, demon hunters sworn to defeat the Sons of Darkness and their demon minions. He should be back there, fighting. His brothers and sisters of the Realm were right now engaged in battle with demons, and he was deserting them, running off with the woman he'd been assigned to terminate.

There was so much fucked-up about this scenario. He'd never walked away from a fight before.

But he had something more important to do. Instinct told him this was the right thing—the only thing he could do, given the circumstances.

He glanced over at Isabelle slumped over in the passenger seat. A woman he barely knew, yet he was screwing his entire future for her—okay, mostly for her. Unconscious, her head resting against the window, she looked so innocent, almost angelic. Her hair fell in soft waves over her shoulders; her lips were half open as she breathed rhythmically. Her hands rested in her lap. There was no fight left in her—unlike a short while ago when she'd battled like a demon.

Because she *was* a demon. Half demon, anyway, and a part of the Sons of Darkness.

Dalton had been ordered to destroy her, and he couldn't do it. Which was why he was heading away from the battle instead of standing side by side with the other hunters. He'd been told to remove Isabelle from the scene because her sister, Angelique, was there, and Lou, the Realm's leader, didn't want Angelique to witness Isabelle's destruction.

Lou had ordered Dalton to take Isabelle away and kill her.

But how could he? He was responsible for much of what had happened to her. He'd started this chain of events that had led to Isabelle's downfall. He'd handled it all badly, from the time he stole her diary, to making love to her when he shouldn't have. It hadn't been part of his mission, yet he'd found her irresistible.

Hell, he hadn't wanted to resist. There'd been something about her that called to his dark side. Now he knew why. It still didn't excuse what he'd done.

When he fucked up, he fucked up big, didn't he?

So instead of terminating her, he was ignoring Lou's

orders, taking Isabelle away, abandoning the Realm of Light.

All to save Isabelle.

He could never go back to the Realm now. They'd come looking for him and Isabelle. They'd want to destroy her, to do the job he couldn't. She represented a danger to the Realm. Yeah, there were other half demons within the Realm, but they had proven they could control the demon side of themselves. The others had never taken that step into darkness like she had. Isabelle had embraced the demon within her, had tried to kill her sister, Angelique. Isabelle had sided with the Sons of Darkness. To the Realm of Light, she was nothing more than another demon now.

To Dalton, she was more. He didn't understand it all himself, but as soon as Lou had given him the order, he'd known it was wrong. For a second back there when he'd stood in front of Isabelle, she'd changed. He'd seen the human side of her warring with the demon side. In an instant, he'd known.

She was just like him. Straddling both light and darkness. He'd seen her look of helplessness, the pleading in her eyes. What he would have given for someone to offer him a second chance all those years ago. It might have made a difference in the turn of events, the direction of his destiny. Now he had the chance to offer Isabelle what he hadn't been. And at that moment he'd known he'd do whatever it took to bring the human part of her back.

Now he just had to stay one step ahead of the Realm, had to keep the two of them moving and in hiding long enough to come up with a plan to save her. If he could bring Isabelle's humanity back before the Realm of Light caught up with them, they'd never hurt her. He'd prove to them that the demon inside her had been banished.

Isabelle stirred, moaned, reached up to her temple with her fingertips.

"Isabelle?"

He was prepared to pull over, had a weapon at his side. He hoped he wouldn't have to use it.

Her eyes drifted open. She frowned, angled her face in his direction, then looked at him like she had no idea who he was.

"Are you all right?" he asked.

She opened her mouth, her bottom lip trembling. Her gaze drifted to the laser lying across his lap. Her eyes widened and he saw recognition in them. She snapped her gaze to his.

Tears filled her eyes. She shook her head, shrank against the window.

"I'm not going to hurt you, Isabelle. I'm taking you away from all of this. From them. Do you understand?"

She drew her arms across her chest as if to ward off an attack.

Shit.

Dalton pulled over to the side of the darkened country road. He put the car in park and half turned in the seat, sliding the laser to his left side, out of her sight but still in reach. He didn't know yet whether he could trust her. Her eyes were clear—human clear—but he knew from experience that could change in an instant.

"I needed to get you away from there. Do you remember what happened?"

She studied him for a few seconds, then gave a quick nod.

"We're going to get out of here. Just you and me. And then we're going to figure it all out. I'm going to fix this. Understand?"

She looked so petrified he wanted to fold her in his arms and comfort her. That would be such a bad move right now. Or ever.

"I'm scared, Dalton."

Isabelle had always been so strong and confident. Now? Lost. Broken. Confused. Her voice, ragged and soft, cut through him like a blade. "I know. I'll take care of you. Trust me."

She shuddered out a sigh. Her lids drifted and her body sagged. She closed her eyes and let her head fall back against the seat.

In less than a minute, she was out again. Obviously, this had all been too much for her to process. But at least she hadn't gone demon on him again. A good sign.

Now he really had to get moving. He mentally processed the To Do list—fake passports, a private flight, access to cash, and making sure their whereabouts weren't tracked. The Realm had their fingers in everything, so he'd have to be careful not to leave traces. He was good at hiding his identity.

He'd already been doing that for a long damn time. He could do it for a few more months.

CHAPTER ONE

NEW ORLEANS

Two weeks later

Dalton felt more at home in the bayou than anywhere else. Moss providing a drapery of darkness, the dank smell of stagnant water, the humidity and the feeling of being closed in all suited his nature. Well-hidden, a place where no one could find him. No one knew about this place, no one would connect him here, so he knew it was safe to bring Isabelle.

The cypress trees bent low in welcome as he paddled the boat through the thick mud of the swamp bottom, keeping watch over the woman who sat ramrod straight on the metal seat in front of him.

For the past two weeks Isabelle had said very little. Like a robot, she'd followed orders, eaten, showered, and slept when he'd told her, but stayed mostly silent. No conversation other than a few verbal affirmations to his questions regarding her comfort level.

He'd hoped to draw her out, to talk to her, to begin the process of healing her. But he'd gotten nothing. Instead, she'd gone further into her shell.

Shock? Maybe. She was probably confused as hell and completely disoriented. He'd circled them around

Europe before chartering a plane back to the U.S. When they arrived in New York, he'd bought a car and driven to New Orleans, not using the direct route to do that, either. Instead, he'd gone east and then south. Good thing he had a stash of cash he could utilize to do everything he'd needed to do. No way could he have accessed Realm money to fund this venture.

The only good thing about Isabelle's silence over the past two weeks was the time it had given Dalton to think, to plan. He'd known then where he was going to take her, what he was going to do. Hopefully, it would work.

Of course there were no guarantees, but at least it would give her a chance, which was more than the Realm would have given her.

"We're in the bayou in Louisiana now," he said, getting used to hearing only the sound of his own voice. But he kept talking day after day, hour after hour, hoping it would help Isabelle, that maybe something he said at some point would trigger a response from her. "A place I used to call home."

Isabelle gave a curt nod in reply, remaining, as usual, virtually motionless. Her fingers held tight to the rim of the metal seat on the boat. She stared straight ahead while he paddled, not taking in the view of the swamp at all. For all he knew, she was completely catatonic.

As the boat broke through the low-hanging moss, the house loomed into view, a great sprawling home well hidden from those who didn't know about it.

The Labeau family was his family. Not blood relations, but they knew him better than anyone. He had no blood family. He'd come from nowhere. He didn't, in fact, exist. No one knew that except for the Labeaus. And now the only one still living who knew his secret was Georgie, and at—how old was Georgie now, forty-five, fifty or so?—hadn't even been born when he'd first met her family. But when he'd contacted the Labeaus a week ago, Georgie had answered. She'd known right away who he was, had told Dalton this place would always be his home.

As always, the Labeaus could be counted on. He had to come back here. There was something he needed from this place and this family beyond the shelter it would provide Isabelle and him.

He drew the boat up to the dock. Several young children rushed to greet them, smiling and waving, their bare feet slapping hard on the wooden dock as they ran and smiled. They moored the boat while he helped Isabelle out.

"Miss Georgie says you should go right to the house."

Dalton grinned at a young girl of about eight with dark hair and serious chocolate brown eyes. "I'll do that. Thank you."

"She sick?" the little girl asked, inclining her head to Isabelle.

He noted the purplish cast under Isabelle's eyes, the drawn look to her face. She'd lost weight over the past couple weeks because she hadn't eaten much.

"No, she's just tired." Dalton slid his arm around Isabelle's waist and led her up the path toward the house.

He liked the old house. Reminiscent of a plantation home, the house was rectangular, two stories with a wraparound porch. It always looked like it had been freshly painted, white with green shutters at each of the windows, cheerful flowers climbing up out of pots sitting on the porch. The house was a sprawling mansion, at least what he would call a mansion, though there was nothing fancy about the place. But it was huge, it was clean, and to Dalton, it was the only home he had. More important, as soon as he took the first of the five stairs heading up to the porch, the tension within him dissolved.

He felt safe here, and Dalton rarely felt safe.

The screen door opened and a woman stepped out, wiping her hands on a kitchen towel. Her skin was flawless, the color of cream-flavored coffee. Her hair was cut short and her full lips lifted in a smile as she waited for them with her hands on her hips, her colorful ankle-length skirt swishing around her as she shifted back and forth. She looked a lot like her great-grandmother, that same kind of strange magic radiating in waves off her. It had been years since he'd been here, but he knew her. And she knew him.

"Dalton."

"Georgianne."

She held out her arms and he walked into them. She hugged him, and despite how much older he was than her, he was the one who drew comfort from the embrace. He pulled back and turned. "This is Isabelle."

"*Bienvenue à notre maison,* Isabelle. I'm Georgianne. Welcome to the Labeau home. We're so happy to have you here."

"*Bonjour,* Georgianne."

"Everyone calls me Georgie, and if you're a friend of Dalton's then you're practically family."

"*Merci*, Georgie," Isabelle said, dropping her chin to her chest. "*Je suis désolée.*"

"Now don't you go apologizin'," Georgie said. "There's nothing to be sorry for. We love having visitors here." Georgie slung her arm around Isabelle. "Come on, let's go inside for something cool to drink. It's blisterin' hot out here today."

Isabelle nodded and went in with Georgie. Dalton noted Isabelle was having trouble making eye contact, as if she was uncomfortable.

Maybe she was just tired. But on a good note, she'd spoken more words to Georgie in those few seconds than she had to him in weeks.

The kitchen was exactly as he remembered. Linoleum floors, still scrubbed to a gleaming shine every day, no doubt. The one thing he remembered most about Celine, Georgie's great-grandmother, was the woman always scrubbing something. She kept a seriously clean house and God help you if you tracked mud into her kitchen.

Gingham yellow-and-white curtains covered each window, open today to let what little breeze there was blow through the house. Georgie motioned to the old wooden table where Dalton had eaten many a meal. It could seat twenty, with wide benches on either side and chairs on each end that reminded him of thrones. It was a lot more scarred now than it had been on his last visit, but still sturdy as a hundred-year-old oak.

He climbed over the bench and took a seat next to Isabelle.

"Lemonade," Georgie said, setting glasses down and filling them with ice before pouring lemonade from the pitcher. "Loaded with sugar, too, because girl, you look like you need some nourishment."

"I haven't been very hungry," Isabelle said, her head bent down and her eyes averted as she grasped the glass and brought it to her lips. She sipped, then her lips curled in a hint of a smile. *"Bien, merci.* This is very good."

"Drink it all. You look like you're about to fall down."

Isabelle exhaled. "I feel that way."

"Then you should eat. There's soup on the stove." Georgie stood.

Isabelle raised her head enough to peer at Georgie through her half-lidded gaze. "Please, don't trouble yourself."

"*Chère,* it's no trouble. What's trouble is you passing out on my kitchen floor." She scooped seafood stew into two bowls and laid it in front of them.

Dalton inhaled, the memories taking him back. "Your great-grandma used to make this soup."

"Yeah," Georgie said with a wide smile. "She and my mama taught me how to cook."

"I was sorry to hear of your grandmother's passing," Dalton said. He'd known Georgie's grandmother well. Marie had a twinkle in her eye that had always made him laugh.

Georgie nodded. "*Merci.* She lived a happy life. We were blessed to have her as long as we did."

"I'm sorry, too," Isabelle said in between spoonfuls of soup.

Isabelle was eating. That was good. He hadn't been

able to coax her into much more than a few bitefuls at each meal.

"*Grand-mère* was ready. It was her time and she was in pain. Though we tried, there was nothing we could do to help her. Even magic can't fight disease."

Isabelle paused, looked at Dalton, then at Georgie. "Magic?"

Georgie slanted a look at Dalton, then smiled at Isabelle. "Voodoo."

Now Isabelle's head raised fully and her eyes widened. "You practice it? Seriously?"

"Of course. It's part of our lives, our culture. It's who we are and as natural as breathing."

"Georgie comes from a long line of voodoo priest-esses," Dalton explained.

Isabelle shuddered, laid the spoon in the bowl and placed her hands in her lap. "Sounds like the dark arts."

Dalton caught the fear in her eyes. He knew she'd had her fill of darkness. Feared it. He couldn't blame her for that.

Georgie rose, moved around the table, and sat on the bench next to Isabelle. She grasped Isabelle's hands in hers. "Oh, no. You have it wrong. Voodoo is white magic, *chère*. What you see in movies, read about, they have it backward. This is holy magic, as pure as Christianity. Our practice parallels the Christian rites in many ways."

"I don't know anything about voodoo. I've only heard..."

Georgie frowned. "You heard wrong. There is no evil practiced here. No blackness allowed. Only white light, clean. You have nothing to fear here. You are protected."

Isabelle turned to Dalton, who nodded but didn't say anything further.

Georgie rose and went to the sink. "You'll stay down at one of the cabins while you're here. It will give you some privacy to do what you need to do."

"What you need to do?" Isabelle asked. "And what's that?"

Isabelle's gaze was focused on Georgie's back, but Dalton knew she asked the question of him.

Georgie turned to face her.

"To remove the demon inside you."

Isabelle's heart slammed hard and all she heard was her own blood pounding in her ears. Had Dalton told Georgie everything about her? She'd spent the past two weeks in a fog, trying her best to fold inside herself, to keep from remembering everything that happened that night in Sicily.

All she wanted to do was forget.

But it kept coming back to her in bits and pieces, especially when she slept. Nightmares, mostly, of that night in Italy. What she'd done. What she'd become. The vivid images of her hands like claws, digging into her sister's throat, were impossible to escape. And the evil that had wrapped itself around her, crawled inside her, become part of her . . . how much she'd enjoyed the power . . .

Even now, she still felt that evil, trying to claw its way to the surface. It had taken every ounce of strength she possessed to push it deep inside. But Isabelle knew it remained, ever ready to burst free.

Had that really been her? She found it hard to believe, and yet she knew it had happened, could happen again.

Those men dressed all in black, surrounding her, telling her she was one of them. She hadn't even fought them. Where was her grit, her determination to remain human and pure despite their soul-tainting efforts? Oh, no. Instead, she'd embraced their evil like a warm, welcoming blanket. She'd reveled in it, been consumed by it.

And she could still feel it. How easily evil had taken her over. She was so weak. What did that say about her soul?

That she was damned. That's what it said.

So she tried not to sleep much, just lay awake at night staring into the darkness, certain they were going to come for her, afraid to turn to Dalton for comfort.

She had no one to lean on anymore. She'd tried to kill Angelique. Her sister no doubt hated her, the Realm of Light probably wanted her dead, and Dalton . . .

She had no idea why Dalton had brought her here.

To save her, Georgie had said. Why? Why would he even want to? They barely knew each other. They'd shared one night in Italy, a wild, passionate night on the yacht, but then he'd betrayed her by stealing her mother's diary. He'd used her to find out her secrets. She shouldn't trust him.

Then again, he shouldn't trust her, either. Not after discovering what she was. She could have killed him that night.

She still might. She was unstable; there was a demon lurking around inside her, ready to pounce. Who knew what could happen?

She shivered, wrapped her arms around herself, dread and confusion like a spiderweb, spinning thicker and thicker and clouding her mind. She had no idea what to do.

"You cold, *chère?*"

She lifted her head, glanced at Georgie. She shook her head. "I'm fine."

"I know you're confused, maybe a little angry. You don't know why you're here. You're probably scared. Just relax and make yourself at home. Nothing is going to happen here to hurt you."

Isabelle didn't want anything to happen. She wanted to go back to a year ago when she was blissfully ignorant about who and what she was, before she'd found her mother's diary that revealed everything. She wanted to hunt for treasure, live the life she'd always wanted without any knowledge of demons.

"I'd like to forget who I am."

Georgie graced her with a bright smile. "You can never go back, Isabelle. Only forward."

She inhaled, shuddered it out. The future seemed dismal, a dark and frightening place with no hope.

"It's been a long day," Dalton said. "I think we need to get to our cabin and unpack, let Isabelle rest."

Georgie nodded. "You know the way to the cabin. I'll let you take care of it. I have things to do."

Georgie bent in front of Isabelle and took her hands. A surge of warm energy zipped through her. Isabelle almost jerked her fingers away, but Georgie's grip was firm, holding her in place.

"Don't be afraid of me, of anything that happens here, Isabelle. You are protected."

She smoothed her hands over the top of Isabelle's, then straightened, moving down the long hallway. Dalton went with Georgie, his head bent toward the petite woman's as they whispered together at the doorway. He returned within a few seconds.

"You ready to get unpacked?" he asked.

"I guess." It wasn't like she had much choice. She no longer had freedom to come and go as she pleased. Where would she go if she did?

She was hunted and she knew it. She had no money, no family, no job, and nowhere to go. Both the Realm of Light and the Sons of Darkness wanted her. She couldn't run, and if she did, where to, and for what reason? Her life was in Dalton's hands, at least for now. She had questions and needed answers. Why had Dalton brought her here? Why wasn't she dead? Did the Realm of Light have something to do with this, or did he do this on his own? And if so . . . why? What did he want?

Too many questions—the sheer volume of them exhausted her. It was easier to block them all out, like she'd been blocking everything else out for the past two weeks—not think about them. Not yet, anyway.

She remembered feeling so powerful not so long ago. Where had all her vigor gone? The Sons of Darkness had promised her . . .

They'd promised her a lot. And then they'd abandoned her. She was completely human again, no traces of the power she'd wielded a short time ago. Just like so many other times in her life, she felt used and discarded.

She bit back a laugh. How gullible was she, anyway? Was it stamped in big neon letters across her forehead? *Hey, everyone, victimize me!*

"Isabelle."

She jerked her head up at the sound of Dalton's voice. "What?"

"Let's go."

She nodded and followed him out the door, sucking in huge breaths of hot, humid air. She glanced up at the palm fronds adjacent to the big house. They weren't flapping. No breeze at all. The smell of the swamp made her wrinkle her nose. They walked down the front steps and Dalton led her around the side of the big white house, along a well-worn path of dirt and flagstones, then across the lawn.

"Where are we going?"

"There's a cabin separate from the house. We'll stay there. It's quieter, more remote. It'll give us more privacy."

"It's great that we have a place to stay."

"It's not exactly the Ritz-Carlton, but I think you'll like it. And it's quiet."

Whatever. The last thing she needed was more time alone with her thoughts. Or her nightmares. A big house filled with people would have been a nice distraction.

And how far were they going to walk, anyway? The path seemed to wind on forever, skirting near the edge of the swamp. There were probably alligators lurking just under the surface of the murky water, sizing her up for their next meal. Low-hanging moss whapped her in the face as they traversed the narrow trail; the trees seemed to be alive and reaching for her. Her skin prickled like she was being watched, though she didn't see anyone on the porches of the few cabins they passed by, nor was anyone outside. She felt like Alice, only this was no Wonderland. It was just freakin' creepy.

Yeah, and maybe she needed to start sleeping at night, before her delusions started hitting daylight. Though her demons weren't really delusional, were they? They were real.

Dalton finally led her down a gravel path toward a small, one-story cabin near the water's edge. Cute, if a bit rustic-looking, all dark wood like a log cabin. Tall trees surrounded the place and there were some bushes along the porch and a few hanging pots with flowers and greenery spilling over. Still, it was small. Really small.

"We're both staying here?" she asked as they stepped up onto the porch.

"Yeah." He turned the knob and pushed open the door.

Not locked. That made her feel oh, so secure. Dalton flipped on the light, then stood out of the way while she walked in.

Okay, so it wasn't so bad. All warm polished wood with area rugs, rustic furniture, a fireplace, a tiny kitchen, and two small bedrooms with a connecting bath. Even a claw-foot tub that sat underneath a shuttered window. It was cozy and quaint. Maybe she could relax here. Her suitcase sat on top of a quilt-covered bed.

"Unpack, then I'll show you around."

She jumped at the sound of Dalton's voice, his breath

sliding over the back of her neck. She whipped around to face him.

"Jesus! How do you do that?" she asked, tilting her head back to look into his face.

"Do what?"

"Sneak up on me. I didn't even hear you." She looked down at his feet. He wore those thick boots, and on a hardwood floor it wasn't like they were stealthy. Did he float on air or something?

One side of his mouth lifted, as if he found scaring her amusing. Dickhead.

"It's my job to walk without noise. Sorry. I'll stomp in the future."

"You do that." She waited, but he didn't move. "Is there something else?"

His gaze was intense as he studied her face. The tiny bedroom suddenly got smaller, her breathing grew shorter, and her senses decided at the wrong damn moment to come alive. She had way more on her mind, crises to deal with—sexual attraction was going to have to go to the bottom of the list. Or even better, completely off the list.

Now tell that to her body, which suddenly decided to warm and moisten in all the most inappropriate places. Dammit.

"Well?" she asked, hoping her surly attitude would get rid of him before she did something really stupid like kiss him. Body contract, passion, to touch and be touched . . . it all sounded really good at the moment. And totally catastrophic at the same time.

"No." He pivoted and walked the short distance from her room to his and closed the door behind him.

Isabelle exhaled, sat on the bed, and rubbed her temples, trying to massage away the dull pain that seemed to constantly seethe in her head.

She was tired. So damn tired she wanted to cry. It made thinking so much harder, and she knew she needed to start engaging her brain if she was ever going to drag herself out of this mess.

She missed Angelique, needed her sister's counsel, her warmth, more than ever. But she could no longer turn to Angie, could no longer count on her sister to help her.

She slid onto the bed, turned to face the window, watched the bend and sway of tree limbs as a breeze picked up. So giving, so flexible, so adaptable.

She'd never been able to do that, had been rigid in her goals and what she'd gone after. Like an unyielding tree branch, she'd snapped. It had destroyed her.

Her eyelids were so heavy. She yawned, fought sleep, knew what waited for her there. But maybe she could get five, ten minutes. If she was lucky, the dreams wouldn't come.

Maybe the demons would stay away. She thought of all the wonderful things in her life, thought of her mother and how sweet she'd been when Isabelle and Angelique were children. She thought of Angie—her sister's smile, how they'd played together as kids. She thought of every single positive thing she could, hoping it would help keep the monsters away as she slept.

She'd no sooner drifted off than they came for her.

Dalton stayed in his closed room long after the five minutes it had taken for him to unpack.

Coward.

Yeah, some tough demon hunter he was. He could kick ass with the best of them. He feared nothing.

But he couldn't face one woman.

One minute in a small room with her and he'd been toast. Not that this was the first time he'd noticed it. But there was definitely something different about Isabelle, and it was more than just being attracted to her. Every time he stood close to her, every time she gazed up at him with her gold-flecked green eyes, every time he breathed her in, it was like being struck by lightning. He felt it—he felt *her*—all the way through his bloodstream, from his scalp down to his toes and all the important parts in between. It was like she'd entered his senses, his nerve endings, twining around inside him.

Yeah, way more than physical attraction, though heaven knows that was there, too. She made his dick hard, and he was a master at ignoring women, had been doing it a damn long time.

He couldn't ignore Isabelle.

So what was it about this woman—this flawed, screwed-up woman—that made him want to fold her in his arms to protect her one minute, and throw her down and fuck her brains out the next? What made him want to drag his mouth across hers, to bare her body, to touch and kiss and lick every part of her, to bring out the passionate side he'd witnessed only once but craved to see again?

Did he think that was going to save her? He knew damn well it wouldn't; in fact, it would only complicate things even more. He had to be her friend, not her lover. He might have to hurt her, not care for her, in order to save her.

This was messed up. What the hell had he been thinking bringing her here? What made him think he knew what was best for her?

But what was the alternative? Destroying her?

He'd eliminated plenty of demons, hadn't given it a second's thought.

Isabelle was a demon. He'd seen the darkness in her, knew there probably wasn't hope to save her. So why the hesitation? The Realm of Light knew what they were doing. What the hell made him think he knew more than they did?

Because you do. Because you need each other. Because she might be able to save you, too.

Okay, maybe. If he didn't kill Isabelle in the process, or kill himself trying for this redemption he placed in such high esteem.

He hoped to God it was all worth it. It had to be. It was all he had left now.

It was a chance. She was his chance.

And he was going to take it. Even if it killed them both.

CHAPTER TWO

NEW YORK

Sequestered at one of the Realm's secret headquarters, Michael leaned against the doorway of the operations center and surveyed his new team. They were deathly quiet, some whispering in small groups, others staring down at their hands, alone with their thoughts. And he knew damn well not a single one of them had their minds on work. Weapons hadn't been touched since that night in Sicily.

It was time that changed, and he was going to have to be the one to kick their asses. He was their Keeper now, assigned to them since their leader, Lou, had been killed. He knew none of them were overjoyed they had a new Keeper. At least one of them wasn't at all happy that it was him.

In the two weeks since Lou's death, he'd tried to give them all space to mourn. They'd had a funeral, of sorts, though there wasn't much left of Lou to bury after the hunters had blasted him with laser fire in order to destroy the demon that had insinuated itself inside him.

Lou had done what was necessary to destroy a powerful demon, one that could have wreaked havoc against the Realm. Michael knew these hunters felt guilt that Lou had died by their hands, but there had been no other choice. Lou had wanted it that way, knew his people would get the job done, no matter the cost. Lou was a hero to the Realm. So were the hunters who had done their jobs.

But from the pain ravaging their faces, he could tell they were hurting, and Mandy seemed to be taking it the hardest. She had been brought into the Realm when she was a young teen, had been practically raised by Lou. Lou was like a father, and she'd had to take part in his destruction.

This would be a lot easier if they would all look upon this as their job and quit taking it so personally. He'd lost people, too. A lot of them. But he picked up and went back to work. Death was part of the business of being a hunter. You had to harden your heart.

Michael had seen death too much. He knew how to avoid the heartache. It was his job to teach his new team how to overcome the pain.

Might as well start now.

"Okay," he said, moving to the front of the ops room. Eyes snapped to attention. "Let's talk about what we know."

Gina stood, tossing her dark ponytail over her shoulder. "Dalton used fake identities for both Isabelle and himself, switching passports each time they entered a new country throughout Europe. He moved them through Italy and into France, then Spain, and on to Portugal before they hopped a flight to JFK. From the scans we got it looks like they altered their appearances, but we have a pretty good idea it was them."

"And?" Michael asked, casting his gaze around the room.

Blank stares. His frustration level grew. He leaned against the desk and crossed his arms. "So I'm trying to decide if all of you just don't give a shit enough to push this investigation, or if you're deliberately trying to let Dalton go free."

"That's bullshit," Punk said. "We do our jobs."

Michael smiled. "Doesn't look to me like you're doing much of anything these days, other than feeling sorry for yourselves."

"That's a low blow, Michael," Mandy grumbled from the back of the room. She sat with her bare feet propped up on the table. "Even for you."

"Lou's the one who died," he reminded them. "Not any of you. So maybe it's time the rest of you came back to the land of the living and started working for the Realm of Light again."

"What the fuck?" Derek pulled his long, muscled frame out of the chair and dragged his fingers through his hair. He shoved the chair back with his legs and pressed his palms on the table, his eyes spitting fury. Gina grasped his arm.

"Don't, Derek."

"We don't need this shit, Michael," Derek said.

Undaunted by the fury pressing in on him from all sides, Michael kept his voice level. "I can appreciate that you all cared for Lou. But we have a job to do. It's time to go back to work."

"Last time I looked we have been working," Trace said. "We got this far, didn't we?"

Michael didn't bother to state the obvious, that it was mostly the tracking work he and the Realm of Light had done that brought them to New York. Instead, he stayed silent, staring them down. They knew.

"You've lost an entire team before, Michael," Derek said, barely even moving, his dark gaze boring into him. "How much downtime did you take?"

Ignoring the pangs of remembered guilt, Michael said, "None. My job isn't to mourn fallen comrades. My job is to track and kill demons, to find and destroy the Sons of Darkness. I don't have the luxury of time, and neither do any of you."

"Your heartfelt emotions move me to tears." Mandy's sarcastic tone almost made him smile. Almost. But he didn't think that would help the situation.

He knew he was going to provoke angry responses, but that was his intent. Even anger was better than apathy.

"Look, I understand your pain. Lou was a Keeper, a valued member of the Realm. His loss is felt deeply among us all and I share your sorrow. But the bottom line is, you are hunters and we need to hunt. We have to find Dalton and Isabelle, and it's not like the demons or the Sons of Darkness are going to take any downtime just because you're grieving. Lou wouldn't want you to stop doing the work he fought so hard for. In fact, knowing Lou, he'd be damn angry to find you all moping instead of getting out there and continuing to fight. Do you want his death to count for nothing?"

He paused, letting his words sink in before continuing on. "As I see it you have two choices. You either light a fire under your asses and start working again, or I'll wipe your memories of your time with the Realm and you can leave here, go out and live a normal life, free of all responsibilities as a demon hunter."

"You're certainly a lot different from Lou."

That from Olivia, petite, always quiet and soft-spoken. She had been one of Lou's newer recruits. He'd spoken highly of her keen observation skills, her intelligence, and her amazing physical abilities that belied her size. Of course Lou had always recruited the best.

"I'm not Lou. Get used to it."

"No, you're definitely nothing like Lou," Mandy said.

"So who wants out?" Michael asked, ignoring Mandy's retort. "This is your chance, because it's the one and only time I'm going to offer. After this, you take what I dish out—you work for me and you do what you're told."

"Wow, spoken like that, who could resist?"

He was going to have trouble with Mandy. Then again, he already knew that from their time together in Italy. She was going to challenge him at every turn, didn't believe he had what it took to lead. Good thing he thrived on challenge. And maybe if he kept her blood boiling, she would get over Lou faster.

"Anyone?" he asked again, ignoring Mandy.

No response.

"Good. Then let's get to work. Based on information we've received from the Realm, there are several possibilities for where Dalton and Isabelle went next. There are no verifiable purchases of airline tickets, so we need to check rental car receipts and automobile sales, possibly train and bus tickets by anyone who might fit their descriptions."

"That could be thousands of people," Trace said.

"Yes," Michael said. "So we're going to have to rely on psychic signatures. Perhaps, Shay, you can help us in that regard."

"I'll do what I can," Shay said, sliding her hand in Nic's.

"We'll all do what we can," Nic said.

"Good. Because this isn't going to be easy. Dalton isn't an amateur. He knows what he's doing and he can hide from us well, if that's his intent. It's taken us two weeks to get this far, and he could be anywhere by now."

"Do you really think he's taken up with the Sons of Darkness?" Shay asked.

Michael shrugged. "I don't know him as well as the rest of you do, but people change. Or can be changed, even against their will."

"You believe Isabelle did something to him."

Michael shifted his gaze to Angelique, Isabelle's sister. "I didn't say that."

"You didn't have to." Angelique lifted her chin.

"Don't let this get personal, Angelique. We need you to stay focused, because you can be our biggest help of all. I need you to concentrate on Isabelle, see if you can tune in to her."

"Don't you think I've been trying? There's been nothing. I've felt no connection to her since that night in Sicily."

Tears glistened in Angelique's eyes. Michael knew she had been through a lot with Isabelle. Seeing her sister

take that step into darkness had been devastating for her.
Ryder slung his arm around Angelique's shoulders. At
least she had Ryder to comfort her. To lose someone you
loved to evil like that...

He didn't even want to think about it. He had no
family anymore, made no friends, formed no attach-
ments for this very reason.

"Keep trying," Michael said. "Let me know if you
pick up anything."

Angelique nodded.

"As far as the rest of you, I have assignments. See me
individually and we'll get started. We don't have any time
to waste. It's imperative we find Dalton and Isabelle."

"What do we do when we find them?"

Mandy leaned her hip against Michael's desk. She'd
purposely waited until last, until it was just the two of
them in the ops room. He didn't even bother to glance
up from his carefully organized paperwork to look at her.
So she took her time to scan the oh-so-neat piles on his
desk. Everything in its place, not a spec of dust to mar
the dark surface.

A part of her wanted to lean over and sweep everything off his desk, to muss it up a little. To muss *him* up a
little, to mar that air of haughty remoteness he seemed
to carry around with him.

The thought of it shocked her. Why did she even
care? Michael was a pain in the ass. Cold, so different
from Lou.

Her stomach twinged, just as it did every time she

thought of their former leader. She missed Lou, missed his counsel, his warmth, the way he would brush his hand across her hair, or utter a soft word or two to comfort her whenever things got too rough.

Now she was alone. Oh, sure, she had the other hunters, people she thought of as her family, but it wasn't the same. It would never be the same. Lou had been there for her since she was a kid and had been thrust into this world of the Realm of Light, in shock, orphaned and fully aware that demons existed. Lou had had no choice but to sort of... adopt her. And she'd grown to love this life, to love the man who was like a father to her, who had taken her under his wing and taught her everything she knew.

Until she had to turn her laser on him. Destroying the people you love wasn't part of the deal. Weren't they on the side of the good guys?

Now she was stuck with this man. So cold, so remote, so unfeeling...

She glared down at Michael, who still hadn't answered her question, his head down while he scanned his precious paperwork.

"Michael."

He lifted his head. "Oh. Sorry. I was absorbing these charts and I didn't hear you."

Yeah, she'd like him to absorb some charts, all right. Right up the—

"What was your question, Mandy?"

"What happens when we find Dalton and Isabelle?"

He leaned back, frowned. "I can't answer that question without knowing all the parameters."

Parameters. Whatever. "Do you really not know, or has the Realm already decided what to do and you're just choosing not to tell me?"

"Why do you think I'm hiding something from you?"

Because I don't trust you. She shrugged.

"I don't know what's going to happen when we find them. It depends on their state."

"You mean it depends on what state Isabelle is in."

"Yes."

She still didn't believe him. Dalton had betrayed the Realm. She knew the deal. The Realm had already decided what to do about Dalton and Isabelle.

"I won't kill another member of the Realm, Michael." Dalton was family, just like Lou had been. She wasn't going there again. "And don't think anyone else will, either."

"I think you might surprise yourself with your capabilities, given certain situations."

She rolled her eyes. He talked like one of the Realm's freakin' scientists, all full of himself. "I think you might be surprised by how many of us won't be willing to do the Realm's dirty work."

He steepled his fingers, studied her. She hated that. It made her feel like a lab rat under a microscope.

"Do you really believe the Realm wants to kill Dalton?" he asked.

"Yes."

"Then maybe you *are* in the wrong line of work, Mandy. Sit down."

"I'd prefer to stand."

"You'd prefer to be contrary."

"Pot, meet kettle." This was getting them nowhere. "Do you have an assignment for me or not?"

"Considering your current emotional state, I'm not sure that's a good idea."

"For the love of God, Michael, give me a break. I can still do my job." She needed to work, needed to do something—kill something—demons, preferably. Anything other than sit around and do nothing but think about Lou, revisit the night of his death over and over again in her mind. It was making her crazy. Inactivity never sat well with her. She wasn't a thinker, preferring to leave that in the hands of the upper echelon of the Realm. She was a doer.

He studied her with that dark, unfathomable gaze of his that made her feel like she was being assessed, graded—only in secret. She crossed her arms, tapped her foot, quickly losing patience.

"Mandy."

"Michael."

"Losing your cool with me and throwing off attitude isn't going to win you points."

"I wasn't aware I was trying to score points with you. I want to be given an assignment, to be treated the same as you treat every other member of this team. For some reason you have a problem doing that."

"Maybe it's because you have a problem acting like a member of my team."

Emphasis on *my*, she noticed. Why did Michael have to be assigned as their new Keeper, anyway? She thought he was based in Italy. Now they were stuck with him and she had issues with that. Big issues.

"I've always been a team player. Ask anyone." And why was she bothering selling herself to him, anyway?

"I'm worried about you."

She snorted. "Don't be. I've been taking care of myself for a long time."

"Lou's been taking care of you."

His voice went low, quiet and soothing like Lou used to do when he wanted her to pay attention. "You can't take his place. Don't even try."

"That's not my intent. Lou and I manage differently."

"So I noticed."

"You want to work for me or do you want me to assign you to a different team?"

He would do that, too. Rip her away from the rest of the team—the rest of her family. Asshole. "I'll work for you. Never said I wouldn't. Haven't I been standing here waiting for an assignment?"

He continued to gaze up at her for a while, then nodded. "All right. You'll work directly with me."

Oh, great. This was some kind of punishment. "Are you serious?"

"Yes. You're like a ticking time bomb and I can't afford to have you explode somewhere. We're headed south, first thing in the morning. Be ready at dawn."

"Yes, master." She pivoted and left the room before she could wrap her fingers around his throat and strangle that smug smile off his chiseled face.

The one thing she thought an assignment would gain her was space from Michael. He irritated her, got under her skin. And she wasn't sure all the reasons for that irritation were bad. The fact of the matter was, she kind of liked the bantering between them. It fed her blood and she looked forward to matching wits with him. He was smart, and not bad looking at all with his dark good looks and that brooding quality that made her toes curl.

Which made distance between them imperative. Mandy wasn't all that experienced with the male species. Linc was her best friend, but she'd known him since she was a kid. He was like her older brother. Someone like Michael—he was an unknown factor.

Not that he liked her or anything. He definitely didn't like her. Though sometimes, the way he studied her . . .

Oh, hell. What did she know? She couldn't tell the difference between a guy who liked her and one who hated her.

And he'd just become her partner.

Things had gone from bad to worse.

CHAPTER THREE

Isabelle woke with a start and shot straight up in bed, the nightmare fresh in her mind. She dragged both hands through her hair, searching through the darkened room for a clock. No clock. What the hell time was it? She'd only meant to lie down for a few minutes. It was dark outside now. How long had she slept?

Too long. Long enough for the nightmares—the demons—to come.

She blinked, swung her legs over the side of the bed and headed into the bathroom. After a quick shower she felt a lot better, the nightmare just hanging on the fringes of her memory now, like always. Only bits and pieces remained, never enough for her to examine, to put all the parts of the puzzle together. After putting on shorts and a tank top, she opened the bedroom door and went in search of Dalton.

He wasn't in any of the rooms, including his bedroom. Had he gone up to the main house to talk with Georgie? She started toward the front door, but a flame and a plume of dark smoke out the back window caught her eye. She turned and went in that direction instead, opened the back door and stepped outside. The smell of something cooking greeted her. For the first time in a long time, her stomach rumbled. She was hungry.

Dalton stood over a brick grill. He looked up and smiled. "Have a good nap?"

She slid into a chair and pulled her feet up. "I never sleep well. What are you cooking?"

"Fish and some vegetables."

"Anything you need me to help with?"

"No. I've got it covered. They're almost done. You can pour us each a glass of wine. It's uncorked and on the table."

He motioned with his head to the picnic table next to her, where he'd spread out their plates and glasses. She grabbed the bottle from the cooler and poured wine into the two glasses. Instead of taking a seat back on the chair, she stayed where she was at the table in the darkened corner. She could watch Dalton this way and he couldn't see her.

He kept his attention on the food, flipping, staring, not once turning to see what she was doing. He was definitely focused. She liked the way he wore his hair—a little long, the kind of hair a woman could sink her fingers into and hold on.

Her stomach tightened, her thoughts drifting to the bedroom, to sliding along cool sheets with a hot man—with this man. Naked, sweaty, Dalton moving inside her. She loved his mouth. His bottom lip was full, and when he'd kissed her that one time his kiss had been filled with deliberate, focused passion and determination. Dalton was a fierce lover. She wanted that again.

Right now.

She rose and moved toward him, her breathing stilted, sweat beading between her breasts. Her nipples grew tight, her sex moistening as animal heat consumed her. She lifted her arm, reached for him.

"I know, you're probably starving. I'm just scooping it off the fire now. You ready?"

She blinked, realized she was only inches from Dalton, but had no idea how she'd gotten there. Dumbfounded, she lowered her arm and nodded. "Yes."

He lifted his lips in a smile. "Great. Let's sit down."

Swallowing past the dry desert in her throat, she followed him to the table and sat, grabbed the glass of wine, and took a long drink. Then another.

She remembered watching Dalton. Then . . . nothing. No, that's not right. There had been something. What was it?

"You're not eating."

She looked up at Dalton, then down at the plate, not even aware it had been set in front of her. "Oh. I'm sorry. Of course." She picked up her fork and moved it around the plate.

"What's wrong?"

"Nothing. This looks wonderful." She made an attempt to eat. She'd been really hungry earlier. She remembered that much. The fish had smelled so good. What happened to her? Where had she gone in those brief moments that she'd lost time? She lifted the fork to her lips and took a few bites, not even tasting what she ate.

"Isabelle."

She glanced up again. Dalton was staring at her. "What?"

"Tell me what's wrong."

She didn't want to. What would she say? But she had to confide in someone, and right now Dalton was all she had. "I lost time just now."

He frowned. "What do you mean?"

"When you asked me to pour the wine, I did, then I sat here at the table. I was watching you cook, and next thing I remember I was standing behind you over at the barbecue."

He glanced over his shoulder at the grill, then back at the wine bottle, then at her. "You don't remember anything?"

She shook her head.

"That was about ten minutes' worth of time."

Damn.

"Is that the first time this has happened?"

She shrugged. "I don't know. It's the first I'm aware of." She reached for her wineglass and emptied it in one long swallow. Dalton refilled it.

"You need to eat."

She nodded, scooped up the tender fish with her fork and forced herself to eat at least half of what was on her plate. Dalton was right. She needed to rebuild her strength. Think. Remember.

They finished eating, cleared the plates, and did the dishes, all in silence, then returned outside to sit on the back porch. It was still balmy, but at least a breeze had started to kick up. She lifted her hair, letting the air blow over the back of her neck.

"You want more wine?" Dalton asked.

She shook her head. She was fuzzy enough without too much alcohol muddling her brain. Why couldn't she remember? She leaned back in the chair and stared out into the night, into the swamp. "I hate not being in control."

Dalton lifted his lips. "That's a shocker."

She glared at him. "What does that mean? You think I'm a control freak?"

"Yeah. But who isn't? Who doesn't want to be in charge of their life, their own destiny?"

"Sorry," she said, pulling her knees up to her chest. "I didn't mean to be so defensive."

"You have a lot of things to be angry at me about, Isabelle. Don't be sorry."

"You mean because of my mother's diary?"

"Yeah."

She shrugged. "Somehow I think everything would have happened the way it did regardless of you finding the diary or not. In fact, you might have saved my life because you found it."

"How?"

"The demons would have found me, taken me eventually. If you hadn't found me when you did, if the Realm and Angie and everyone else hadn't been there that night..."

"You think the Sons of Darkness would have finished what they started with you."

"Yes. And we wouldn't be sitting here right now having this conversation. I wouldn't still be human." She'd be wholly demon, one of the Sons of Darkness.

"That's not what happened. Don't think about it."

"How can I not think about it? I was one of them. I am one of them. Their blood runs in me. I . . ."

"What?"

"Nothing."

He stood and came over to her side of the table, straddling the bench. "Isabelle, if we're going to make any headway, you have to talk to me. You have to tell me everything. What you're feeling, what you see, what you experience. I can't help you if I don't know what's going on."

She still didn't understand how he could help her at all. He was just a man. A human. He had no power. "I appreciate the offer, Dalton. But there's nothing you can do for me."

He cocked his head to the side and his lips tilted. "You might be surprised what I can do to help."

Isabelle frowned. "Like what?"

"This and that."

"Now who's being vague and uncommunicative?"

"Okay. Let's just say there are things I can do to help you."

"What? Do you practice voodoo like Georgie?"

His lips quirked. "Not really my area. But I have other talents."

She rolled her eyes. "I don't understand how the whole voodoo thing pertains to me and my situation anyway. Blood is blood. It's in me. I'm a demon. Nothing can change that. No one can take it away."

"You've already changed it. You're human right now."

She swung her legs over the bench and stood, feeling

cornered, needing space so she could pace back and forth. She wrapped her arms around herself. "For how long, though, Dalton? I don't feel human."

He studied her. "How do you feel?"

She didn't look at him, just kept pacing. "Unsettled. Not myself. I feel like at any time I could revert back to the demon I was. I feel shaky, like I'm barely holding on."

"Do you have some kind of sensation inside you, some kind of feeling that makes you think that?"

"No."

"Then what?"

"I don't know," she snapped back at him. "It just is. And the dreams."

"What dreams?"

This time she stopped, looked at him. "Every damn time I try to sleep, even if I drift off for a few seconds... the demons come."

He stood and came toward her. He reached out, laid his hands on her shoulders. She wanted to pull away. But she also wanted to walk into his arms, wrap herself in the comfort of someone holding her. She needed that. At the same time she feared it, felt if she gave into her emotions, if she let go of the tight string holding herself together, something would snap inside her and the demons would take hold.

"What happens in your dreams, Isabelle?"

His tone wasn't accusatory. It was gentle. She took a deep breath. "I don't really know. By the time I'm fully awake I've forgotten what happens. I can only grab hold of remnants. I just know they come for me when I fall asleep."

"They?"

"The demons."

"Are you having the same dream every time?"

She shrugged. "I think so."

"But you don't know in what way."

She shook her head again. "I wish I could remember all of it. Most times I want to shake it off as soon as I wake up."

"Maybe it's time you start to remember."

She tilted her head back to look at his face. "Why?"

"Because it might help unlock this mystery about the hold they have on you."

"Do you think they know where I am?"

He shook his head. "Doubtful. If they knew they'd have come for you already. For us. I don't think they do. I think you're blocking them."

Despite the heat of the night, she shivered. "Then why would I want to remember? Isn't it better if I forget, to keep forgetting?"

"I don't think so. The more we know about what you're dreaming, where it's coming from, the better armed we'll be when they do show up."

She backed away from him. "They'll come for me, won't they?"

"Eventually, yeah."

Honesty was supposed to be refreshing. Maybe it would be better if he lied to her. "When will they come? When I remember? When I stop blocking them?"

Dalton inhaled, let it out. "That depends on you. You're in charge of more than you think, Isabelle." He slid his hand in hers, pulled her back to the table, and sat them both down on the bench.

He didn't let go of her hand. This time, she didn't mind. It felt good. His hand was so big, like the rest of him, and calloused from hard work. It signaled strength. She needed to draw on some strength right now. She'd always been independent, strong on her own, never needed anyone else.

Not right now, though. She felt weak and she hated it.

"I know you're afraid," he said. "I know you're confused. There's a lot unsettled right now, a lot we both don't know. All I do know is that I'm not going to let anything bad happen to you, Isabelle. I won't let the Sons of Darkness take you. Not again."

For the first time in a long while, she felt hope. Maybe it was lame to take that hope from Dalton's words alone, but she'd always been on her own, and now she felt like she had an ally. She had to believe he'd protect her, that he'd do whatever it took to keep the Sons of Darkness away from her.

"Thank you. I'm not used to . . . needing anyone. This isn't easy for me. But I do need you."

"We need each other."

"You need me? How?" What could she possibly offer him?

He looked away for a second, then back at her. "What I meant was that I feel like I owe you after stealing your mother's diary, setting all this in motion. Let's just say this is my chance at redemption."

Somehow she didn't think that's what he meant. But as long as he was on her side this time, it was a start.

Dalton mentally cursed himself. He was going to have to watch what he said. He'd slipped a couple times tonight with Isabelle. He couldn't let her know that he needed her, what his plans were for her. She wouldn't understand. Not right now. Maybe never. It was best that she just believe he was trying to help her, that he'd brought her here because he thought Georgie could assist her.

They'd talked for a while, then she'd started to yawn, her eyelids drooping. He could tell she fought it, but she eventually gave in and went to bed. He waited an hour or so, slipping her door open to make sure she was asleep.

He went up to the main house and found Georgie sitting out front in her great-grandmother's old white rocking chair.

He'd had a few conversations with Georgie's great-grandmother while she rocked in that chair.

It had been so long ago.

"Thought you might come by tonight," she said.

Dalton smiled and leaned against the railing. "You psychic, too?"

"Oh, I have many gifts, Dalton. I know what you're about."

"Do you."

She nodded. "You have big plans for that girl down there," Georgie said, her palms flat on the wide arms of the rocker as she rode it gently back and forth. "She know about them?"

"Not yet. She's had a bad time of it."

Georgie's gaze drifted down the path toward the cabin. "She's got a lot of darkness in her."

Dalton stared down the road. He wished he could see the cabin from here. He shouldn't have left Isabelle alone. The urge to go back there grew stronger. "Yeah, she does."

"So do you."

He snapped his gaze back to Georgie. "What are you talking about?"

"My grandmother filled me in from what she knew, what my great-grandmother told her. The rest I can sense."

"What can you sense?"

"There's conflict in you, Dalton. And within me."

He frowned. "What are you conflicted about?"

"Whether to help your Isabelle or not."

She wasn't *his* Isabelle. He'd need to make sure Georgie understood that. "Why wouldn't you help her? Help me? Your great-grandmother did."

"Those were different circumstances, and you know why. We owed you. Now you want help for Isabelle. Why?"

"Because what happened to her isn't her fault."

Georgie studied him. "But maybe her destiny. And something you shouldn't interfere in."

Dalton sucked in a breath. He'd interfered before, and it had cost him dearly. "I'm right about this, Georgie. I know I am. Isabelle doesn't deserve this."

Georgie folded her hands in her lap, seeming to contemplate while rocking. Dalton knew better than to push it, so he waited for her to speak. When she looked up, her gaze was penetrating.

"I think you need to take some time while you're here. Search your heart, Dalton, and determine whether you're really out to save Isabelle's soul. Or your own."

CHAPTER FOUR

Isabelle knew she had slept some, but it wasn't a good, deep sleep. She felt ragged and cranky when she woke near dawn, gray light filtering through the blinds in her bedroom. The nightmare that always seemed to latch on to her evaporated almost immediately, its fuzzy edges still attached like tentacles to the shadows of her mind. Despite Dalton's advice to remember, she wanted to shake it loose permanently, so she slid out of bed and got dressed, brushed her teeth and wound her hair up in a ponytail, then went out into the kitchen to make coffee.

Dalton was already up, coffee made. She inhaled the scent of caffeine and picked up her step. Coffee would banish the demons.

Dalton sat at the table, drinking in the still-dark kitchen.

"Don't you sleep?" she asked, filling a cup and sitting.

"Not much. I'm used to being on a hunt. I can do with just a few hours."

"So this is like vacation for you."

He arched a brow. "Uh, yeah."

"I'll bet you hate downtime."

"I'm not used to it."

"Me, either." She took a long sip of coffee and waited

for the caffeine to surge. "I'm used to starting digs before dawn and working until sunset. Doing nothing is going to make me crazy."

He nodded. "You're not here to do nothing."

"Good. What am I here to do?"

"First thing is to get you strong again."

She practically inhaled the first cup of coffee and went to pour another. "And you're going to help me with that."

"Yes."

"How?"

"Battle exercises for the physical. You're not a demon hunter."

"You planning to make me one?"

"When the Sons of Darkness show up, I want you prepared. But not just physically."

She took a seat across the table from him and cupped the mug of steaming coffee. "How else?"

"Mentally. Working on your psychic skills. Try to get you to clear the cobwebs."

"What am I supposed to do—sit around and channel my inner demon?"

"That would be helpful."

She laughed. "I don't think you really want me doing that. I thought the idea was to keep the demon away."

"Maybe. Maybe not."

"Which means what exactly?" She hated when he got vague and mysterious like this.

"It means that the more we know about what's going on with you and the Sons of Darkness—what kind of hold they have on you—the better prepared we'll be to fight them."

Why did she feel like a guinea pig here? She didn't like this. "So you want me to bring out the demon?"

He shrugged. "We'll just take it as it comes, one day at a time."

She rolled her eyes. "So not helpful. A plan of attack would be better."

"You can't plan for what you don't know, Isabelle." He pushed back from the chair, refilled his cup, and started dragging bowls, pots, and pans out of cabinets. She rose and went to the refrigerator for eggs, bacon, and butter, working silently alongside him fixing breakfast.

It felt...good. Normal. Cooking and eating together. They even did the dishes side by side. And she found it all enjoyable, which was strange since she hated all this domestic stuff. A few months back she'd dreamed of being successful enough to have servants to do all this for her, or to live out of hotels and eat in the finest restaurants. Now she just wanted a chance at having a normal life where she could cook and do dishes. Funny how one's outlook could change so drastically. What used to be so important to her wasn't anymore. She'd once wanted to be rich, famous, a successful archaeologist.

Now she just wanted to be human. And alive. She wanted to do dishes.

"So when do we start?"

Dalton wiped his hands on the dish towel. "Feel strong enough today?"

She nodded. "Definitely. Anything's better than sitting around doing nothing."

"You'd better change clothes." He glanced down at her khaki shorts and white tank. "You're going to get dirty."

"I can handle getting dirty. Clothes are washable." Besides, none of these were her clothes anyway. Everything she wore now Dalton had bought for her along the way from Sicily.

He shrugged. "Okay. Put on boots and I'll meet you in the back."

After putting on socks and her boots, she met him outside. He'd changed into camo pants and a muscle shirt, along with those heavy shit-kicker boots he liked to wear. Those things must have weighed ten pounds each. Isabelle didn't know how he walked in them, let alone managed to sneak around like a ghost.

"So what are we going to do today?" she asked.

"See those woods back there? We're going to hike."

She tilted her head. "Hike? That's it?"

His lips curled. "Yeah. That's it. Come on."

They set out down the walkway from the front of the house, side by side along the path leading east. Away from the main house, into the dense trees and foliage of the woods where there was no path, where it looked like no one had been before.

Isabelle found herself behind Dalton, stepping wherever he stepped, because soon they were in the thick of overhanging cypress and gnarled bushes with thorns, and she suddenly wished she'd worn long sleeves. Though the thought of it made her sweat even more than she already was. She was thoroughly drenched through her bra and tank top, and her shorts clung to her. The humidity was unbearable, and the sun had long ago disappeared from under the canopy of treetops bunched close together overhead. She couldn't imagine how bad it would be if the light and heat were blasting down on them from above.

But despite the discomfort, Isabelle was happy for something to do to occupy herself. It was mindless effort and she found herself enjoying the push of her boots against the mushy swamp soaked earth, stepping up over a twisted branch every few feet, keeping her focus sharp for roots coming up from the ground so she wouldn't trip. Dalton kept a brisk pace so she had to hustle to keep up. And he didn't say much, which was fine with her since she had to use all her lung power just to keep moving.

All in all, this was quite a workout. Physical activity felt great after so many weeks of sitting around alone with her thoughts. Being lost in her own head was a scary place these days. She wanted to spend as little time there as possible. Outside, she could focus on the sounds of birds, the whistle of tree limbs in today's hefty breeze—and thank God for the breeze that had kicked up an hour or so after they'd started this trek. She wasn't sure she'd survive it otherwise. She could smell the damp earth sinking into her nostrils, feel her muscles tighten and ache from inactivity. It was awesome.

Dalton finally stopped after a couple hours, turned to her and pulled his backpack off, then reached in for two canteens.

"Water. Stay hydrated. Don't drink too much."

She unscrewed the lid and took a small sip, watching

him as he rested against a wide fallen tree trunk. "This strikes me as survival training."

He put his own canteen away, then hers. "You're right. I've chased a few demons through jungle like this, or been chased by them."

She imagined trying to run from demons out here in this tangled jungle, then shuddered at the possibility. "Do you think that could happen to us? Out here?"

"It's possible. I can guarantee that if demons show up here, we won't be standing still or fighting them within the confines of the house. Plus I'm going to want to lure them away from Georgie's place."

She nodded, looked down at her feet. "I understand."

He tipped her chin with his fingers. "No, I don't think you do. They won't be coming just for you, Isabelle. They'll be coming for me, too."

She blinked. "You? Why would they want you? Why not just me? I'm who they want."

He paused, his gaze so intense her body heated up a few more degrees.

"Because I'm a demon hunter and they want us all dead."

"Oh. Of course."

"Which means you need to familiarize yourself with the area. First, in case we have to set out in a hurry, and second, in case we get separated. I don't want to worry about you getting lost out here. You need a sense of direction, to know where you're going."

"Does it matter which way I go if demons are chasing us?"

"Yeah, it does. You don't want them hunting you

down and trapping you in a corner, like a snake-infested swamp."

"Oh. Good point." That's why he was the expert at this.

"I know this area; I've hiked it before. You don't. You need to know the landmarks so you can find your way around."

She nodded. "Okay." She glanced around, but it all looked the same to her. Then again, she'd mapped desert regions before on a dig. She could do this. "I don't suppose you have a GPS handy."

"Actually, I do have something that might help," he said with a slight smile. "A couple units that will allow us to keep track of each other."

"Handy."

"Very. Plus comm units that we can use to stay in verbal contact."

She was going to enjoy this. "You have all kinds of fun tech stuff."

"Babe, you have no idea. Wait til we get to weapons."

"Now I'm drooling."

He laughed. "Come on, let's get moving again."

This time, she made note of where she was, where the sunlight filtered in through the treetops, tried to memorize twists and turns in the landscape of the path they traversed. Somehow, it made sense, at least to her, which was really all that mattered. But could she do this at night? She didn't know, wouldn't know until it came time to do it. But if she was on the run from demons, she'd damn well do whatever it took to get away.

She even knew when Dalton circled and headed

back. By that time, she could have led them, and she bit back a triumphant squeal because she actually knew where she was going. He brought them around to the back of the house where they pulled off their muddy boots and soaked socks. Isabelle sat in a chair on the porch and watched him.

His shirt was soaked, clinging to his chest and back. Dirt smudged his face and his hair was dripping wet.

Oh, man, did he look sexy. She shook off the visual of licking the sweat beading against his neck.

"I'd say that's enough for now," Dalton said.

"I can do more."

He shook his head. "It was a tough hike and you're not used to the exercise. Go take a bath. Relax your muscles. There'll be more to do tomorrow. I don't need you so sore that you're useless to me."

She laughed, but didn't argue. He was right. The last thing she wanted was to ache so much she'd have to spend several days laid up and unable to move. She went inside and turned on the water, opened the window over the tub to let the breeze through and pulled the shutters partway closed, then found some bath salts on the ledge. She poured them over the running water, then began to strip off her grimy clothes.

The bath was heaven. She sank in up to her neck and closed her eyes, letting the warm water loosen her tight muscles. She was so relaxed she almost fell asleep, until a strong gust of wind blew one of the shutters open. She sat up and started to close it, but glanced outside, realizing the bathroom overlooked the backyard. The window was just above the bathtub, so she could lie back and look outside. She eased the shutter partway closed, then leaned back, watching Dalton.

He had a long table outside on the patio, and spread across it were weapons that he had taken apart to clean.

He had taken his shirt off. Sweat poured off his back, running in rivers down the smooth muscles outlined there. He was tan, his shoulders broad, his waist slim, and when he turned around she sucked in her breath at the wide expanse of his chest, the sculpted abs and the fine line of dark hair sprinkled across his lower abs and disappearing into his pants.

The water in the tub was only lukewarm, but her body suddenly felt heated. She blew out a breath, knowing she should get out, but she couldn't drag her gaze away from Dalton.

She might have been exhausted, but apparently he wasn't. With every movement the muscles in his back rippled, showcasing his power.

Power. It sizzled around her. Like a jerk of lightning, she felt it enter her, in her veins, surging through her bloodstream. And with every sensation her gaze stayed riveted to Dalton.

Speaking of power...his was strong. Though yards and a building separated them, she felt it emanating from him. She wanted to touch him, run her hands down his back, lick the sweat from his body and absorb some of his power. She wanted to taste him, strip him naked and take him right there in the yard. Her breasts swelled, her nipples hardened, heat filled her. The more she watched, the more she knew she had to have him—right now. Even from in here she could smell him—the raw animal scent that drew her to him like a mating heat.

She rose from the tub and followed that scent, down the hall and out the back door, to the porch. She laid her hand on his shoulder. He pivoted with a smile, then his eyes widened, scanning her body.

"Isabelle. Jesus! What the hell are you doing?"

His gaze shot around the yard. Dammit, she wanted him looking at her.

"I want you." She curled her fingers around his nape, pulled herself up against his body. Touching him was like drawing to a flame—agonizing, painful pleasure, but she sought it out, wanted more. "I need you."

He reached for her arm. "Let's go back inside. Now."

She held firm, took his hand and laid it on her naked breast. The heat of him sizzled against her skin. Her heart pounded furiously against his palm; her nipple puckered against the deliciously rough calluses of his flesh. "Touch me, Dalton."

She didn't wait for his answer, just held his hand there and drew his head to hers, using every ounce of strength she possessed. She *felt* powerful, too. She was a queen. She could have anything she wanted, and she wanted Dalton. He was hers for the taking. She could see it from the way he couldn't take his gaze from hers. A woman could get lost in eyes that sexy.

But now she had to have his lips on hers, his mouth to her mouth. If she didn't she might die, the thirst to have him was so great. The shock of her lips touching his was like a lightning bolt, a fusion of their strengths, a sexual torrent transferring from her to him.

She might not survive it. She didn't care. She wanted this man more than she'd ever wanted anything before. He was power. He was hers.

At the first touch of Isabelle's lips to his, Dalton felt the shock, like being struck by an electric current. But it was more than that. It was a physical rocking of his senses. Never mind that a gorgeous, naked woman stood in the backyard molding herself against him and wordlessly begging him to fuck her right there. Her mouth was magic. Soft, yielding yet demanding. She knew what she wanted. She wanted him. He'd never felt more desired, more needed.

But in the back of his sex-soaked brain there was a small voice that knew this was wrong. This wasn't really Isabelle in his arms. Something had happened. Something bad. He had to think with his head, not with his dick. And that was going to be damned difficult to do given the circumstances, because she was crawling all over him and he was rock hard and ready to do whatever the hell she wanted.

But he finally drew enough strength to pull her arms away, jerk his mouth from hers. Oh, that mouth. Christ, she was sexy, her lips puffy and parted, her eyes druggingly half-lidded and sexy as hell. And of course, she was naked, and her body was perfection, from her full, pert breasts to her slender waist, curvy hips, and athletic legs.

He wanted her, wanted to be inside her, would have

no problem throwing her down on the ground and doing it right there.

But he'd made that mistake once before. And it had cost Isabelle. He wasn't going to let it happen again.

One of them had to have some common sense, and right now it sure as hell wasn't the hot woman rocking against him.

He grabbed her by the shoulders, focusing only on her face. "Isabelle!"

She stared at him, almost right through him.

"Isabelle, wake up. Now."

She blinked a few times, then frowned. "Dalton?"

She was coming back. He could almost see her eyes clear, as if a veil had been removed from them.

"Yeah. That's it. Come on."

He saw it then—the focus, the reality slip back into her eyes. She looked at him, around the yard, then down at herself, her gaze shooting back to him as she realized she was standing in the yard stark naked. "Oh, shit. Oh, God. Oh, my God, Dalton." She wrenched away from him and covered herself. Dalton grabbed his discarded T-shirt from the ground and helped her put it on. She was wobbly, looked confused, so he slid his hand around her waist.

"Let's go inside."

He helped her into the house and toward the bathroom. The tub was filled with water, now cold. Isabelle stared into the water, then up at him.

Now he saw confusion soaking her features. He wanted to drag her into his arms and comfort her.

Really bad idea considering what had just happened. He kept his distance.

"I was taking a bath," she said. "That's all I remember until I found myself outside. With you." She dragged her hands through her hair. "What did I do, Dalton? God, I'm drenched in sweat."

What should he tell her? That she stalked out there naked and tried to have her way with him? He was pretty sure that's not what she wanted to hear right now. She was emotionally fragile, barely holding it together. Telling her she'd stormed out into the yard bare-assed naked and tried to seduce him wasn't going to help her.

Then again, she couldn't help herself if she didn't know the truth. And after everything, he owed her that.

"Let's both get cleaned up, then we'll talk," he said.

She nodded. He turned to go but she grasped his forearm. "Don't leave."

He swallowed, but nodded. "Okay."

"I'll just rinse off in the shower. It won't take me long." She moved away from him, turned on the shower in the tiny stall, and with her back to him, pulled his T-shirt off and stepped inside, shutting the door behind her.

Dalton leaned against the bathroom counter and tried to remind himself that Isabelle was in shock. Admiring the beauty of her naked body was the wrong thing to do in this situation. Thinking about anything having to do with her body was a bad idea. Watching her silhouette through the smoky glass shower door wasn't helping his situation any, either. He decided the best course of action was to bend down and unlace his boots, then find Isabelle a towel.

He held it up for her as soon as she turned off the water and stepped out. She offered up a tentative smile and wound the thick fabric around herself.

"Thanks. Your turn now. Do you mind if I just hang in here while you shower?"

This was some kind of punishment for his misdeeds. "No, it's fine. I won't take long."

He shucked his pants and turned the shower back on, hurried inside and closed the door, then buried his face under the water, concentrating on soap and washing, not on Isabelle. When he finished, he turned the water off, realizing he'd have to step out naked. He blew out a breath and opened the door. Isabelle was combing her hair. She stopped and stared as he walked by. He grabbed a towel in a hurry.

"Are you feeling better?" he asked.

She nodded. "Yeah."

"Good. I'm going to get some clothes. You going to be okay?"

"Yes. I'm fine now."

Fine his ass. She gaped at him as if she was pondering licking him all over. Dalton was a man. He recognized sexual hunger in a woman. So did his body. He needed to get out of this bathroom—and fast, before things started to become . . . obvious.

"Great. I'll meet you in the kitchen." He pivoted and went into his bedroom, shut the door, and blew out a breath. Christ, that had been difficult. What was with Isabelle? There had always been an attraction between them, but this was different. There was something powerful going on between them, and he was being counted on to be the strong one and resist.

Well, goddammit. He wasn't that strong. Isabelle was beautiful, desirable. He'd wanted her from the beginning. Why was he required to be so fucking noble and push her away?

He grabbed a pair of shorts and a shirt and got dressed, then dragged his hands through his hair. It was time to figure out what was going on.

Isabelle was already in the kitchen, sitting at the tiny round table. Her hair hung in damp tendrils down her back. She looked up when he walked in. The hunger he'd seen earlier was gone. Now he saw only curiosity. Misery. Confusion. Those emotions wringing her dry made him feel like hell.

Great job thinking with your dick, Dalton.

"Thanks for the tea." He pulled up a chair and took a long swallow.

"I figured you'd be thirsty. It was hot out there today. You need to replenish."

He laid the glass down. "So do you."

Her lips lifted. "It felt good to do something physical for a change. My muscles were atrophying from sitting around."

"We still have a lot to do, so plan on working those muscles even more."

"Good. I like physical work. Keeps my mind occupied on something other than myself."

She was avoiding the topic. So was he. He wasn't even sure how to bring it up.

"What's happening to me, Dalton? It's not like me to

walk out naked in the backyard. What's worse, I can't re-member anything. Can you tell me what I did?"

She asked for the truth. He owed it to her to give it to her. He cupped the cool glass with his palm and looked at her. "I was cleaning weapons on the patio. You came up behind me, so I turned around. You were naked."

She blinked, then nodded. "Go on."

"You...uh...pressed yourself up against me. Said you wanted me, needed me. You asked me to touch you. Then you kissed me."

Her cheeks turned pink. She palmed them. "Oh, God. I don't remember that. I swear, Dalton, I don't re-member doing that."

"It's okay."

"You stopped it. You pushed me away, didn't you?" He saw tears glistening in her eyes.

"Yeah."

She leaned back in the chair, wrapped her arms around herself, and laid her chin on her chest, closing her eyes. He could feel her pain and embarrassment.

Dalton wanted to move, gather her up in his arms, drag her onto his lap and comfort her. But somehow he knew that touching her right now would be the wrong thing to do. For both of them.

"Isabelle. Look at me."

She did.

"I didn't want to stop you."

She inhaled sharply. "What?"

"You're beautiful, the most desirable woman I've ever known. And when you kissed me, touched me...oh, hell no, I didn't want to stop you."

"You didn't?"

"No. If it was you, really you out there, I wouldn't have stopped you. We wouldn't be having this conversation right now."

"We wouldn't?"

"No. We'd be in bed."

"Oh." Her cheeks pinkened even further. And he hardened, thinking about having her in that bed. Naked, under him. Christ. Wrong thing to think about.

"But it wasn't you out there. We both know that."

She lifted her chin and nodded. "Yes. You're right." She finally seemed to relax. "We have to figure out what's going on with me." She seemed to ponder it for a minute or two. "Do you think I'm possessed?"

"I doubt it. It's you . . . but not you. It's not like it's someone else taking over your body. When you were out there in the yard with me, you were definitely Isabelle. You reminded me of that night we spent on the yacht together."

Her lashes drifted down. "When we had sex."

"I meant the look on your face. Intense. Driven. It still seemed like you in many ways, but deep down I knew all of you wasn't there."

"Oh."

"Does that make sense?"

"Yes. And obviously I know I wasn't all there. And this isn't the first time it's happened to me since we left Sicily. I just don't know what triggers it."

"Do you remember any other times it's happened?"

"Besides the nightmares?"

"But that's pretty common. Most people can't remember their dreams."

She leaned forward, cupped her hands around her glass of tea. "These aren't dreams, Dalton. It's like I'm really there. Like the demons come for me as soon as I close my eyes and drift off. And it's so real when I wake up, as if they're trying to hold on to me and don't want to let go. But I lose memory of what happened as soon as I'm fully awake. It's more real than dreaming. I can't explain it."

He nodded. "Okay. Any other times?"

"Just the one time . . . the night before."

He cocked a brow. "What do you mean?"

"I'm not sure how to explain this. But since we've been here . . . this is really embarrassing, Dalton."

"Tell me, Isabelle. Don't be embarrassed."

She blew out a breath. "Okay. There's been a couple times I've lost it when I find myself staring at you in . . . that way."

"What way?"

"God, are you dense? In the way a woman stares at a man. When she wants him."

"Oh." He was dense. And flattered as hell. And worried. "Well, thanks. I think."

She laughed. "You're welcome. I think."

He pulled up the chair next to him and placed his foot on it. "So it's in your dreams. And it's focused on me. Or at least tapping into your sexual desires."

"Great. So we're at least pinpointing something. Now what do we do about it? How do we stop it from happening? Because I'd hate to jump you in the middle of the night when you're sleeping and defenseless."

He snorted. "Yeah, that would be awful, wouldn't it?" Just the thought of it had him quickening, his mind whirling with the possibilities. Really, he needed to get a grip. And the best way to do that was work on getting Isabelle past these nightmares—or daymares—or whatever it was that had ahold of her.

"We're working on building you up physically. Now we need to focus on your mental and psychic strength. The stronger you are, the more you'll be able to push past whatever's causing you to have these nightmares or episodes."

"Okay. How do you suggest we do that?"

"Intense exercise. Just like we do for your body, we'll do the same for your mind."

"Again. How?"

"Well, I'm not sure what I have in mind is a good idea right now."

She frowned. "Why not?"

"Because of what's happening to you, and between us."

"Just spell it out, Dalton."

He dragged his hand through his hair. "It's going to require us to get . . . close."

CHAPTER FIVE

FLORIDA

Mandy stared out the hotel window at the cool blue water and white sand beach, longing to be out there. This was one of those days that she hated her job—they never got vacations, dammit.

She wasn't going to get one now, either, no matter how appealing that ocean was. She'd love nothing more than to throw on a bikini and hit that beach, slather on a ton of lotion and bake her body, then play in the waves for a day. A week. A month. Maybe with a hot guy by her side.

Michael was definitely a hot guy. However, the word *vacation* probably wasn't even in his vocabulary.

She'd checked out of her room and waited for Michael to finish packing up his things. With great reluctance she turned away from the streaming sunlight. "Wouldn't it be nice if we could take a few days to lie around on the beach, soak up the sun, do a little surfing?"

Michael laughed. "I don't remember the last time I did anything like that."

"You need to lighten up, Mike. Life's short."

"Don't I know it. Unfortunately, we need to get moving."

She scrunched her nose and mentally cursed the man

she'd had to follow around like a trained dog for the past few days. Granted, Michael knew his business. As a Keeper, he was damn good at hunting. He wasn't one to waste time; he knew how to track and kept them moving. And since Mandy loved her job, she always admired those who did it well.

But Michael wasn't Lou. And she missed Lou so much her heart ached. Ever since Sicily she'd refused to let herself wallow in grief. Instead, she'd worked out, practiced with her weapons, beat the shit out of a couple of punching bags. Basically done everything she could to keep her mind and body occupied so she wouldn't have to think, or feel, or break down. Because she was afraid if she did, she'd never get up again.

And Lou would have been disappointed in her if she let that happen. So she simply never stopped. Fortunately, Michael was a great slave driver, kept them moving every day and almost every night, stopping only when necessary to eat and fall into a dead sleep. She was reaching exhaustion, mentally, emotionally, and physically, and she knew it. Still, she'd push on. It was her job. It kept her occupied. Occupied meant she wouldn't have to think, to dwell.

Michael shoved the last of his things in his bag and turned to her. As tall as she was, Mandy normally towered over or stood eye to eye with many of the guys she worked with, other than Linc, an obscenely tall, hulking warrior who was her best friend and fellow hunter. But with Michael, she had to tilt her head back to look at his face. It was unusual and somewhat disconcerting.

Even more was Michael reaching out to sweep his

thumb across her cheek. "You have dark circles under your eyes. You haven't been sleeping well."

She fought the shiver caused by the warmth of his touch, and took a step back, unused to affection from anyone she thought of as a...man. The other hunters were like brothers. Lou had been like a father. Michael was...she didn't know what he was or how she felt about him. He gave her butterflies in her stomach and he pissed her off at the same time. He made her feel weird and she didn't know what it all meant, so she decided to keep her radar up and her sarcasm high. "Are you monitoring my sleeping habits now?"

His lips curled. "No. I'm worried about your effectiveness if you don't rest."

"I'm plenty effective. Wanna try me?"

"I don't want to pay the hotel for broken furniture, so no thanks. Not here."

"Some other time, then. I'll be happy to prove to you that, sleep or no sleep, I can still do my job."

"It's okay to grieve, Mandy, to mourn Lou's loss."

"That's not what you said before."

"That's not what I meant before." He scratched his nose. "You can feel the pain of loss. We wouldn't be human if we didn't. If you bury it, it can affect you to the point where you shut down. The sooner you face it head-on and deal with it, the sooner you can move forward."

"I mourned him. I'm done now. Are we ready to leave?" She picked up her bag.

Instead, he stood firm to the spot. "I know all about refusing to face your emotions."

She arched a brow. "You have emotions?" She looked

around either side of him. "Where? Show me where they're hiding."

Michael shook his head. "You're killing me, Mandy."

"Well, not yet, but given the right opportunity . . ."

He rolled his eyes and grabbed his bag. "Smart-ass. Let's go."

They headed out to the car, tossing their things into the trunk. They were on Dalton's trail, tracking him from New York all the way south into Florida. Now they had a line on a car rented by a couple who matched Dalton's and Isabelle's descriptions. GPS on the vehicle indicated it had headed east into Georgia before being turned in, so that was their next destination.

"I need to stop at a bank before we head out," Michael said.

Mandy buckled up and nodded.

Michael drove to the city and headed downtown. Traffic was heavy since it was the tail end of morning rush hour. He pulled into the parking lot of a large bank, choosing a space near the back.

"It shouldn't take me long," he said. "You want to come inside?"

She shook her head. "I'll wait here."

He nodded and got out. Mandy unbuckled her seat belt and opened the door, getting out to stretch her back muscles, knowing they were going to be driving for a while today and not wanting to sit any more than necessary. She leaned against the front of the SUV and surveyed the area. Her vantage point gave her a clear view of the sidewalk and street as well as the alley. She watched busy people walk by dressed in business suits, carrying briefcases, cutting across the street and through the alley. Tall buildings surrounded them, so high she couldn't see the top floors. Everyone was in a hurry, juggling cups of coffee or talking on their cell phones.

It was a lifestyle completely foreign to her. For as long as she could remember she'd been with the demon hunters, moving from city to city, staying hidden. No place was home, yet every place was home, because the people she was with were family.

Lou had been her family. The only father she had known, since her own parents had been taken down by demons. She remembered that night so clearly, as if it had happened yesterday instead of ten years ago. The darkness, the shock at seeing the creatures. Her parents—what those monsters had done, killing her father and taking her mother away. The hunters had shown up, but it was too late. Mandy had hidden; otherwise, she was sure, she'd have been either killed or taken, too.

And in the darkness a hand had reached out for her, a comforting voice telling her she was safe now. She had grabbed on to that hand like a lifeline. That hand had been Lou's.

She knew he'd had other options. He could have wiped her memories, left her somewhere—a shelter or orphanage or something. But instead he'd taken her in, cared for her, and eventually made her one of them. He had accepted her, hadn't turned her away, had patiently answered all her questions honestly, had put up with her tantrums and her anger and her grief over the loss of her parents. He'd held her through the nightmares and had entrusted her with the Realm's secrets. He'd made her into what she was now. She'd loved him fiercely, had held on to him like any child would to a parent.

And then he was gone. Just like her other parents.

Now she was alone again.

She was an adult now. It shouldn't matter.

That it did annoyed her. Lou had always told her she was a marshmallow. She'd worked hard to prove him wrong.

The hot sting of tears clouded her vision. Oh, no. Not here, not now. She blinked them back and slid on her sunglasses, surveying the bustling crowds once again, forcing her mind to empty.

Watch the people. Think about their lives. Where are they going? What are they doing?

Her gaze wandered, scanning the crowd until it captured a tall, thin man darting into a darkened alleyway. With her special sunglasses on, her eyes quickly adjusted to the darkness there, outlining him as he paused. What was he doing? Curious, she pushed off the car and moved toward the alley, staying in between the cars in the parking lot so he wouldn't see her. She paused at the corner of the brick building, peered around, and saw the man. Nice-looking, mid-thirties with thick sandy blond hair and a dark blue business suit. He carried a briefcase. He just stood there, though, looking out toward the other side of the alley, watching people go by.

The guy darted behind a filthy Dumpster. What the hell did he do that for? Wouldn't his suit get dirty? Mandy started into the alley, but stopped dead in her tracks when a mist began to form around the man, starting up from his feet.

Oh, shit. Mandy couldn't believe what she was seeing. This couldn't be happening.

She crouched down behind a couple trash cans and watched.

The mist lifted up, surrounding the suited man. His eyes began to glow a pale blue. The mist covered him completely and he disappeared.

Fuck! She ran back to the SUV just as Michael came out of the bank, smiling.

He frowned when he saw her. "What's wrong?"

"I just saw a demon."

His eyes widened. "What?"

She motioned with her head. "Back there, in the alley."

"What kind of demon?"

"Guy in a business suit. He crossed over from the street, slipped into the alley. Just stood there for a few, then ducked behind a Dumpster. Mist coated him, then he disappeared."

Michael frowned, turned and looked over at the street. "It's sunny over there."

"Yes."

"You know demons can't handle sunlight."

"Allegedly, yes. But apparently this one could."

"Are you sure of what you saw?"

She folded her arms over each other, irritation beginning to boil inside her. "Do you think I'm delusional?"

"No, of course not. But it could have been something else. Steam, for example."

She rolled her eyes and grabbed his arm. "Come on."

They moved into the alley, behind the Dumpster.

Mandy led Michael to the exact spot where she'd seen the demon disappear. "Right here. See, no steam vent."

Michael crouched down and inspected the ground, the wall, the Dumpster, before rising and wiping his hands. "This makes no sense. Demons can't walk in daylight."

"Correction. They couldn't walk in daylight before. Apparently now some can."

He shook his head. "Not possible."

"Right. Neither is the existence of demons to nearly all the world's population. Do you think I'm making this up?"

"Following this would delay searching for Dalton and Isabelle."

"Oh, come on, Michael. Even I can't put off the inevitable. Besides, I believe in Dalton. The sooner we find them, the sooner we can prove his innocence. There's a damn good reason he took Isabelle and ran. But right now, we need to figure out what the hell happened here."

"We can't stay here, Mandy."

She blew out a hard breath. "You go on ahead, then. I'm not leaving until I figure out what's going on."

He seemed to consider the idea. Fine. He could leave if he wanted to. This mystery was too good to pass up. And they were demon hunters, weren't they? Their job was to hunt demons. There had been a demon standing right in this spot less than five minutes ago. And where there was one demon, there had to be more. Mandy didn't like the idea of leaving the area crawling with the Sons of Darkness' minions.

"Twenty-four hours," Michael said. "I'll give you one

day. We'll check things out. If nothing comes of it, we're back on the road."

She nodded. "Fine with me."

"Okay, Mandy. You saw the demon, so I'm putting you in charge. Where do we start?"

She'd never been in charge before. This was new. Lou had always told her that some day she'd get to lead a team. Now was her chance. Of course said team consisted of just her and Michael, but still, it was a start. Excitement drilled through her veins. "This is the downtown business district. My first thought when I saw the demon was, what was he doing down here? What does a demon need with a business environment in a major city?"

"Good point. And if a demon can pass as a businessman, anything's possible," Michael said as they made their way back to the SUV. "The Realm has always feared that the Sons of Darkness would someday, somehow make inroads into our world. That they'd figure out a way to have their people live among ours."

Mandy opened her car door and slid inside, turning to Michael as she slammed her door shut. "Infiltrating the human realm could have disastrous consequences. Commerce, politics, technology...think of the influence they could have in so many areas, Michael."

His grimace said it all. "I'm trying not to. That's why I'm hoping you're wrong."

For the first time, she hoped she was, too. The possibilities were endless. "Demons running our world...It's unthinkable."

"If the Sons of Darkness have somehow managed to

create demons that look human, who can walk among and interact with other humans without detection . . ."

"How would we ever be able to identify them . . . to destroy them?" Mandy asked.

Mandy didn't like the worry she saw on his face.

"I don't know. I guess we'll have to start figuring that out. If there are demons passing for human out there, we'd better start hunting them. Which means we need to find one so we can figure out what they're capable of. I pray you're wrong, that you didn't really see what you thought you did."

"I know what I saw, Michael."

Suddenly this mission had become more important than finding Dalton. She wanted to prove to Michael that she had seen a demon, but at the same time she really wished she hadn't seen it at all.

It could change everything.

Isabelle sucked in a breath, ignoring the pounding of her heart. Dalton was right. Getting close to him in order to figure out how to dig into her mind and drag out her demons—literally or figuratively—might spell disaster, given what had been happening to her lately.

"Any idea how we're going to do that?"

He offered up an encouraging smile. "It won't be painful, I promise. We'll just talk."

"Talk? That's it?"

"At first. You have to admit we haven't done a lot of that."

"True enough. But I don't see how just talking is going to help."

"It's not just the talk, Isabelle. It's the topics."

"Oh."

"I need to find out what you can remember, especially about those dreams you've been having. And then we need to delve into the . . . daydreams, or whatever they are."

"So you're going to push me."

He nodded.

"Is that wise?"

"The more we know, the stronger you'll be. You can't fight what you don't know, what you can't see. Right now we're fumbling around in the dark and I don't like it. I know you don't like it, either."

He was right. She felt like she wasn't in control, that someone or something else was pushing her buttons. She'd do whatever it took to change that, even if it meant opening up the Pandora's box of her mind, her soul, or whatever held her captive.

"Okay, so when do we start?"

"How about some dinner first?"

Of course. It was getting late. She'd been so used to eating very little that the thought of food never occurred to her unless prompted by Dalton. She hadn't even thought about the time.

Time, that elusive thing that seemed to slip by her a lot lately.

"Come on. You need some company besides me. We'll go eat dinner with Georgie and her family."

He was right. She could use the distraction.

But as they walked up to the house, she tensed. Maybe it was the way Georgie looked at her, as if she knew all her secrets. Which was funny, now that she thought about it, because even Isabelle didn't know the answers. What made her think Georgie did?

She had to calm down. It was just dinner.

So why did she feel like she was on her way to an inquisition? Georgie had seemed nice enough the first time she met her. Hardly imposing. She was a slight thing, and friendly.

"Would you relax?" Dalton said as he pulled open the screen door and held it for her.

She walked through, inhaling the sweet scent of something cooking. She followed it into the kitchen in the back of the house. Georgie and a few other women were in there, surrounded by several children.

"Evenin'," Georgie said as they walked in. "Grab something to drink and have a seat. Dinner will be on the table shortly."

"Can I help?" Isabelle asked.

Georgie shook her head. "Almost finished here, *chère*, but thank you."

Isabelle went to the counter and filled her glass with iced tea, then made one for Dalton. The tea was already sweetened; she licked her lips and savored the sugared brew. Okay, so far so good. No one had pounced on her or given her funny looks the minute she walked in the door.

Georgie introduced her to the other two women— Anabelle and Laticia, cousins who also lived on the property. The few children scurrying around belonged to them. Georgie had a daughter named Celine, after her great-grandmother. Three men came through the back door as soon as the women started serving food. Georgie introduced one as her husband, Frank, the other two as Anabelle and Laticia's husbands, Thomas and Jerome. The men worked the small farm on the property.

Dinner was a raucous event, filled with lively conversation, everyone talking over one another and lots of laughter. Isabelle settled in as an observer, happy to stay silent and watch the interplay between the families. The children were well behaved, but allowed to intermingle in the conversations. The parents weren't overly indulgent, but not too strict, either. They all engaged Isabelle and Dalton in their conversations, but didn't pry into anything too personal. The children seemed fascinated by Isabelle's career as an archaeologist, and of course wanted to know if she'd ever dug up dinosaurs. When she said she had, the kids were excited and filled with questions, which she was delighted to answer.

When the meal was finished, everyone helped clean up, so the chore was done in a hurry. Anabelle and Laticia scooted off with the kids, and the guys headed out the back door, leaving Georgie alone with Isabelle and Dalton.

"Now," Georgie said, wiping her hands with a towel before sitting down at the table. "You two getting settled over at the cabin?"

Dalton nodded. "We're fine. Took a nice hike today to get Isabelle familiar with the area."

"Good." She looked over to Isabelle. "But that's not why you're here, is it?"

Isabelle's glance shot over to Dalton.

"I'd like Georgie to weigh in on what's been happening to you, see if she can offer some insight," he said.

Great. Isabelle shifted uncomfortably. How many people needed to know who and what she was?

"She knows, Isabelle. Georgie is gifted with incredible insights as well as magic. And she knows about the Realm of Light and Sons of Darkness. There are no secrets here."

Wow. That was a pretty big secret. "Okay," she said.

"I'll be happy to help in any way I can," Georgie said.

"Isabelle's having some problems."

Georgie turned dark eyes to her. Isabelle resisted the urge to scoot away from the woman's mesmerizing gaze.

"What kind of problems?"

Dalton slanted his gaze to her. "Go ahead, Isabelle."

She supposed saying "I don't wanna" would be a bit childish. She turned to Georgie. "I have these memory gaps. And during these gaps, I do things."

Georgie's expression didn't change. She simply nodded and said, "Go on."

"I have nightmares. Every time I sleep, demons come for me."

"Is it like you're awake? You can feel their presence, feel them touching you?"

Isabelle nodded. "Yes. It's exactly like that. It's almost like as soon as I fall asleep, they get some kind of signal to come for me."

"Do they take you somewhere, or come to where you are?"

"I don't remember. That's the problem. As soon as I

wake up, everything is foggy. I know the demons have been with me, because I sense them descending as soon as I fall asleep, but I can't recall exactly how or where."

"That's all right," Georgie said. "What else?"

Isabelle shifted her gaze to Dalton, who nodded. "It's okay. You can tell her."

This part was going to be tough. It was personal. Humiliating. Confusing. She looked at Georgie. "It's about Dalton. There's something about him that... draws me."

Georgie looked at Dalton, then back at Isabelle, her lips lifting in a knowing smile. "Yes, I can see that it would. Is that a problem?"

"It's a problem when I can't remember what I'm doing."

Georgie frowned. "What do you mean?"

"I was taking a bath. I remember glancing out the window and seeing Dalton. I was...uh...admiring him, if you know what I mean."

"Yes. I understand," Georgie said, smiling at her as if she knew exactly what Isabelle meant.

"Next thing I knew, I woke up and was in the backyard with him. Naked. Practically draped around him. I must have left the bath and walked right outside."

"And you don't remember how you got there?"

She shook her head. "And apparently I offered up some rather provocative invitations."

Georgie didn't even blink, just nodded. "Has it happened before that incident?"

"Sort of. Though not as flagrant."

"And you can't recall what happened during these periods?"

"No. Only that there seemed to be a period where I was almost asleep, or I suffered some kind of memory loss, because I don't remember how I got from point A to point B."

Georgie came over and sat on the bench next to Isabelle, smoothing her fingers over Isabelle's hands. Georgie's hands were warm. Isabelle's felt like ice.

"You're blocking them," she finally said.

"Excuse me?"

"They're trying to find you, and you're fighting them. I feel them near you."

"Them being the demons?" Dalton asked.

"Yes," Georgie said without taking her eyes off Isabelle's face. "This is hard for you. It's causing you stress, pain, emotional upheaval. You're very strong. So are they. This battle of wills is taking its toll on your psyche."

Isabelle wasn't even aware of a battle taking place. "I'm not doing anything. I'm just trying to exist."

"Trust me. It's happening. You're fighting them, but that just makes them try harder to get to you."

"Okay. I can accept that I don't want them to take me again. It makes sense that I would subconsciously block them. But that doesn't really explain my behavior," Isabelle said. "With Dalton."

"Actually, it explains more than you think. Dalton is the reason you still live. He is—at least in your mind—your one and only ally against them. Also, you are drawn to him, and he to you. But you fight that attraction."

Georgie turned her gaze to Dalton. "So does he. It creates much conflict within you both."

"Which means?" Isabelle hated to be dense, but she still didn't understand.

"You're at war within yourself, Isabelle. You're fighting an internal battle with demons who want to know where you are. You seem to be trying to focus your attention there. Your full attention. At the same time, you're also battling your attraction to Dalton. Part of you refuses to give in, very much wants to remain distant. The other part of you wants to join with him, needs to join with him in the most basic of ways."

She exhaled. So much of what Georgie said made sense.

"Also, I'm not sure it's the human part of you that seeks him."

That was not good. Isabelle tensed again.

"Oh, great," Dalton said. "So what you're saying is the human side of Isabelle can resist me just fine. It's the demon side of her that wants to jump my bones."

Georgie smiled. "In a way, yes."

"So when I went out in the yard—the part I couldn't remember—that was the demon part of me . . ."

"Coming out to play," Georgie finished for her. "Yes, I believe so."

Isabelle laid her head in her hands to combat the dizziness. "I don't understand this. It's all so confusing. You're talking about parts of me that don't seem real to me." She lifted her head, looked at Dalton, then at Georgie. "I don't feel like I'm battling anything. I feel human. All of me."

"For now," Georgie said. "Soon enough, that will change. The demon side of you will grow stronger, will fight for dominance."

"How can I avoid that?"

Georgie laid her hand over Isabelle's. "You can't. You're going to have to face it. It wants to take you over. *They* want that part of you to take over. If you want to win, you have to be ready to do battle." Georgie's face changed then, her expression fierce, like that of a warrior as she looked at both Dalton and Isabelle.

"You're both going to have to fight."

"Tell me what I have to do," Isabelle said, determination filling her. "I don't want them to take me again. I won't let them take me again." She looked to Dalton, communicating her desires without words. He would understand what she meant.

She'd rather die than let the Sons of Darkness have her.

"You have to break through these losses in time. Work with Dalton on your memories. Allow him to get closer. You're going to need him in this battle."

How much closer? If the demon part of her wanted Dalton, shouldn't she keep him as far away as possible?

"I know the question you're not asking," Georgie said. She stood and moved toward the sink, put a few dishes away, then turned and crossed her arms, staring down at both of them. "The answer is no. Don't keep Dalton away from you. Draw him near. He is all that is good within you. You are all that is good within him. But you have to sift through the darkness together to find the light within each other. Search, until you discover it."

CHAPTER SIX

Isabelle was floating, sinking into a blissful, dark silence. She felt weightless, as if she were sailing on a cloud in the moonless sky, no destination in mind. Nothing in front of her, nothing behind her. She reached out, sensed only misty, cool air surrounding her. She'd never felt more at peace.

Until she landed with a hard thud, jerking her out of her sense of well-being. She moved, but was restricted by walls on each side of her. She tried to find her bearings, but it was so dark she couldn't see. Where was she?

She couldn't move. Not an inch on any side.

She was trapped. She raised her arms above her head, but felt nothing. No handhold. The coolness around her evaporated, her sense of air cut off. Something fell on top of her. She inhaled, breathing in dust, dirt as it rained on top of her in a fine, unending mist. It coated her skin, her lungs, as it continued to pour in on her. Despite covering her mouth and nose, she couldn't hold it back as the downpour of dirt continued, filling up the tiny hole she was trapped in, burying her to her ankles, her knees, her hips, wedging her in this grave.

"Help me!"

No one answered.

"Dalton, help me!"

Dalton didn't answer. He wasn't there. She was alone. Panic hammered at her and she began to shake. She clawed at the sides of the hole. More dirt fell in, trapping her arms at her sides. Now she couldn't cover her mouth and she breathed in dirt. It filled her nostrils, poured into her lungs, choking her. She couldn't breathe.

Oh, help me. Someone, please.

She was dying, smothering, unable to suck in life-giving oxygen. They were burying her alive and no one would ever find her. She opened her mouth to scream, but the scream was empty, silent, filled with dirt. As consciousness faded, she heard their laughter, their voices. Dark, evil, twisted.

You're ours, Isabelle. We control you. Your air, your breath. When you die, you will still be ours. You cannot run. You cannot hide. You cannot put us off forever. Your soul belongs to us.

Isabelle shot up in bed, her mouth open, nothing coming out but a panicked rush of air as she fought for breath, fought for the scream that wanted to erupt but couldn't.

In the half darkness she saw a shape to the side of the bed. Panic rushed at her, her body filling with heat. She pushed away, ready to run.

"Isabelle."

Dalton's voice was low, soothing, as he reached for her hand. "Isabelle, it's me. You're here, in your bed. You're all right."

She couldn't catch her breath. Sweat drenched her body, her clothes, the sheets around her. She couldn't speak, fought to control the overwhelming nausea.

Dizziness made the room tilt. The dream was still so real, she was caught between it and the darkened bedroom.

"Breathe, honey. Slow and easy. In through your nose, out through your mouth."

Dalton's voice helped. She did as he instructed and the dizziness began to fade. But this time, she kept the dream in the forefront of her mind, refusing to let it disappear. She wanted to remember, even though the thought of it made her throat constrict.

She shivered. "I'm all wet," she managed, her voice still hoarse. She could still taste dirt in her throat, shuddered at how real it all was.

He smoothed his hand over her hair. "You were sweating. I heard you moaning, came in to check on you. You were thrashing around on the bed. I debated whether to wake you..."

"I'm glad you did. I need to take a shower." And brush her teeth. And gargle. She had to get the taste of dry earth out of her mouth.

"Do you want me to come in with you?"

Yes. No. She didn't want to be alone, but knew she had to do this by herself. She refused to become dependent on Dalton. "I'll be fine."

He nodded. "I'll wait right here for you."

"I'll only be a few minutes." On shaky legs, she slid off the bed, grabbed some clothes and slipped into the bathroom. She turned on the water and while it warmed up, scoured her teeth and used mouth rinse. Feeling immensely better after that, she hurried through her shower, washing off the sweat coating her body. True to his word, Dalton was still in her room when she came out. In fact, he was making her bed.

"I changed the sheets. They were drenched."

"Thank you. For that, and for hearing me, for waking me." She turned her head as a low rumble sounded off in the distance, followed by a flash of lightning.

"Storm's coming," Dalton said in reply.

She nodded, shivering as goose bumps prickled her skin.

"Let's go sit in the living room for a while."

"What time is it?"

"About four A.M."

She tossed her damp hair over her shoulder. "I'm sorry, Dalton. I don't sleep much these days."

"Don't worry about it. Neither do I. Come on."

He went into the living room and sat on the sofa. Isabelle hesitated. For some reason she needed the contact of Dalton's body but felt uncertain asking for it.

Dalton patted the cushion beside him. "Sit with me."

Relieved, Isabelle curled up next to him and pulled her legs behind her.

"Do you remember the dream?" he asked.

"Yes. This time I forced myself to stay in the here and now, to remember. At first I was floating, like on a cloud or in space. It was wonderful, very freeing. But then I fell, plummeted into a hole or a grave, and dirt came raining down on top of me. I couldn't crawl out, and more dirt came in, choking me. I couldn't breathe. I was being buried alive."

Dalton put his arm around her and drew her closer

to him. She didn't mind that at all, still chilled despite the warmth in the room.

"When it felt like I was dying, I heard their voices."

"Whose voices?"

"The Sons of Darkness. Tase, the one who was their leader."

"What did he say?"

"Something about how I belonged to them, and they control everything about me. That even in death, I would be theirs, including my soul. And that's when you woke me."

Dalton arched a brow. "That's pretty intense."

"Yeah."

"No wonder you were in bad shape."

He smoothed his hand down her arm and back up, settling at her nape to massage the tension nestled there. She shivered, but this time it wasn't from being chilled.

"It's better now. Thank you for sitting with me."

He looked down at her. "Are you ready to go back to sleep?"

"No. I'm pretty much done with sleeping for the night." The thought of closing her eyes again brought about vivid images of being closed in, of dirt pouring on her, of being unable to breathe. She couldn't sleep anymore. She might not be able to again for a long while. "You can go back to bed if you want to. I'll be fine out here."

"So will I." He shifted so she could slide into the crook of his arm. She felt sheltered there, and he wrapped his arm more securely around her. She drew her knees up to her chest, settled, and finally relaxed. She could almost fall asleep this way, except Dalton kept moving his hand up and down her arm and shoulder, and slid his fingers into her hair to massage her head. The sensations he evoked had her wide awake and wired, her emotions and physical reactions tuned into him completely.

"Are you deliberately trying to provoke a response from me?" she finally asked.

"Huh?" His voice sounded lazy and tired. He even yawned.

"Never mind."

"What are you talking about?"

She sighed, staring at the darkness through the front window. Normally after a dream like the one she'd just had, the dark would scare her, but sitting in the pitch-black room with Dalton didn't bother her at all for some reason.

"You're touching me."

He didn't stop, his fingertips gliding over her arm. "Does it bother you?"

"Yes and no. I'm just trying to figure out your intent."

"I'm relaxing you."

"I'm fine."

"True enough. You haven't gone all demon on me."

She snorted. "So do I get a cookie?"

"You're a bit of a smart-ass, Isabelle."

"So I've been told. And you didn't answer my question."

"What question?"

Men. Always talking in circles to avoid answering. "Are you trying to provoke the demon?"

"Maybe. The demon is part of who you are. You can't avoid it forever."

She shifted, facing him. She could see his face despite the darkened room. There was enough gray light sifting in from the moonlight that she could read his expression. But she couldn't tell if he was teasing her or he was dead serious. "Won't waking up the demon part of me alert the Sons of Darkness to our whereabouts?"

"I don't think so. Because as Georgie said, there's a part of you that doesn't want to mix it up with the Sons of Darkness again. You're doing a fine job of fighting their attempts to find you. I don't think bringing out your demon side is going to alert them."

Easy for him to say. He wasn't having the kinds of nightmares she had, the feeling that the demons came for her every night, took her somewhere, had power over her. She started to pull away, not liking the direction this conversation—or his intent—was heading.

"Don't."

Her gaze shot to his. She wished there was more light so she could see his eyes. "Why?"

"We need each other."

She didn't understand that. She knew why she needed him—right now he was all she had, a lifeline to grasp on to. Otherwise, she'd be facing this nightmare alone. But why did he need her? "What do you mean?"

He hesitated. "I have to prove to the Realm of Light that there was a damn good reason I ran off with you."

Things were becoming more clear. "You saved my life that day. You weren't supposed to, were you?"

"No."

She didn't know why it had never dawned on her before. Maybe she hadn't wanted to think about the possibility, to voice it. "You were ordered to kill me, weren't you?"

"Yes."

She let that soak in for a second, though for some reason the knowledge didn't surprise her. She was a demon now. She had become a threat to the Realm. It made perfect sense for them to want her dead. What didn't make sense was why she still lived. "Why didn't you?"

"Because for a second that night, when you looked right at me, I saw you. Not the demon. And I saw something in you that I—I saw something in you that was still human. That was worth saving."

Dalton really did save her life that day in Italy. He'd not only rescued her from the Sons of Darkness; he had traded in his life with the Realm in order to keep her alive. "I don't know what to say."

"You don't have to say anything. I did what I thought was right, Isabelle. The others didn't know you like I did. They didn't see what I did. I made a choice."

"You made a choice that cost you your career, your friends."

"The hunters are—were—my friends, yes. Still are, I hope. We'll get this thing with you figured out. Once we do, they'll understand. And we'll make it right with them."

He made it sound so simple. Isabelle didn't think it would be that easy. He had broken some policy or one of their sacred laws or something. Surely there would be consequences. She didn't want him to be hurt because of her, because of what she was. "I'm sorry."

"Don't be."

Other than Angelique, she didn't have friends or anyone she could count on. She'd always been on her own. No one had her back, so she'd relied only on herself. And she'd never made sacrifices for others. She had always been too into making sure her own needs were met. She didn't understand why Dalton had given up so much for her.

"Why are you doing this, Dalton? For me?"

He didn't answer for a while. She waited, not wanting to push him.

"I know how much it hurt you when I read your mother's diary. I saw it on your face that day on the yacht."

She remembered that day so clearly, seeing Dalton with her mother's diary in his hands, knowing he'd read it, that he knew her secrets, knew her own mother thought her evil... She'd never wanted anyone to see that. "I wanted to burn that diary but I couldn't."

"It's good that you didn't. It gave the Realm insights into who you are."

She snorted. "Even I don't have those. And all it did was give the Realm ammunition to use against me."

He shook his head. "Not true. It'll take time for you to realize that the Realm is not your enemy. That's why I'm doing this for you. My taking your diary was a catalyst for a lot of bad things happening to you. I felt responsible. I figure I owe you."

She shook her head. "You don't owe me anything. The Sons of Darkness would have found me, anyway. You've said so yourself."

"Yeah. They probably would have." He looked at her,

and it was growing light enough now that she could see his eyes. Like mirrors. Beautiful, and truly open to her. "But I hurt you."

Her lips lifted. "No, you didn't hurt me. I did more damage to myself than you ever could."

"How?"

"Self-hatred is a powerful weapon, you know."

He swept her hair away from her face. "You have nothing to hate yourself for."

She laughed. "I'm part demon, Dalton. I tried to kill my sister."

"No . . . *you* didn't."

"My claws were at her throat. I raised my hand to strike. I—"

She realized then that she was remembering. Everything. Including that moment when Dalton stopped her, when he told her he'd take her away. When the human side of her had come back, because she had forced it out. Part of her had wanted to come back long enough for him to see it.

"You remember that night in Sicily, don't you?"

"Yes."

Dalton had seen it. The human part of her had wanted to live that night, had wanted to triumph over the demon inside her. She hadn't wanted to hurt Angelique—God knows she'd hated hurting her sister. She hadn't wanted to be a pawn of the Sons of Darkness. That wasn't Isabelle. She was a human being. Not a demon. She carried a demon's blood inside her, but that's not who she was—not who she wanted to be. She refused to let them turn her into one of their slaves.

Besides, Dalton had sacrificed everything for her. She couldn't let him down.

"You're right," she finally said. "I have to fight this— fight them. They can't win."

He nodded. "And I'll fight with you. For you."

She grinned, hope surging for the first time. "Like my own personal knight in shining armor."

He laughed. "Trust me, honey. I'm no knight. And my armor is kind of tarnished."

"Even better. I hate perfection. Makes me feel inadequate."

"So we're two imperfect people struggling together."

"That works for me."

He went quiet then. The whole room was dead silent except for the two of them staring at each other. She studied his face—almost too beautiful for a man's, and yet rugged and angled in all the right places. But it was his eyes that captured her. They always seemed to study her, as if he could see inside her soul. It was both comforting and disconcerting at the same time. She wasn't used to being examined this way, and yet she couldn't help but enjoy being looked at by him. What woman wouldn't?

Isabelle was in awe of this man who would give up so much of his own personal freedom, the life that he was comfortable in, for someone he knew so little about. It still didn't make sense to her. Why would he do that when she could give him nothing in return?

Unable to help herself, she reached up and palmed his cheek, let her hand slide down, shivering at the contact of her skin against the stubble there. His expression turned wary and that made her smile.

"What are you doing, Isabelle?"

She didn't answer, instead leaned into him, lifting her face to his. She remembered what it was like to kiss him. It was fireworks and magic and volcanoes with melting lava. When he kissed her and touched her, she forgot everything except what it was like to be a woman.

She wanted that right now. While it was the human Isabelle fully in charge, not the demon side of her taking control.

And the human Isabelle knew exactly what she wanted.

Their lips were only inches apart, and Dalton didn't seem to be going anywhere, just studying her cautiously. Of course he didn't seem to be in any hurry to make the first move, either. So she'd have to do it.

She didn't mind. She leaned in and brushed her lips across his, felt the tingle in her toes and other points in her body, felt warmth sweep through her as she moved her mouth over his. She sighed against him, laid her palms flat against his chest and deepened the kiss.

He tasted of orange juice—they'd had some when they first came out here to the sofa. She licked along his bottom lip, savoring the oh-so-male flavor of him, a spicy yet sweet scent that drew her to him like no man ever had before. The fact that he wasn't grabbing her and tossing her under him on the sofa was even more appealing. It made her want to take charge. She held his shoulders and climbed onto his lap, straddling him.

Dalton wasn't unaffected. She felt that solid evidence

as she settled against him. Her gaze drifted down and she admired the hard ridge of his erection against his shorts, her mind awash in all the things she wanted to do with him. But not just yet. She enjoyed where she was and what they were doing. She glanced back up at him and smiled. And still, he stared at her, as if questioning what she was going to do. She didn't think it required explanation, so she said nothing, instead drifted toward him and kissed him again. He had such a great mouth. Full, yet firm. And he held still while she explored, so she grasped his head and pressed more firmly, surging into him to press her breasts against his chest. She could feel his heart pounding against her.

It took her all of a minute and a half of wonderful kissing to realize he wasn't touching her, wasn't kissing her back. She pulled away.

"What's wrong?"

"We shouldn't be doing this."

She wiped her lips with the back of her hand, suddenly mindful of her wanton, oh-so-bold position on his lap. But dammit, he had an erection. It's not like he wasn't into this.

"You want me to stop."

His lips curled into a hint of a smile, devastating to her senses. That smile held promise. "Parts of me definitely don't want you to stop. Only the logical part."

She glanced down at his lap.

"That's not the logical part," he said.

"Clearly." She climbed off his lap and gave them both some distance, dragging her fingers through her hair, trying to shake off the effects being so close to him had on her. She grabbed the glass of juice and drained it, then set it down and turned back to him. "I thought you wanted to wake the sleeping demon."

"Not that way. If your sexual attraction to me makes the demon take front and center, then we should probably—"

"Yes. I understand." She stood.

"Isabelle." He grasped her wrist, holding her there.

She looked down at him, equal parts embarrassed and still needy for something she obviously wasn't going to have. "It's okay, really. I'm hungry. I'm going to fix us some breakfast."

He let go of her and she went into the kitchen, needing distance. "I'll help you."

She stopped, turned. "Please don't. I need some space, Dalton."

"Okay. I'll go take a shower, then."

"You do that."

She turned her back to him and opened the refrigerator, not exhaling until she heard the bathroom door close. She shuddered out a sigh, blinking back the hot sting of tears that broke through and slid down her cheeks despite her best efforts to force them back. She wrapped her arms around herself when she discovered she was shaking.

Idiot.

"Well, you took that rejection well, Izzy." She shook her head and began cracking eggs into a bowl, needing to keep her hands busy.

Dalton was right. Being together would have been a really bad idea. She had no clue what even happened to her when she fell under one of those weird spells. And if she was going to be with Dalton again, she'd definitely want to be in the present, so she could remember.

All things considered, there were too many strikes against them.

But oh, it would have been so, so good.

Dalton stood under the cool water, hoping it would chill the heat in his body.

Eventually he turned the shower off, realizing he was still on fire. Cold water hadn't helped. Not that he'd expected it to. From the time he leaned over Isabelle's bed and shook her out of her restless sleep, he'd known it was going to be tough to remain in this house with her.

Not impossible, but damned hard.

Just like his condition most of the time around her. Pathetic, really. One would think he could control his libido after all these years, but just being around her, listening to the sound of her voice, looking into her mesmerizing eyes, and he was hard as granite and ready to throw her down and bury his cock inside her.

And he'd wager that's just what the demon part of her was hoping for. Her demon side had a goal: temptation. And he wasn't going to fall for it. He was the one who had to remain strong, because if he gave in, he wasn't sure what would happen.

He'd wanted to test the demon side of her, and maybe that had been a bad idea. She really seemed to crave affection of any kind. But was that Isabelle, or the demon?

Maybe he shouldn't think of her as two entities. After

all, she was both human and demon. The confused human Isabelle and the seductive demon were one and the same. He needed to remember that. His goal was to integrate them, not destroy one of them. She could learn to live with and control the demon side of herself, just as Derek and Nic—the other hunters who were part demon—had done.

The key was in figuring out how, because even though he'd like Isabelle to be just like Derek and Nic, she wasn't. Her demon side was a hell of a lot different from theirs. It was stronger, and the Sons of Darkness knew it. He was going to have to tread lightly, and think before he made any moves.

Which wasn't easy when living with a beautiful seductress who wanted to have sex with you. A man could only be noble for so long.

He groaned and got dressed, staring at himself in the mirror. It was times like this he missed Lou and the other hunters. Lou would have advice for him, could tell him what to do. How easy would it be to just pick up a phone and call him. He really would like to talk to someone.

Maybe he could get Lou on the phone. He could rewire a disposable cell with an untraceable number, figure out the Realm's reaction, and at the same time get Lou's advice on what to do about Isabelle.

Risky, but worth it. He needed to find out if he was walking down the right path with her.

Because the wrong choice could lead to both his and Isabelle's destruction.

CHAPTER SEVEN

"Your twenty-four hours are almost up, Mandy."
Michael cast an impatient look in her direction. Mandy ignored him. They'd spent the past twenty-four hours without sleep, barely eating. Instead, they'd scoured the city, searching for any sign of demons. So far, they'd found nothing. They'd been downtown, to the beach, had even driven around the suburbs. Michael had used his tracking system while Mandy drove.

"They aren't going to appear on your super-secret decoder map there if they aren't hiding out underground. I told you, the guy I saw wore a business suit. He walked in the sunlight. He didn't appear different from any other human walking the streets downtown."

Michael didn't look up from the infrared sensors and whatever gadgetry the Realm had them using. "You just keep driving and let me worry about the technology."

She shook her head. "Whatever. But there's got to be a better way to do this. I say we hang out near the alley where I first saw the guy. It's nearly the same time we were here yesterday. I might be able to pick him up again."

"Drive over that way and see if you can spot him," Michael said.

They were only two streets away. Mandy turned and headed in that direction, parking on the street this time. She got out and fed the parking meter, then climbed back in the car and waited, convinced she was going to see him again.

Michael kept his head down and scanned his laptop.

"Anything?" she asked.

"No. I don't think I'm going to see anything on the scans here." He looked up at her. "There's nothing to see. There are no demons here, Mandy."

"You want me to be wrong."

He nodded. "Yeah, I do. But not for the reasons you think."

"I understand." She really did. She wished she hadn't seen it, hoped it was an illusion. But she knew what she'd seen. It was real. She stared out the window.

And spotted him. She blinked, looked again, needing to be sure.

She grasped Michael's wrist. "There he is!"

"Where?"

"Navy blue suit, pale blue shirt, red tie. He's just crossing the street at a pretty hefty clip, at the light." Mandy had her hand on the door handle, her backpack crushed in her hand.

"All right. Let's cut him off."

She slid her comm unit into her ear and slammed the car door shut. Michael climbed out on his side and met her on the sidewalk.

"I'm heading through the alleyway," Michael said. "We'll intercept him there. Stay in touch via the comm."

She nodded and headed fast down the sidewalk,

trying to appear normal, like she was late to work. Fortunately, the people she brushed by were intent on their own destinations. They were probably used to this morning rush of bodies zooming past them and didn't even notice her fast pace. Even if they did, she didn't care. Mandy's attention was focused on the man, who was also in a hurry. He was about a hundred feet ahead of her. No way was she going to lose this guy. Not this time. She quickened her pace to a jog, her heart thumping with the adrenaline rush. Finally, she was beginning to catch up to him. Now she had to hope he didn't turn around and notice her, though he kept his attention straight ahead, obviously with a specific purpose or destination in mind.

"I'm just inside the alley entrance. Where are you?" Michael commed.

"He's about a hundred yards from where you are. I'm twenty-five feet or so behind him."

"Hurry the hell up."

"I'm not going to stroll hand-in-hand with him, Michael. Trust me. I've got the timing covered."

For every one step the man took, she took two. The alley loomed closer and she knew she was only going to get one chance at this. Fortunately, the crowds had thinned. She'd have a few seconds at most to get this done, and hopefully no one would notice.

Almost on his heels, she slowed her pace, keeping her head down but her gaze fully on her quarry. A few more steps and he'd be at the alley. As soon as he crossed it she'd have him. She had to watch everything now. Nobody was around them as he stepped into the alley.

She made her move, quickening her step as if she was going to pass him, then seemingly losing control of her backpack.

"Oh, sorry," she said, knocking into him. As soon as he was off balance, bending over to reach for her fallen backpack, she gave him a shove, pushing him farther into the alley. He stumbled and fell and she checked to see if anyone had noticed, but no one was paying attention. Nothing like an eagle-eyed public keeping watch over one another. She almost laughed. She darted into the dark alley, where Michael was waiting.

The guy was on his hands and knees, glaring up at Mandy. "What the fuck!" he said.

"You sure this is him?" Michael asked.

"Positive."

Michael didn't hesitate, just plunged a syringe filled with clear liquid into the guy's neck. His eyes widened with surprise. He jerked a few times like he was having a seizure, his eyes rolling into the back of his head. Finally, he went pale as death and dropped to the ground.

"Did you kill him?" she asked.

Michael shook his head. "No. Let's get him out of sight."

They dragged him into the darkness of the alley, behind some boxes.

"Hang tight while I go grab the SUV."

Mandy nodded, pacing back and forth in front of the unconscious demon for what seemed like an eternity until Michael pulled in and popped open the back of the SUV.

Michael grabbed his upper body and Mandy went for

his legs. Even through his clothes she could tell he was icy. "This guy's cold."

"He was that way before I injected him. As soon as I put my fingers on his neck I knew he wasn't human."

Mandy didn't feel the need to mention she'd been right. They loaded the guy into the back of the SUV. Michael threw a pile of clothing and bags on top of him and pulled the shield over the back, then closed the hatch. They climbed into the SUV and Michael took off.

"What did you inject him with?" she asked as Michael turned onto the highway, heading out of town.

"A freezing agent. It'll drop his temperature to a near coma state."

"So basically, he's dead."

"For the most part, yeah. But I don't want him dead. Not yet, anyway."

"Where are we going?"

"To a Realm headquarters. We've never caught a demon alive before. And since this one can wander around in the daylight, we need to find out more about it. And ask some questions."

"You don't really think he's going to give you any answers, do you?"

Michael shrugged. "Having a live demon to examine will give us more than we have now."

"Yeah, if we can keep him from disappearing into a mist."

"We'll make sure he doesn't disappear."

But they'd made it past the initial hurdle. They'd captured the demon. Mandy hadn't been wrong. This could be a huge breakthrough for the Realm.

For the first time since Lou's death, Mandy felt a spark surge inside her. She was working again, hunting demons instead of one of their own.

It felt good.

Dalton left Isabelle with Georgie that day, saying he needed to make a run into town for some supplies, which was fine with her. And fortunately, Georgie seemed to instinctively know she wanted time to herself, so she kept busy in another part of the house and left Isabelle alone.

Isabelle needed some distance after everything that had happened between them early this morning. Dalton had been pleasant enough, acting as if nothing at all had happened between them, which was nice of him, all things considered.

She just couldn't handle being near him. It made her feel hot and itchy, like she constantly needed to take a cool shower.

There were a few magazines and books lying around, so she flipped through a couple but she couldn't concentrate. She'd asked Georgie if she could help around the house, but Georgie told her to rest and relax. She didn't want to rest. She always preferred doing something more physical rather than sitting around. She wasn't a television watcher—not that there was one to be found even if she was. When she wasn't out on a dig, she was typically on her laptop, researching. Right now she could do neither, which meant she spent the day pacing the house, bored out of her mind.

By late afternoon she'd had all she could handle of

being cooped up inside. She wandered through the house in search of Georgie, but didn't find her, so she headed outside toward the docks.

Ugh. It was hot, sticky, so humid just breathing took effort.

She found a shady spot by a group of trees near the dock and took a seat on the ground, content to be outside, even if she was sweating. She'd mostly worked in desert heat. Dry heat, not this unbearable humidity that threatened to suck the very air from her lungs.

She closed her eyes and thought about what Dalton had told her, about working her mind. If she was honest with herself, the idea frightened her. The thought of setting the demon inside her free . . . the havoc it could cause . . .

She hated not having control over herself—all of herself. But maybe if she practiced, a little bit at a time, strengthened her mind, tuned into her psyche, she could do it. She really wanted that control back.

She leaned her head against the tree, closed her eyes and took several deep breaths, reminding herself that she was human, that she was strong, that she could do this. She had done many important things on her own and she could do this, too. She could be triumphant. She was powerful . . .

Isabelle.

She stilled at the sound of her name, opened her eyes, and looked around.

No one was there. The water was calm, lazily lapping against the old wooden dock. The back of the house was quiet and when she looked up and down the walkway, she didn't see anyone.

Maybe she'd imagined hearing her name. She shrugged and leaned back, closed her eyes again, employing the same focus and mental exercises, visualizing herself as strong and powerful.

Isabelle.

Her eyelids shot open and she leaped to her feet.

Okay, she wasn't insane. Someone had definitely whispered her name. And it was coming from across the water, where the thick woods hid darkness.

She shivered. Great. Now she was scaring herself, and probably for no good reason other than her overactive imagination.

"Is someone there?" she yelled, then waited.

Nothing.

She crossed her arms, irritated with herself. She was not going to be scared. She slid back down the tree and sat again, this time keeping her eyes open, chanting to herself that she was strong, that she needed no one, that she could do this on her own.

Isabelle.

It wasn't real. She didn't hear it.

Isabelle.

Oh, God, yes she did. And she knew that voice, finally recognized the lilting, sickening sweet quality of Tase's voice calling her name.

Tase, the leader of the Sons of Darkness.

Stricken with fear and unable to move from her spot on the ground, she inched her gaze in either direction, afraid at any moment she'd see his black-clad form materialize in front of her, that he'd sweep her away to Hell before she ever had a chance to change who she was.

Come with me, Isabelle.

Her heart pounded, adrenaline pumping. Tears pricked her eyes but she refused to give way.

"You can't have me. Not this time."

A soft laugh, so evil it made her shiver. She raised her knees to her chest and buried her face in her hands, ashamed to feel such fear.

I'm not strong enough to fight this.

"Isabelle!"

Dalton! She looked up. He was there, at the back door, searching for her. In her spot against the tree he hadn't yet seen her.

He will kill you. We can save you.

No. She would *not* listen to Tase. He was evil. She had to move and do it now, no matter how afraid she was that they were going to snatch her the minute she left her place there on the bank.

"Dalton!" she screamed, panic blanketing her as she pushed off the ground and tore off running.

He saw her, the smile dying on his face immediately. He pushed through the door and flew off the back stairs, running to meet her. Her legs shook so badly she could barely put one in front of the other, but she had to. She had to get to Dalton. Falling apart wasn't going to help her get out of this mess.

He can't help you.

She shuddered, the voice like a snake slithering over her.

They wanted to scare her. It was working. She couldn't allow it.

Behind her, she heard laughter. Dark, demonic, coming closer.

You'll never get away from us, Isabelle. We're always with you.

Her breath wheezed in and out, her throat desert dry as she fought to swallow. She had no saliva left. Her fear had sucked it all up.

But only a few more feet and Dalton would be there.

That's it, run. More laughter. *We're coming for you, Isabelle.*

She took a diving leap and fell into Dalton's arms, panting from exertion and utter terror.

"Isabelle. Christ, what happened?" He wrapped his arms around her.

She couldn't speak, her throat raw, her heart pounding so hard she was afraid it would leap out of her chest. All she could do was stare up at Dalton's concerned face and thank God she was safe.

They hadn't gotten her.

Not this time, anyway.

"I was bored," she said, trying to breathe normally again. "I came out here to sit underneath the shade tree and work on my . . . mental exercises. I heard someone call my name. At first I thought it was you. But it wasn't. It was like a voice in my head, but not in my head, if that makes sense."

"No, not really. But I understand."

He probably didn't. "You think I'm crazy, that I'm hearing things."

He looked down at her. "Honey, you're not crazy. If you heard it, then it happened."

It was nice that he believed her. Especially since she wasn't certain she believed herself. "I don't know, Dalton. Part of me thinks the voice was just in my head. Then again, it seemed like it was all around me."

"Did you see anyone?"

"No. I looked everywhere. No one was around. And I thought it had to be my imagination, especially when I realized it was Tase's voice."

His face was grim as he nodded. "Let's get you back to the cabin."

They went inside the house. Dalton grabbed a bag and went to talk to Georgie for a minute. Then they walked back to the cabin.

"I'm sorry I left you today," he said, sitting her down on the sofa.

"It's not your fault."

"Are you sure it was Tase's voice?"

"Yes."

"What did he say?"

"That he wanted me to come with him. That you were going to kill me, and that only they could save me."

Dalton blew out a breath.

"Do they know where we are?" she asked.

"No. If they did, they'd come for you."

"But didn't they just do that?"

He swept a tendril of hair away from her face. "No. Their contact with you is on a psychic plane, not tangible."

"So it's like making a phone call but the number is blocked. They can reach me but they don't know where I am."

He smiled. "Something like that, yes."

She stood, paced the living room. "I was scared out there."

He watched her. "I don't blame you. They're hoping to frighten you, weaken you so they can penetrate your defenses."

"They don't think much of humans, do they?"

His lips lifted. "No, they don't."

She inhaled, blew it out. "They think we're cowards, that we scare easily. That pisses me off."

"Good. Your anger will give you power over them."

She dragged her hands over her sweat soaked hair. "I didn't say I wasn't afraid. I think I'm more pissed at them than afraid of them, though."

"Good. Keep it that way. I'm going to take a shower."

Isabelle needed one, too. A fresh start, for both her body and her mind.

While Isabelle was showering, Dalton worked on modifying the disposable cell he'd purchased in town. He intended to make a call to Lou tonight, especially considering what had happened to Isabelle this afternoon.

Damn Sons of Darkness, the relentless bastards. Why couldn't they go pick on someone else?

You know why. They want her. And probably you, too.

There wasn't much he could do about that, other than fight them when the time came. And the time would come. He only hoped the Realm of Light would be there to back him up. Or, if he was lucky, he'd find a way to make the Sons of Darkness lose interest in Isabelle, and the only way to do that was to take away the threat of her turning into one of their strongest demons.

Which meant he needed to talk to Lou.

"What are you doing?"

He looked up at Isabelle. Her hair hung in soft wet curls over her shoulders, her skin pink from her shower. She pulled up a chair at the kitchen table and Dalton inhaled her scent, the clean washed smell of her shampoo and soap, and felt the tightening in his gut from being near her.

Deciding that focusing on work was better than drooling over Isabelle, he said, "I need to call Lou."

"The Realm? Why?"

"A couple reasons. I trust Lou. I want to feel him out, find out what's going on there."

"You mean, related to me."

"Yes."

"Won't they be able to track us down once you call him?"

"No. I've rigged this cell phone so it's untraceable."

She looked at the phone and frowned. "You hope."

He offered an encouraging smile. "I know."

"I guess you know what's best."

"Trust me."

"Famous last words."

He laughed, but he realized he was asking a lot of her. "I've brought you this far. I won't let you down."

"I know you won't. And I do trust you. I'd be dead if not for you."

The way she looked at him, like he was wholly responsible for her life, made him decidedly uncomfortable for a lot of reasons. So he focused on the phone instead, finished rigging it and put the pieces back together, then stared at the buttons.

"Are you going to call him?"

He lifted his gaze to hers. "Yeah."

She pushed her chair back. "Do you want me to leave?"

He reached out and grasped her hand, holding her there. "No. I don't have any secrets from you." Which was a huge lie, but he could only reveal so much. She wasn't ready. Not yet. She'd already dealt with enough.

He punched in the buttons, dialing Lou's number, then brought the phone to his ear, listening to it ring once, twice, three times, then four.

"Hello?"

That wasn't Lou's voice.

"Hello?"

It wasn't anyone's voice he recognized. None of the other hunters.

"Is someone there? Who is this?"

Dalton clicked to end the call and laid the phone on the table.

"What's wrong?" Isabelle asked.

"I don't know."

"Did Lou answer?"

"No. Someone else did."

"Who?"

He dragged his fingers through his hair. "I didn't recognize the voice."

"Is that unusual? I mean, for someone else to answer his phone?"

"Yes. Lou's a Keeper, in charge of other hunters. He always had to remain in contact with his team. He would never leave his cell unattended or give it to someone else.

He's a decision maker. It would be one thing for him to not answer if he's indisposed, another entirely for someone I don't know to answer it."

"Maybe they've brought on new hunters since you've been gone."

He sidled a glance at her. "I haven't been gone that long. And I know all the hunters on Lou's team."

He stared down at the phone again.

"Tell me what you're thinking."

"I'm thinking I need to call Derek." Before he changed his mind, he picked up the phone and dialed Derek's number. It rang once, twice . . .

"Yeah."

Dalton hesitated.

"Hello?"

"Derek. It's Dalton."

Now it was Derek who hesitated. "Dalton. Where the hell are you?"

"I'm not ready to tell you that just yet. Where's Lou?"

Derek didn't say anything.

"Dalton, you need to come in. Are you okay?"

"I'm fine. I tried to call Lou's cell but someone else answered. A voice I didn't recognize."

"Shit. Dalton, you really need to come in. Where are you?"

Ignoring Derek's plea, he asked again, "Where's Lou, Derek?"

"Lou's dead."

CHAPTER EIGHT

What?" Dalton's chest tightened. He wanted to believe he'd heard wrong, that Derek hadn't said what he thought he'd said.

"He's dead."

"When? How?"

Dalton felt Isabelle next to him, her hand squeezing his.

"That night, after you took Isabelle away. The black diamond held a demon inside it. Lou took the diamond and coaxed the demon out of it. It . . . absorbed inside him."

Dalton fought to control his breathing, concentrating instead on Derek's voice. "The demon went inside him?"

"Yeah. It was a powerful demon. Equal to the Sons of Darkness. The only way to kill the demon was to . . . destroy its host."

Dalton pushed back from the chair and paced the room, his heart pounding. This couldn't be real. "How did it happen?"

"We had to do it," Derek said, his voice low.

Shock lanced him. "What?"

"We had to do it," Derek said again. "All of us. With lasers."

"Why?"

"Because Lou asked us to."

"Christ." That had to have cost them all, emotionally. "He's gone? He's really gone?"

"Yeah, man. He is."

He couldn't process this. Lou, gone.

"Dalton, come in."

He shook his head. "I can't talk right now." He clicked off and laid the phone down, and immediately felt a warm body pressed against his back.

"Lou's dead?" Isabelle asked, her voice soft.

"Yes. The night we left Sicily. There was a demon inside the black diamond and Lou took it on. To destroy the demon inside him the hunters had to kill Lou."

She laid her head against his back. "Dear God. I'm so sorry."

Sadness emptied him from the inside out. Lou had been so understanding, so wise; he had been Dalton's mentor. Incredibly kind and smart, he knew demon hunting, had understood the Sons of Darkness with a keen insight. Dalton had always been able to go to Lou with anything.

Lou had been his friend.

Devastation tore a hole in him.

"Come sit down with me."

Warm fingers entwined with his, an equally warm body pressed up against his side. Like a robot, he followed Isabelle to the sofa and sat. He looked over to find her sitting next to him, tears filling her beautiful eyes.

"I'm so sorry, Dalton."

Even though Lou, as Keeper, had been instrumental in ordering Isabelle killed, she still mourned his death.

Dalton turned and pulled her against him and she snuggled close, laying her palm against his chest.

"It hurts to lose someone you care about."

He didn't say anything, had no answer. She was right. Despite trying not to care for anyone, it had happened.

A human quality—caring. And when he cared, people died. It would have to stop.

"I need to go out and get some air."

He stood. So did she.

"I'll go with you."

He shook his head. "I appreciate it, but I really just need to take a walk. By myself."

"If it was me this happened to, would you let me go off alone?"

He looked at her. "That's different."

She slipped her hand in his. "No, it's not. You don't need to be alone right now. You don't have to make small talk or even say a word, but I'm not going to let you go wandering off by yourself. I'm going with you."

He gave a curt nod. "Let's go."

They headed out the front door and down the walk. The night was cloudy, muggy; it was hard to catch a breath since there was no wind.

True to her word, Isabelle said nothing, just held tight to his hand as he wandered the path leading away from the cabin and into the darkness. He didn't even know where he was going, only that sitting in the house, feeling the walls closing in on him, would make him crazy. He needed to be outside where he could wander, lose himself in the swamp and the trees and hear the night sounds, where every thought wouldn't be about Lou.

They walked a long way, deep into the woods before he turned them around and headed back the way they'd come, guiding them back toward the cabin. When they reached the front of the cabin, he directed her to the two wicker chairs. "I'm not ready to go in just yet. Have a seat."

Isabelle stared out toward the swamp they'd just returned from. "Didn't it scare you to be out there, so remote, in the darkness?"

He smiled. "No. There's nothing to be afraid of out here."

"Are you sure?"

"Yes."

"What if demons had showed up?"

He reached behind him, lifted his shirt, and pulled out a laser pistol. "I'm not stupid. I never travel without being armed."

"Oh."

"That was one of the first things Lou taught me. Always have a weapon close at hand. You never know when you'll need it."

"Sounds like Lou was a smart guy."

"He was. A good leader, too."

"And a friend?" She reached for his hand again.

"Yeah." The guilt poured over him. "I should have been there."

"What could you have done?"

"I don't know. Something. I left the team—I just should have been there. It was my responsibility."

"To do what? To help them kill Lou? Or do you think you could have stopped it from happening?"

He pulled away from her, laid his head in his hands, and dug his fingers in his hair. "I don't know. Nothing would have changed. You can't change someone's destiny. What's meant to be can't be altered without screwing up a lot of things. I of all people should know that."

"What does that mean?"

He lifted his head. "Nothing."

"Dalton, why do I feel you're keeping something from me?"

"It's nothing. I'm just rambling." He stood. "Let's go inside."

She stood, but instead of going inside, took a few steps off the porch, then turned to face him. "No. Tell me what you meant. You're talking about me, aren't you?"

"What?"

"The whole changing of destiny and not altering things. That's what you did with me, and look how it's messed everything up."

"That's not at all what I'm talking about."

"Yes, it is. I was meant to be with the Sons of Darkness. Or destroyed by the Realm of Light. What you did changed that. And now Lou's dead and it's my fault."

Wow. Women and their leaps in logic. How did she manage that one? He walked down the stairs toward her, grasped her by the shoulders, and looked her in the eyes. "No. Lou's dead because he made the choice to absorb a demon, knowing what the outcome would be. That would have been the same no matter what happened to you. And no one is meant to be a demon. That's not your destiny. I don't believe it any more than I think you do."

"Don't I? You have no idea what my life has been like.

You've only known me a short period of time. You don't know the impulses I've had, the darkness that's buried just under the surface."

"You think you're the only one who has dark impulses? That's human nature."

"Is it? Is it human nature to set fire to a bungalow with people inside? Or try to kill my own sister?"

"It was never proven that you were the one who set the fire your mother mentioned in her diary."

"I had the matches on me. My mother said I smelled of smoke."

"Do you remember doing it?"

She shook her head.

"Then how do you know you had anything to do with it?"

"Oh, come on. You've seen my memory lapses. Who knows what I'm capable of. It fits, doesn't it? I was always different, Dalton. I hurt people. And I hated Angelique my whole life."

He smoothed his hands over her shoulders. "I think you're normal, Isabelle, with normal human frailties. Maybe you were selfish and self-absorbed before. Lots of people are. That doesn't make you evil."

She lifted her gaze to him. "You just like to see the good in people."

His lips lifted. "Sometimes. And often there isn't any. With you, there's plenty of good."

"You were there the night in Sicily. You know what I am, what's inside me."

"And that's the only time I've seen evidence of the demon inside you. The night the Sons of Darkness took you over and controlled you. So why are you damning yourself because of that one act?"

She put a fist against her stomach. "Because it's still in me. I feel it, fighting inside to get out."

"If you were truly evil, don't you think the demon part of you would be winning? We wouldn't be having this conversation. You'd be trying to kill me."

"I'm trying to fight it."

"Which proves what I said. You're not evil."

"I wish I could believe that. Why do you believe in me?"

"Because I know what's inside you, what you're capable of, even if you don't see it."

"You think my humanity is my salvation."

"Yes."

"Prove it."

He frowned. "How?"

"I'm human right now, Dalton. This is me, the human Isabelle. No demon in sight. Prove that you believe in me."

She tilted her head back, her golden-green eyes mesmerizing. The fullness of Isabelle's lips drew him, and suddenly tasting her became more important than breathing.

Really bad idea. Taking what he shouldn't take and letting human needs get the best of him had been his downfall. He couldn't let it happen again.

He was stronger than his own desires. He hadn't been before. That's where he'd made his mistakes. Thinking with your emotions and your heart got you in trouble every time. Logic always won out if you listened to it, and logic told him any involvement with Isabelle other than what he was here to do spelled disaster for both of them, no matter what Georgie had suggested.

But feeling Isabelle so close to him made his blood pound. It was as if they were connected, and he could hear her heart beating, sense the blood rushing in her veins. He picked up her scent, sweet and musky—a heady combination that entered his senses and drove him crazy. He dragged his fingers through his hair.

"Tell me what you're thinking." Her voice had gone soft.

"Nothing."

"You're a really bad liar, Dalton."

"Am I?" He used to be really good at it.

"Yes."

"And what do you think I'm lying about?"

"Your thoughts. You're thinking about me."

He let his smile show. "Isn't that a little vain, Isabelle?"

"No. I could almost feel it, like you were touching me."

Shit. "What do you mean?"

She shook her head. "I can't explain it. I could feel your thoughts like a whisper across my skin. It happens when I think about you. Weird, huh?"

Weird, no. Uncomfortable as hell, yes. And her telling him this wasn't helping his resolve to be stoic. His supposed impenetrable wall of reserve was buckling. The night was hot, and so was the woman in front of him. What harm would it do to—

He felt something wet and lifted his head. The first fat droplets fell on his arm, then his face.

"It's starting to rain. We need to get inside."

She didn't budge. "I don't mind getting wet. And I'm not going to let you run from me this time."

"I've never run from you."

"Haven't you? You keep telling me you trust me, that you think of me as human, but here I am, Dalton, asking you to prove it to me. This is your chance."

The rain came down harder now, soaking them both, the wind picking up and whipping her hair around her cheeks. Her clothes were wet and stuck to her skin, outlining her breasts, her nipples. Dalton grabbed her hand and they ran onto the porch. He stopped, turned to her, his gaze raking every inch of her rain-soaked body.

She followed where he was looking, then lifted her gaze to his eyes. She wasn't smiling, but he read every emotion on her face, from interest to desire to invitation.

She licked her lips. "Dalton."

"Ah, hell," he said, moving in on her, caging her against the front door with his hips. He threaded his arm around her waist and did what he'd wanted to do for days.

He kissed her.

CHAPTER NINE

Isabelle absorbed the shock of Dalton's kiss. Her toes curled, her hair stood on end. She sizzled all over as if she'd experienced a lightning strike. And oh, it was the sweetest lightning ever.

Actual lightning pulsed just beyond them, along with a driving rain that seemed to feed off her needs. The primal energy of the storm surrounding them matched her own rising passion.

She knew it was going to be like this with Dalton—a wild maelstrom of intense heat turning her insides to liquid. Her nipples hardened against his chest, tingling every time he shifted to press closer against her. The length of his cock, hard and insistent along her hip, whipped her into a fury of desire. She slid her hands around to his back and lifted his shirt, needing to press herself against his bare skin. She wanted much more than this, but just to be able to touch him was going to have to do for now.

As it was, she was dizzy under the assault of his mouth as he performed magical things, his lips sliding against hers in a slow, tender dance. Could a woman faint from being kissed? She was losing her mind, every nerve ending in her body sizzling. She needed to quench this fire, and the only one who could do that was Dalton.

A kiss wasn't going to be enough. She needed more. She lifted her leg, wrapped it around his hip, and surged against him in an effort to get closer, to communicate her needs. Dalton dragged his lips from hers and kissed her jaw, then reached behind her and grasped her hair, jerking her head back to bare her neck so he could lick the side of her throat.

God, the sensations were intense, like fire licking along her skin. He kissed her neck, her shoulder, still holding on to her hair so she couldn't move, couldn't look at him. She was stretched in an impossible position, her back arched, yet she wasn't uncomfortable at all. Not with the way he took possession of her. She wanted more of his mouth and his teeth grazing over her skin. When he bit lightly into the tender skin between her neck and shoulder, she shuddered.

"More. Please, Dalton, hurry." She lifted her hips, searching out the hard, hot part of him that would give her the greatest pleasure.

"Not yet," he growled against her neck, then moved up and took her mouth in another kiss that blindsided her, left her breathless and clinging to sanity. She palmed his back, then moved her hands forward to touch his abdomen, feeling his muscles flinch there, loving that he reacted to her this way. When she moved her hand lower and dipped it inside the waistband of his shorts, he dragged his mouth from hers and pulled her head forward to look her in the eyes.

She gasped at the darkness she saw in his eyes, the

hunger. He barely looked human. A normal woman could almost be afraid of a look like that, because it meant he'd lost control, that he was ready to take what he wanted.

She wasn't a normal woman, and she wanted to give him whatever he wanted to take. And then she wanted to take from him. Whatever she wanted.

She wanted a lot.

"Yes," was all she said, and Dalton scooped her up in his arms, pushing the front door open and kicking it closed behind him.

She thought he'd carry her to one of their beds. She was wrong. He marched the short distance into the kitchen, swept the napkins and a few other things off the kitchen table with one swoop of his hand, and laid her on top of it, then nudged the chair out of the way and loomed over her.

Her body prickled with desire. She felt like a feast. His feast. She bit down on her lower lip to keep from whimpering, then raised her hands to his wet shirt, dragging it up. He lifted, jerked the shirt off, then reached for her top, spreading both his hands underneath it, using his knuckles to raise it inch by inch over her stomach, her ribs, finally baring her breasts.

"Too damned beautiful," he murmured. She sensed he wasn't all there anymore, like he was in some kind of trance. She didn't care, as long as whatever had taken hold of him took them where they needed to go, where she'd needed to go for a long time with him.

He cupped one breast and took her nipple into his mouth, devouring it like a man starved. He sucked, licked, rolled his tongue over the taut bud, teasing the piercing there until the sensations were like shooting fireworks, all heading south to that spot that burst with crazy need. Then he tormented the other nipple with the same sweet pleasure. She tangled her fingers in his hair and held on tight, certain she wasn't going to survive Dalton's lovemaking. It was equal parts tender and torturous, ratcheting up her desire to explosive levels. She felt like she was climbing a ladder one rung at a time, and unable to see the top. She knew there was nirvana up there, but she couldn't quite make it. She needed help.

"Dalton." His name left her lips on a ragged gasp as he slid his hand over her belly, delving into her shorts to cup her sex. He parted the folds of her moist and needy flesh, dipping into her core, exploring her with soft, deliberate strokes that sent her spiraling into oblivion. She'd gone too long without and this was exactly what she craved, but she wanted to hold on, to take him with her.

But Dalton was relentless, using his fingers to stroke her into madness. He dipped, caressed, demanded her response that she couldn't hold back. She climaxed with a blinding cry that Dalton absorbed with a deep kiss, shattering her completely. He held her while she rocked against him. She was too drugged with passion to do anything but hold on to him and tremble against his lips.

Her orgasm only served to whet her appetite for more. But when he removed his hand, he pulled her to a sitting position and backed away, dragging his hand through his hair. She saw apology in his eyes, regret, all the things she didn't want to see.

Shaking from the aftereffects, she slid her legs over the table. "What's wrong?"

He shook his head. "Nothing. I just . . . don't think it's a good idea to go further."

"Why?"

"Because we should take this slow."

The heat of embarrassment and anger suffused her face. She'd asked, and he'd answered. She'd wanted this tonight for so many reasons. To comfort him, yes, but also because she'd thought they were growing closer.

Obviously, she was wrong. He still thought of her as a demon, not a human. Not a woman. Oh, sure, he could get the hots for her, but he couldn't see it through, because bottom line, she had demon blood. He could talk a good game about trust, but he really didn't trust that she wouldn't sprout fangs while in the middle of sex and try to kill him.

Could she blame him for that?

She jerked her T-shirt down to cover herself.

Dalton leaned against the counter, shirtless, his shorts riding dangerously low on his hips. The evidence of his desire was still outlined for her to see, to want. She was consumed with this inexplicable need to leap off the table and throw herself at him. Her body throbbed all over.

"I'm sorry, Isabelle. This is my fault. I got carried away."

Un-freaking-believable. He couldn't handle the demon side of her. He wanted a human lover, not a freak show. It was all too clear. She just wished he'd figured it all out before she'd become emotionally invested.

Way to go, Isabelle. One mistake after another.

"I don't feel well. I'm going to bed."

"Isabelle . . ."

"Save it, Dalton. You've said enough." She hopped off the table and dragged the remnants of her dignity out of the room before she did something stupid. Like cry in front of him like some . . . girl.

She shut the door to her room and turned her back to the door, blinking back the hot splash of tears she couldn't seem to will away.

She used to be a lot stronger, used to be the one in control of men and relationships. When did that all change? When had she gone weak in the knees over a man? How could she let him manipulate her feelings like this?

How could she have let her heart get involved?

Damn him.

Well, that went well. There were so many reasons to go after Isabelle. Dalton wanted to explain why he'd pulled away. All the reasons why he hadn't wanted to stop. But really, what would be the point? He'd already hurt her enough. It was best to just let her go.

He should have never started in the first place. So much for his self-control, for his determination of logic over lust. One look at her outside, wet from the rain, one whiff of her sweet scent, and he'd gone after her like some kind of wild animal with one intent in mind. He'd wanted her. That's all he'd thought about. Not the repercussions. Not all the reasons he shouldn't. Just the one reason he should.

Because he wanted her. And he'd had her, coming apart under his hand, breathing in the scent of her desire, feeling her moist heat clenched around his fingers and knowing in seconds he could be inside her, joined with her.

And then he'd stopped. Which was a good thing.

Right?

Shit. He went to the fridge and grabbed a beer, popped the top off and took a long pull, letting the icy cold liquid slide down his throat. Maybe it would chill out the heat Isabelle had caused.

She hadn't seemed demonic at all when he'd kissed and touched her. She'd told him she was fully human, had asked for his trust in her. She'd been with him, in the moment, clearheaded and all female. His balls were twisted into knots remembering how she responded to his touch, to his mouth. Though he knew he shouldn't, he still wanted her with a fierceness that defied all reason. It wouldn't take much for him to stalk into her bedroom, take her into his arms and show her with his mouth and body how much he really did need her.

Which was what really shocked him, his need for her. He'd never needed anyone before, but the thought of being without Isabelle left a hole inside him.

Maybe that's what scared him. They weren't lovers; she didn't belong to him. She was here because he'd made it his mission to help her, to integrate the demonic side of her with the human side. He hadn't brought her here to love her. But touching her, being with her, brought something magical out of him.

She also touched his dark side. Something about her made him . . . hungry.

He'd lost control with Isabelle once in Sicily, had done something he knew he had no business doing. Something that wasn't in the Realm's plans. She tapped into a part of him that made him defy what he was, what he had pledged to be.

If he had any chance at redemption, he couldn't go there again. Which meant he had to be hands-off with Isabelle. He couldn't trust who he became when he was with her.

Wind howled, lashing limbs against the windows. Lightning lit up the sky like midday, and thunder crashed all around.

Yeah, that fit his mood. Dark, brooding, and just plain pissed off.

He grabbed his jacket, put on his shoes, and headed toward the main house, ignoring Mother Nature's warning blasts against him as he fought his way along the path. He entered the back of the house, pulled off his jacket, and went in search of Georgie. She was in the library, reading a book by candlelight. She looked up when he entered, seemingly unsurprised to see him.

"There's tension in you. Something else." She studied him, her lips pressed firmly together before turning down in a disapproving frown. "Passion. What did you do?"

He dragged his wet hair away from his face. "Nothing. I don't know. Something, maybe."

Georgie laid the book on the table and laid her hands in her lap. "Come sit down and tell me."

He did, taking a seat in the chair across from hers. It

was old, but still well cushioned, and he sank into it with a sigh. He'd like to stay here and hide, but he was no coward.

Then again, maybe he was.

"I feel something for Isabelle. But it's like dynamite when we're together. Tonight, we came close . . ."

"You sense danger when you're passionate with her?"

Did he? He thought about it. "No. Before, yes, but tonight, no. She was human when we were . . . together." This wasn't the easiest thing to talk about.

"Then why the hesitation?"

"I don't know."

"Dalton, I can't help you if you aren't honest with me." She leaned forward and held out her hands. He laid his palms over hers, feeling the surge of heat that he'd felt with her great-grandmother whenever she'd touched him.

Georgie closed her eyes and hummed, rocked slightly back and forth. Dalton knew not to disturb her when she went into this kind of trance.

"You're not afraid of Isabelle," she said, tenderness and concern reflected in her chocolate brown eyes. "You're afraid of yourself."

He let his hands slide from hers. What could he say to that? She was right. "I pushed her away tonight, Georgie."

"Did you want to?"

"No." Hell, no.

Georgie nodded. "By protecting yourself, you're hurting Isabelle."

"I know." He had seen that in Isabelle's face.

"Wanting to help her is noble. But you need to make

some decisions. Either decide to help her and keep your distance, or decide you want to be more to her than just her savior. What you're doing to her now is confusing her. You're doing more harm than good, Dalton."

And here he thought he couldn't feel any worse. "You're right."

"But don't be with her out of guilt," Georgie said, her lips curving into a knowing smile. "A woman can always tell. She needs you, Dalton, in ways even you don't yet understand. You just need to be clear in your motivations. Either help her get through this with all you have—and by that I mean body, heart, and soul—or leave her alone."

Dalton already knew which way he had to go, because the thought of never touching Isabelle again caused him physical pain.

He was going to have to figure out how to deal with this—having her and still doing what he needed to do. He wasn't sure how he could do both, but maybe an honest approach was a good way to start.

It would sure be a first for him.

Tase sat in the darkness, smiling.

Isabelle's power was strong. He only had to keep pushing her, to bring the darkness within her to life again, and watch it grow.

Oh, she still fought him, but her resolve weakened. And Tase felt her. Every time the dark side of herself tried to emerge, he felt her. And the more the demon blood in her surged, the happier Tase became.

Because with his guidance, her human side had no chance to win.

It would only be a matter of time now. Soon the Isabelle he wanted would surface completely. Then he'd have his Queen of Darkness again, under his control and ready to do his bidding. The human Isabelle was weak. His queen would be powerful, a half-human puppet whose strings he could manipulate as he desired.

And her first task would be to bring about her lover's downfall. Tase looked forward to the day when Isabelle destroyed Dalton.

The Master would be pleased by that coup, the bringing in of not only Isabelle, but Dalton, too.

Tase's smile slid into a wide grin, and he let the flames surrounding him explode into a shower of orange and red fire, enveloping him like a blanket.

CHAPTER TEN

Mandy and Michael had brought the demon into one of the hidden Realm of Light locations—this one fully equipped with a lab—so they could run some tests on the creature.

The demon had a wallet on him, with all the usual things a normal human would have, including a driver's license and credit cards.

The demon's "name" was James McAdams. He lived in the suburbs with his wife, no kids. Drove a nice car and had a job as a real estate developer, income in the mid six figures. He had a ton of credit cards with high limits.

"So who is this guy, really?" Mandy stood outside the lab now, pacing in front of the two-way mirror while they hooked up the demon to more wires, more IV's, stuck more tubes and needles and doodads in the damn thing.

"Obviously a demon," Michael said.

"But the I.D. was legit. Do you think this guy used to be human?"

"He has a full background. His fingerprints match his military record. I'd say that the demon in there is the same body that used to be the human James McAdams."

Unbelievable. There was so much they didn't know.

"This is bullshit," she said to Michael. Poking and prodding the comatose demon was doing no good. How were they going to find out anything if they kept it unconscious? "Wake it up and let me go in there fully armed. Give me five minutes alone with that thing and I'll get some answers."

Michael shook his head, braced his feet in a wide, military stance, and faced the two-way mirror head-on. "Not the way it works around here, Mandy, and you know it. There's protocol."

She scrunched her nose and stopped pacing, mimicking Michael's stance as she, too, turned toward the mirror. "My way is more fun," she grumbled.

Michael's lips curved.

"Careful, Mike. You might have just smiled."

He kept his focus on the activity in the lab. "Tell anyone and I'll have you vaporized. I have a reputation to protect. My team needs to believe I'm an asshole."

She snorted. "No worries there. I'm sure they'll have no trouble buying into that."

"With your help."

"Of course."

She studied the creature. It looked so human. She hated that.

"So what are they doing to it?" she asked.

"Testing blood and tissues, running MRIs and CT scans. Basically a full external and internal workup. We've never had a live demon to examine before. We want anatomical and physiological makeup on it, to see how, or even if, it varies from human."

"And if it's not at all different?"

He shrugged. "Then we'll go at it another way."

"Interrogation?"

"Yes."

Groovy. Maybe she could help. She really liked interrogation. "Won't it be able to disappear once it's conscious, though? They have the ability to vaporize."

"I know. We're working on that."

Leave it to the Realm to figure out a way to keep the demon from evaporating in front of them. If anyone could do it, it was the group of scientists who worked for the Realm.

The door opened and one of the doctors came out, handed Michael a clipboard, and went back inside. Michael flipped through the pages.

"Christ."

"What is it?"

"Preliminary results from some of the tests."

"So what do we know so far?"

"That if the thing lying on the table in there were human, it would be dead."

She arched a brow and peered over his shoulder. "Really?"

"Yeah. All these lab results are insane. All way too high. Sodium, potassium, BUN, creatinine, glucose levels—everything is off the charts. There's no way it should have been up and walking. A human would have been in a coma, or dead."

He flipped the page. "Body temperature way below normal, too. No one with a seventy-five-degree temperature should be alive. And the freezing agent I injected into it wouldn't have lowered its temp that much, so it was already cold."

Mandy made mental notes of all these things that would help the Realm identify a demon. It frightened her to think the Sons of Darkness had come up with a demon that could mix with the human population in daylight. But at least they knew the demons had some characteristics that would allow the hunters to identify them.

"Anything else?" she asked.

"Not yet. Let's hope we can come up with more, because it's not like we can run lab work on every human in the population, or take their temperatures. And if there was one wandering around, chances are there are more."

"In multiple cities."

"Probably. We need to wake this thing up and ask it some questions," Michael said.

"You really think it'll answer?"

He shrugged. "Don't know until we try. Let's just hope we can be persuasive enough that it'll be forthcoming with answers. Nobody wants to die. Not even a demon."

Mandy was looking forward to that part. "So how soon will you wake it up?"

"We don't want to wait too long. They'll finish testing today. After that, we'll figure out a way to keep its body temperature low enough that it can't dematerialize on us, but will still remain conscious."

"I can't wait."

"Neither can I."

"Too bad we can't use some kind of truth serum on it."

Michael turned to her, a gleam of something absolutely wicked in his eyes. "Well, it is human in many ways, isn't it?"

Isabelle did her best to avoid Dalton completely the next day. She made it a point to get up early, then left Dalton a note that she was going up to the main house to spend the day with Georgie. At least the storm had subsided and the power was back on now.

She had to get away from Dalton, couldn't bear to be so close to him again. Not after what had happened between them last night, after what continued to happen between them. Getting closer, and him backing away at critical moments. She couldn't continue to put herself through it.

Never again. She didn't need any more reminders of what she was. She already knew.

Georgie tried to sit and talk with her, but Isabelle hadn't gone there for probing into her psyche or emotions. She had gone to the main house to escape Dalton, and that included talking about him. Fortunately, Georgie didn't push her, just put her to work in the basement stocking shelves of books. That at least kept her mind occupied, thoughts of Dalton pushed aside, if only for a while. She knew eventually she'd have to go back to the cabin and face him, but for now, she was busy and he wasn't around.

"Is all this stuff for real?" she asked Georgie, filling

shelves with books on the history of voodoo, then moving on to candles, cards, necklaces, charms, and incense.

"If you believe, it is. Magic can be very powerful."

"What if you don't believe?"

Georgie stood, smoothed out her generous cotton skirt, and faced Isabelle. "I would think, considering your background, you wouldn't find much of anything unbelievable, Isabelle."

She lifted a few zombie dolls from the box and cocked her head to the side.

Georgie offered an indulgent smile. "Everything has its purpose."

"Zombies? Are there really zombies?"

"Are there really demons?"

"Touché, Georgie." Isabelle placed the dolls on the shelf, realizing she wasn't going to best Georgie in this game of Ripley's Believe It Or Not.

"How come you're so even-keeled?" Isabelle finally asked, leaning back on her heels after the box was empty.

"I've seen a lot, experienced much. In my family, you learn to get over your shock at an early age."

"So as children you're exposed to . . ."

"Voodoo? Of course. You can't fight darkness without knowing it's out there."

"Forewarned is forearmed?"

Again that secretive smile. "Something like that." Georgie pulled up a cushioned footstool next to Isabelle. "Some in my family are born with unique abilities, Isabelle. The ability to touch the other side, to bring forth magic that allows us to see other worlds.

"What we see, what we feel, is never a surprise to us.

Even at an early age. We just accept it as reality and learn to appreciate its strengths and manage its weaknesses."

"So you're saying that's what I should learn to do."

"Those who are born with any sort of gift must learn to adapt. Some do, some don't."

Isabelle didn't quite see how being part demon was a gift. "Those who don't adapt fall into darkness?"

Georgie shrugged. "If you can't control your dark side, it will swallow you up until there's nothing left of the light."

Isabelle understood that all too well; she often felt like she was falling into a hole and being swallowed up. Like her dream. "How do I control it? How do you all control it? If you have these ... gifts, and darkness goes with the light, how do you strike a balance and manage to stay on the good side?"

"It's not something that can be taught, Isabelle," Georgie said, leaning forward. "You simply have to want the light more than the darkness. And then it's up to you to work at it to make sure the darkness doesn't take over."

Isabelle breathed in, let it out slowly. "That doesn't make sense. No one wants to be evil."

Georgie smiled, shook her head. "Don't they? Evil can be so very tempting. Sometimes goodness requires sacrifice. It's not always pleasant. Evil is easier. There's always fun stuff on that side."

Isabelle frowned. "They do that on purpose."

Georgie laughed, the sound like a trickling waterfall, a delight to the senses. "Yes, they do. There has to be a lure. Otherwise, why would people go down that road?"

Isabelle sat on the floor and rubbed her fingers across her forehead, suddenly so tired she wasn't sure she could go on. "I don't know, Georgie. Sometimes it seems like no matter what road I choose, it's the wrong one."

Georgie leaned forward and stroked her hair, not saying a word. The gesture was comforting, as if her touch alone had settled peace over Isabelle. Isabelle tilted her head back and smiled. "Your touch has some magic in it."

Georgie's eyes seemed to twinkle. "Does it?"

"You tell me."

"Sometimes, magic is whatever you wish to believe it is. Your own future can be that way, too, Isabelle. Don't ever give up on yourself. As soon as you do, they'll know. And they'll win."

"I have been fighting this. I know I have."

"You don't have to do it alone, you know." Georgie smiled. "Give Dalton the benefit of the doubt. He is a man, you know. He'll make mistakes."

Isabelle almost snorted at that. "Dalton knows exactly what he wants. And what he doesn't want."

"Does he?"

Now Isabelle was confused. "I don't understand."

"Neither does he. And Isabelle, he needs your help as much as you need his."

"But—"

Georgie held up her hand. "Some things need to be experienced, not explained. Maybe you're talking to the wrong person?"

Isabelle's head was spinning as she made her way back to the cabin at dusk. Now she understood how poor Luke Skywalker felt in *Star Wars*. Having a conversation with Georgie was like talking to Yoda. The woman made no sense at all, talked in circles and left vague clues that Isabelle was supposed to unravel.

She didn't like games, would much prefer that Georgie just slap her upside the head with the truth. Preferably in simple terms that she could understand.

"Some things need to be experienced, not explained," she mumbled as she made her way up the walk toward the cabin. "What the hell does that mean?"

She thought spending the day with Georgie would provide some clarity. Instead, her head and her emotions were more muddled than ever. She needed a bath and a stiff drink. Maybe several drinks.

Dalton wasn't inside when she walked in, which gave her some measure of relief. She wasn't in the mood for confrontation or conversation. She'd done plenty of talking today and had no answers. She searched the liquor cabinet, fixed a vodka and cranberry juice, loaded it down with ice, and took it into the bathroom with her. Then she filled the tub with water and scented bubbles while she stripped. Once the tub was filled with steamy water, she climbed in and sank under the bubbles, lifted the glass to her lips, and took a couple huge gulps.

A stiff drink and a bath—the first things today that had actually helped. Within five minutes she was relaxed, eyes closed, her head leaning against the back of the tub. She emptied her mind of everything bugging her and just let it all go.

Really, she had to make another one of these drinks when she got out of the tub. It really helped. She lifted it to her lips and took another swallow, then smiled as it warmed her from the inside out. Perfect. A little buzz, the sweet smell of the bubbles, and a warm bath. She might just stay in this tub all night long. An empty head filled with some great vodka could do wonders to keep all the evils away.

"Oh. Shit. Sorry, didn't know you were in here."

Buzz kill. She opened her eyes and saw Dalton there, knowing her idea of heaven wasn't going to last. "I'm in here."

"I can see that now. When did you get back?"

She shrugged, not bothering to move. She wasn't certain she could move, she was so content. Not even Dalton's appearance could disrupt her nirvana. "Not sure. Twenty minutes ago, maybe."

He leaned against the doorway and she made it a point not to notice the bulging muscles of his upper arms, or the way his shoulders glistened with sweat, or the streaks of dirt across his cheeks and neck. "What have you been doing today?"

"Did a little work out back for Georgie," he said with a faint smile.

"Good for you." She drained the glass and placed it on the floor by the tub.

"What are you having?" Dalton asked, picking up the empty glass.

"Vodka and cranberry."

"Would you like another?"

She shrugged. "Sure."

He returned a couple minutes later with two large glasses, handing one to her.

"Thanks," she said, taking the glass he offered to her.

Then he leaned against the sink and took a couple long swallows of his drink.

"Uh, Dalton?"

"Yeah."

"I'm taking a bath here."

"I can see that."

She rolled her eyes. "I give up." She downed half the contents of the glass in two swallows. This day was just getting more and more bizarre. Maybe she'd just drink until she passed out. She decided to ignore him. Maybe he'd go away.

He didn't, just continued to lean against the counter, looking damn sexy in his dirt-stained jeans that hugged his muscled thighs, his sleeveless cotton shirt that was filthy and sweat-soaked, and what parts of his body were visible were tanned from spending the day in the blistering sun. At least the parts of him that didn't sport streaks of dirt—which wasn't much of him.

"You need a bath yourself," she said, realizing that she'd been staring at him, and that her body had a definite reaction to looking at him. Even grimy from head to toe, Dalton radiated sex appeal. So unfair, especially since it was obvious he wasn't projecting it on purpose. She didn't think he had any idea what he was doing to her. And it was a damn good thing all her pertinent body parts were hidden under miles of bubbles.

His lips curved, and she nearly groaned, but bit her lip instead.

"Is that an invitation?"

She frowned, looked away. "Don't fuck with me, Dalton. I'm not in the mood."

He drained his glass and set it on the counter, then stalked to the tub, taking his damn sweet time making his way toward her, even though it was only a few feet.

He crouched down and laid his arms on the side of the tub. "I'm not fucking with you, Isabelle."

His face was only a foot from hers. He smelled sweaty, outdoorsy, earthy, and all male. She found his scent not at all unpleasant, and rather arousing.

"Go away." Her voice had lowered to nearly a whisper. She didn't trust it not to waver. Damn him for making her feel like a woman. She should stand up and point him in the direction of the door. But she wasn't all that certain she could, or would, ask him to leave.

Instead, he dipped his hands down the side of the tub into the water. "You don't want me to go away."

"Yes, I do." She didn't sound convincing, even to herself.

"I don't want to go away."

He waved his hands back and forth in the water, hovering so close to her left breast she felt the waves caress her nipple, harden it, and she had to stop breathing to keep from moaning. Really, this was ridiculous.

"I won't ask you again."

He pushed back and stood. "Then don't ask."

She wasn't at all shocked when he drew his shirt off and undid the button of his jeans, then toed off his boots. He shucked his jeans and stood there gloriously naked in front of her, his cock in a semirigid state.

He made her mouth water, and her mind whirled

with a mental list of about forty things she wanted to do with him in this bathroom, right now. But she couldn't find her voice, and her limbs had become like lead. She could only watch as he stepped into the tub and situated himself at the opposite end, sliding his legs alongside hers.

She was pretty sure she'd stopped breathing, at least until he reached for her feet and set them on top of his rock hard stomach. Then she remembered to exhale.

"What do you think you're doing?"

He smiled. "Taking a bath."

"You could have waited until I was finished."

"What fun is that?"

"Dalton, we tried this last night, remember?"

"Vividly."

His low, husky voice tore away at the walls she'd spent all day carefully constructing. She jerked her feet away from his grasp and scooted against the back of the tub. Unfortunately, sitting up lifted her breasts out of the water. She sank back down. Dalton grinned, grabbed a washcloth and scrubbed his face and arms, then dunked his head under the water, splashing it everywhere when he surfaced.

Her bubbles were slowly disappearing. Dalton had a wicked gleam in his eyes that Isabelle found both disconcerting and hot as blazes. She drew her legs up to her chest.

"The water's getting cold."

He leaned forward and turned the faucet on. Hot water streamed into the tub at the same time he pulled the drain plug. "We'll let a little of the cold water out, and refill with hot."

She clamped her lips together, reached for the bubble bath, and poured more in. "You're going to smell like a girl."

He shrugged. "I don't mind if you don't."

"I don't intend to smell you."

"Are you sure?" He started to move forward.

Isabelle held up her hand. "Stop."

"Come on, I'm clean now."

"Quit teasing me." He kept coming. "Dammit, Dalton, I mean it."

That stopped him. He leaned back and laid his arms over the side of the tub. Dirty, he was sexy. Clean and wet, he was devastating. And his legs brushing up against hers, his feet sliding along her thighs and butt, were way too distracting.

"I really think we should get out."

"You go first."

She huffed out a sigh. "Really. You're acting like a juvenile. I'm not playing."

"Maybe you should."

"And maybe you should stop playing games with me."

His expression straightened then. "I'm not playing games, Isabelle. I'm dead serious."

"Were you serious last night?"

He had the decency to avert his gaze for a few seconds before looking at her again, dragging his hand through his wet hair. "I don't know what happened last night."

"I do."

"You do."

"Yes."

"Then tell me."

"Do I have to spell it out? I'm a demon. You're a human. You find me repulsive."

He cocked a brow, frowned, then had the goddamn audacity to smile. And even worse, he laughed. Hard, long, and loud. If she'd had a weapon nearby, he'd be a dead man.

"Okay, we're finished here." She twisted, searching for the bath towel. Naked or not, she was through sitting here being humiliated. She reached for the towel, but Dalton grasped her ankles and jerked her back so hard she almost slipped under the water.

"We're not done, Isabelle. Not by a long shot."

"Are you out of your mind?" She fought for balance, tried to tug her legs out of his grasp, but he had a strong hold on her. He wasn't hurting her, but he obviously had no intention of releasing her. "Let me go."

"No. I'm in here, and we're going to talk." He released one of her ankles, but only to grab hold of the other foot. He began to massage the insole with both hands. God, it felt so good. He had strong fingers, and knew just where the trigger points were on her foot. All she could do was glare, and at the same time melt under the sweet assault of his fingers.

When he finished that foot, he picked up the other and did the same thing.

"I don't hear you talking," she said, tapping her fingers on the edge of the tub.

"Oh, yeah." He smiled. "Sorry, I got distracted." He

lifted her foot out of the water and kissed her toes, one by one. "You have really beautiful feet."

"Stop that." She squeezed her thighs together, trying to banish the sensations evoked by his tongue on her toes. "Talk, or I really am going to get out of the tub."

He released her foot, his expression changing. "Okay. Look, about last night. I'm sorry. I backed off, and I had no reason to."

He had every reason to and she knew why. "I'm a demon. I wouldn't want me, either."

"Would you let me talk?"

"Fine." This was pointless. And she still couldn't believe she was sitting naked in the tub with him.

"I've tried to keep my distance from you."

She cocked a brow.

"Yeah, I know. Let me finish. I wanted to give you space to deal with what happened in Italy, but it was more than that."

"I know."

His lips curled. "No, you don't know."

"I do. It's okay. You have no idea what you'd be dealing with. Before, on the yacht in Italy, when we made love, you thought you were making love to a human. Now, you know you're not."

"What?"

"I'm a demon. I could...well, who knows what I could do in the throes of passion, especially considering what's been going on with me since we got here. The demon could come out when we're in the middle of—"

"Did it last night?"

"What?"

"When I had you stretched out on the kitchen table last night, was it the demon writhing, moaning, and climaxing, Isabelle?"

Damn him for bringing that up, for causing heat to ignite as she remembered how it felt to be laid out on the table, to remember his hand and mouth on her and how he'd made her feel.

"Was it?" he pressed.

"No."

"That's right, it wasn't."

"Then why the hell did you stop?" She met his gaze evenly, refusing to look away, even though it embarrassed her to ask the question.

"Because I was afraid I'd go too far."

That wasn't at all the answer she'd expected.

CHAPTER ELEVEN

Isabelle stared at Dalton, not sure what to say in response to his admission.

"I don't understand." She was being honest. She had no clue what he'd meant when he said he was afraid of going too far. Hadn't they been headed as far as they could go last night?

"I'm no...angel," he said.

"I never thought you were."

He lifted his hands out of the water, dragged them through his hair. "I was trying to be noble, to give you time to heal, to figure out for yourself what was going on inside you. But I hadn't counted on what I felt for you."

Her breath caught and held, afraid of what he'd say, afraid he'd stop and not say it at all.

"And you kept pushing me, when you had those...demon moments, I'd guess you'd call them. But me stopping last night had nothing to do with you being part demon. Last night it was the human Isabelle I was with. And it's when you're human that you get to me, when I really want you. Because then it's just you and me. And it's a little too real." His gaze was so direct, penetrating her defenses.

"Tell me, Dalton."

"You light a fire inside me. Whenever I'm around you it burns high and hot. I backed away from you last night because I'm afraid of what will happen if I let it run wild. Sometimes it seems like there's this darkness inside me, and that if I tap into it I'll hurt you. I'm not afraid of you, Isabelle. I'm afraid of me."

Stunned speechless, Isabelle was at a loss for how to respond. He wanted her. He wasn't repulsed by her or her demon blood. Everything she'd thought had been wrong. To be able to see the passion in his eyes, to know it was for her, was astounding. She'd never felt that special to a man before.

She did now.

And he thought it would frighten her? Oh, hell no. If anything, his need for her, and his reluctance to give her everything, only strengthened her.

As soon as she wrapped her head around all that, she smiled at him.

"Dalton, I'm not at all afraid of you."

He frowned. "You should be. You have no idea what I'm capable of doing."

"You don't know what I'm capable of doing, either. That makes us a pretty even match, don't you think?"

His lips curled. "Maybe."

"I've always wanted to feel close to someone but never allowed it. At first because of selfish reasons, and lately because of fear. Don't you think I'm afraid of what I could do, what I could be?"

"You're safe with me, Isabelle."

"But are you safe with me?"

"I can take care of myself."

She believed he could. If anyone could, it was Dalton. "I need to be close to someone, to feel alive, to feel . . . human. I need to feel as if someone cares for me. And if that caring is only sex, I can handle that."

"I don't know what I can offer you beyond this moment," he said.

She nodded. "Nor do I. But I can tell you that I'm strong enough to handle you. And that I want you, no matter how out of control you think you'll get."

She'd never been so nakedly honest with anyone in her life. It was scary as hell and exhilarating at the same time. It left her shaky, her skin prickling with need.

Isabelle pushed off the side of the tub and stood, bubbles sliding down her skin. "I'm getting all pruny in here. How about we take this conversation somewhere else?"

The heat in his gaze seared her. He started at her knees, his gaze lifting upward, devouring her body with his hungry gaze. When he reached her face, she actually blushed. Dalton's eyes went dark, his intent oh, so clear. He stood, and now it was her turn to look as he stepped out of the tub.

"We've done enough talking." He scooped her up in his arms, lifted her out of the tub, and took her into his bedroom. He jerked the quilt and sheet to the end of the bed, then laid her in the middle of it, coming down on top of her.

Skin-to-skin contact. The shock and utter bonfire consumed her. But he didn't give her time to even breathe before his lips covered hers in a demanding kiss that told her in no uncertain terms that she'd better be ready to accept what was going to happen between them, or let him know now, because this time there'd be no stopping.

She so didn't want to stop. Not with the barely leashed passion that roared inside Dalton, ready to burst to the surface. She felt it in the tension of his muscles as she smoothed her hands over his shoulders, down his arms. She held on to him as he surged against her, letting her feel how much he wanted her. She arched upward, letting him know she wanted him as well, because she couldn't speak—his mouth was doing delicious things to hers, capturing her, mesmerizing her, his tongue licking at hers, rasping its velvet softness in silent demand.

Whatever he wanted, she would give. She had so much to offer it was almost painful. It was frightening and exhilarating, this temptation to bare her soul to Dalton. Part of her wanted to hold back, but she had a hot man in her arms, a demanding man who would take no less than everything. That's what she intended to give him.

He lifted his head, stared down at her, his gaze as demanding as his body moving against hers. "Are you sure this is what you want?"

"How can you ask that? I've been trying to seduce you since the moment we got here."

His lips curled, and he bent, kissing the pounding pulse point of her neck, then licked her until she shivered. "Be careful what you wish for, Isabelle," he murmured against her ear before gently biting her earlobe. "You might just get it."

She tangled her fingers in his hair and pulled, forcing

him to look at her. "So far you've been all talk, Dalton. Let's see what you've got."

He laughed, the rumbling sound full of promise. He grasped her wrists in his hands, spread her arms wide, then used his knee to kick her legs apart before climbing up to his knees, devouring her with his gaze. He lifted her arms above her head and held her wrists together with one hand, using his free hand to caress her hair, her cheek, her neck. She breathed through her mouth when his fingers went featherlight, teasing between her breasts, skiing up and down the valley between the two globes. His touch sent rivers of sensation between her breasts and straight down between her legs. She tried to squeeze her legs together, anything to intensify the feeling, but his body was in the way.

"Like that?" he asked.

"Yes. Touch me."

He circled her nipples, then used the pad of his thumb to skim across each taut bud, lingering at the piercings there, sending her into shivers of delight as he gently tugged the silver rings. She let out a whimper of pleasured response, gritting her teeth when he cupped her breasts and squeezed oh, so tenderly, circling her nipple with his thumb. She gasped at the exquisite sensations, made even more so when he bent his head and captured her other nipple in his mouth, sucking it hard.

She nearly came off the bed, arching upward against him. How could something feel so good? How could he know just what she needed? He rolled his tongue over the piercings at each nipple, which shot pulses of ecstasy to her core until she was mindless with pleasure, all the while rocking against her sex with his shaft until she was drenched with need for him, already so close to completion her body throbbed with it.

Dalton shifted, dropping down beside her to claim her lips again in a potent kiss. She shuddered at the sensual power he had over her, like a drug that made everything hazy. Every nerve ending was alive, everywhere he touched sent her closer and closer to the edge. And when his hand drifted down her belly to cup her sex, slowly massaging the ache inside her that had built to a crescendo, she tensed and whimpered against his mouth.

He lifted his head, looked at her. "Let go, Isabelle."

She did, gasping as she climaxed, letting him see everything, feel everything as she rocked against his hand. He gave her no time to come down from the high, just positioned himself over her while she was still in the throes of these amazing aftershocks, and slid inside her with a powerful thrust.

And oh, it was just what she craved—this possession, this demanding man giving her what she'd wanted from him for so long. He slid one hand underneath her buttocks, lifting her up so her pelvis met his, so he could drive deeper inside her.

Isabelle wrapped her legs around him and held tight, smoothing her hands over the sweat-slickened muscles of his back, memorizing every part of his skin she could touch as he rocked against her, inside her, one with her.

She felt power inside Dalton, and it matched the power inside herself—the part of herself she was afraid to set free.

"Let it out," he said, lifting up on his arms to stare down at her face.

She gasped at the look of intensity, the darkness in his eyes, which almost seemed to glow with feral, animalist hunger. It should frighten her. Instead, it aroused her.

"Let it go, Isabelle. Let me have it."

She knew what he asked for, the part of herself she'd tried to hide. The intensity, the emotion, the deepest part of herself that she'd held locked up. She shook her head, tears welling in her eyes. "I can't."

He lifted against her and she could feel herself coming apart again.

"Trust me," he whispered, bending down to brush his lips against hers. "I'll never hurt you."

She believed him. God help her, she believed him. And she would give him everything. Her heart, her soul, all that she was.

She swept her hand across his cheek.

"It's yours," she said. "Take it."

With a low growl he thrust hard, retreated, powered forward again until she released all she'd held inside. She arched her back as the force of her climax crashed within her, dragged her nails down his arms as she came apart around him. His guttural cry told her that he gave her all he had, too, and it was the most beautiful thing she'd ever seen.

It was like a white light shone around him, nearly blinding her, yet she couldn't close her eyes against such beauty, not when it catapulted her into a place she'd never been before, a place she never hoped to capture.

Shaken, spent, Dalton collapsed on top of her and

she wrapped herself around him, wondering what she had just seen. Imaginings in the throes of passion, or something else? She was almost afraid to ask, didn't want to do or say anything to disrupt this idyllic moment.

It had to have been a figment of her imagination. She probably just had way too many synapses firing.

A pleasure overload, that's what it had been. She'd been so caught in the moment, the sensations, the intensity of everything she'd felt with him. Because there's no way Dalton would have a white glow surrounding him. No way.

He rolled off her and pulled her against him so they faced each other. He swept her hair away from her face, his gaze penetrating.

"Are you okay?" he asked.

She smiled, slid her hand along his beard-stubbled jaw. "I'm great."

"Yeah, you sure were."

She laughed. "Thanks. So were you. I can't remember sex being quite so . . . intense."

He arched a brow and swept his hand along her collarbone. "I'll take that as a compliment."

"You do that."

She nestled her head against his shoulder, utterly exhausted. But a part of her wanted to mention what she'd seen, and that kept her from falling immediately to sleep. Besides, sleep meant demons, anyway, and she was content to just lie here with Dalton for a while.

"You're restless."

She smiled in the dark. "Yes. I tend to avoid sleep."

"Because of the nightmares?"

"Yes."

"Do you want to get up?"

She snuggled against him. "No. I'm fine here with you."

He wrapped his arms around her. "I'll keep the demons away."

"I believe you could." She yawned, trying to fight sleep, but failing. "Your white light could do that."

"Huh?"

She was drifting, barely able to keep her eyelids open. "That white light I saw around you when we were making love. It was so . . . beautiful."

Dalton listened to Isabelle's rhythmic breathing. She was asleep, had passed out almost immediately after uttering the words that had sent him into a cold sweat.

White light surrounding him.

Shit.

He was afraid something like that would happen, but he hadn't known for sure. Not until he'd given all of himself to Isabelle, something he hadn't intended on doing, but couldn't seem to control.

What happened between Isabelle and him was more than just physical. He hadn't counted on his emotional reaction, the involvement of his soul in their joining. He knew he asked her for everything, but at the same time he gave her all he had, all he was.

Huge mistake. What was he thinking?

He wasn't. That was his problem, what he was afraid would happen if he made love to Isabelle. He had suspected after the first time that being with Isabelle would bring out a flood of intense emotions.

But he hadn't counted on this.

Maybe she'd forget what she saw, or chalk it up to some sexual out-of-body experience brought about by a great orgasm.

Yeah, right. He wasn't *that* good. Which meant he'd better come up with a plausible explanation, because chances were she'd ask.

No, he sure hadn't helped himself tonight. All he'd done was remind himself of the darkness inside him, always lurking, the mistakes he could make with her future by making the wrong decision.

Had this been the wrong decision? He might have caused irreparable damage—to both of them. Because he'd allowed himself to care about her, and he couldn't do that.

Not with what was surely coming down the road.

The Realm staff had strapped the demon into a chair, making it sit upright. It was well bound, so no matter how strong it was, no way was it going to get free.

They were also going to try to talk to the demon in a freakin' freezing room, which meant they were all geared up in parkas, gloves, and thermal underclothes.

Mandy couldn't feel her toes and fingers. Her nose was as red as Rudolph's and thank God for lip balm.

She paced, blowing into her gloved hands, watching a white trail of cold smoke filter out through her nearly frozen lips.

Yeah, plenty frigid in here. Demon dude wasn't going to be able to dematerialize. Now all they had to do was wait for it to wake up. The scientists had injected it with just enough of the warming agent to bring about consciousness, but not enough to thaw it so it could turn into mist.

The demon—or should they refer to it as James?—was beginning to stir, eyelids twitching, mouth opening in a grimace.

Good. Mandy hoped it was in pain.

In an instant its eyes shot open, zooming in on her. She grinned and leaned in.

"Have a nice nap, James?"

It struggled against the restraints.

"There's no point in fighting," Michael said, moving alongside Mandy. "You're secure."

Fully awake and aware now, at first it feigned fear. "I don't understand. Why are you holding me?"

"You can knock off the poor captured human act," Mandy said. "We know what you are."

And still, it continued the performance. "Where's my wife? If you've hurt her, I'll kill you."

Mandy rolled her eyes. "They need to give you guys better acting lessons, because you suck at this."

"We know you're not human," Michael said, "so knock off the bullshit. You're not James McAdams, at least not the James McAdams you used to be."

The fear left the demon's face and it smirked. "You have no idea what you're dealing with."

Mandy snorted. She couldn't wait for the chance to go one-on-one with this piece of shit. Her silver-tipped dagger was nice and cold strapped to her thigh. She'd love to plunge it in this bastard's excuse for a heart. But with it tied down like that there'd be no fun in stabbing it. She wanted it free and coming at her so the fight would be fair.

"Why don't you tell us what we're dealing with," Michael said, his voice calm. He was even smiling.

"You think your cold room and these bindings can hold me?"

Michael crossed his arms. "Are you saying they can't?"

James lifted its chin. "Of course not."

"Then go ahead, dematerialize into mist or break the restraints."

The demon shot Michael a look of pure malice. "You're testing me, have me hooked up to wires or something. I'm not giving away my secrets."

"You can't get out of the freakin' chair. Do you think we're stupid?" Mandy smirked at the demon's attempt at superiority.

"Yes, I think you're stupid. All humans are."

Mandy cupped the knife at her thigh. Michael's hand covered hers and patted it gently.

She so couldn't wait for this fight.

Michael cocked his head to the side. "You look human to me."

"That's the idea."

"What's the idea?"

James opened its mouth to speak, then shook its head. "I've got nothing to say."

It wanted to brag. Mandy knew it. It wanted to show them how "advanced" it was to the rest of them.

Michael backed away, leaned against the frozen wall, looked bored, as if he didn't care. "We can just leave you here until you rot."

The demon said nothing.

"They won't care whether you die or not. You're only one of many to them. If they lose you, they'll just make another."

Mandy noticed Michael didn't say who "they" were. But James knew. The Sons of Darkness.

"What did they offer you to give up your humanity?" Michael asked. "To give up your life?"

"Immortality, asshole. They want smart, good-looking humans. In return, we get to live forever, and we get all these cool skills."

"Like shifting into mist, for example," Michael offered.

The demon nodded. "Exactly."

"Is that it?" Mandy asked, already picking up from Michael that they were playing the Good Cop, Bad Cop game. "That's the best you've got? Shifting into mist? Because I've gotta tell you, that's not much."

"Better than what you've got, bitch."

She didn't rise to the bait this time. Oh, but it took a lot of effort. She'd really like to wipe that smart-ass smirk off the demon's face.

"She has a point," Michael said, keeping his voice low and even. "Disappearing is a nice act, but surely there has to be more benefit for what you're asked to do."

"Superhuman strength, immunity to all disease. No need to eat, or sleep, though we do need to feed."

This guy was a wealth of information. The Sons of

Darkness were going to have to work on the discretion thing. This demon was so full of itself it just had to brag.

"You said you didn't need to eat, but you need to feed." Michael made a show of studying his nails, as if he wasn't really all that interested in the answer. "That seems rather . . . human to me."

"Not food, you moron."

"Then what?" Michael asked.

"Life force. Energy."

"And how do you do that?" Michael asked.

"It's so damn easy you wouldn't believe it. Just press your fingers against a human's neck, embed, and suck the life right out of them."

Mandy's gaze snapped to the demon's. "How the hell does that work?"

The demon laughed. "Hell if I know. It just does. And oh, man, there's nothing like the feeling of your victim wrestling for freedom underneath you. The power just pouring into you. It's like you can feel their soul seeping out of them as they die. That's some heady shit."

She'd show it heady. How would it like to have its life force sucked right out of it? Mandy would bet she could figure a way to make that happen.

"That's all you need to sustain your existence?" Michael asked.

The demon gave a short nod. "That's it. We have no weaknesses."

Everything had weaknesses. Everything could die.

"We will rule. You'll find out soon enough." The demon looked them over as if they were nothing but insects. "We are superior over humans and growing stronger every day. There are more and more of us coming on board, and the Masters are turning us at a rapid rate. Soon, we'll take over and you'll bow to us."

"That's pretty big talk coming from someone strapped in and held prisoner," Mandy said.

The demon grinned. "Only a matter of time before I'm out of here."

Mandy snorted.

"Don't turn your back on me, bitch. You'll be dead."

"Knock the thing out," Michael ordered the tech. An injection into its IV and the demon's eyelids closed, but not before it sent Mandy a pale, blue-eyed look of utter hatred.

These demons had emotion. And egos. Too bad it was out cold. Mandy enjoyed the banter. And she really wanted to kill it, but not while it was strapped down like that. She wanted it free and going one-on-one with her.

She'd show it who was superior then. That demon had *overconfidence* written all over it. Which meant it was doomed.

Shivering from the subzero temperatures, Mandy stepped outside the room with Michael, peeling off the layers as she did. She rubbed her arms to get the circulation going again.

"Thinks a lot of itself, doesn't it?" she remarked.

"You could say that. Obviously they assume they're indestructible," Michael said as they strolled down the sterile white hallway and into an office. "That could be a critical mistake."

Mandy slid onto a well-worn leather sofa. "I can't believe it gave us so much information."

Michael pulled up a chair in front of the metal desk, turning the chair to face Mandy. "It doesn't see us as a threat. So it felt safe in boasting about its talents. Obviously the Sons of Darkness haven't taught their new recruits the better part of discretion."

"So what do we do with all that information now?"

"Since we know it feeds on humans, the first thing I want to know is if there are victims, and if so, how spread out are they? I'm going to have the Realm run a search of hospital emergency rooms and morgues, also police records, see if there have been any suspicious attacks, injuries, or deaths in recent weeks. That should tell us how widespread these demons are."

"I hope they're contained."

"I would bet they're not. The Sons of Darkness want to wage their war worldwide. I imagine we're going to see these types of injuries crop up internationally."

Mandy grimaced. "That's a nightmare in the making."

"Yes and no. The fact that these creatures have to feed is a good thing. It means we can spot where they've been."

"After the fact."

"True enough," Michael said. "Not ideal, but it gives us a way of identifying their locations."

"And if they *are* everywhere?" she asked.

His gaze was direct, and she already knew she wasn't going to like his answer. "Then we take them out one at a time, one location at a time. We'll alert all the other Realm cells to know what to look for. We'll figure out how to spot them."

New demons to hunt. Great. But at least having them on human turf made them easier to battle. Sort of.

"How do we kill them? Have we actually been able to kill one yet?"

Michael smiled. "Not that I'm aware of. Ryder and Angelique battled one similar to this one, but it disappeared. We don't know if it was destroyed or not."

"So how are we going to figure out what kills them?"

Michael arched a brow. "We have a nice test subject in the lab."

She smiled back. "We get to do battle with it?"

He leaned back in the chair, stretching out his long legs. "We're not going to keep it around as a pet, Mandy."

She laughed. "I might have underestimated you in the beginning, Michael."

He laced his fingers behind his head, his eyes gleaming with mischief. "Does that mean you're starting to like me?"

"I wouldn't go that far. I don't like anybody."

He cocked a brow. "I'll get to you yet, Mandy. Just wait."

"Famous last words. Many have tried. Most fail."

"I'm not most."

She snorted. "Speaking of boasting..."

"Just stating facts."

"Maybe we should pit you against the demon. You could have an ego match, see who comes out the winner."

"Still a smart-ass, I see." He stood, went around to the desk, and picked up the phone, a smile still lifting the corners of his lips.

Not only did he have a wit equal to hers, he also had

a really nice mouth. Full lower lip, the kind a woman could grab on to with her teeth.

Not that she would know anything about that kind of thing. Or even care. Especially about Michael. Where had that come from anyway? She didn't think about him that way at all.

Though she just had, hadn't she?

Gah. Where had her head gone? She shoved her hands in her lap and laced her fingers together, trying to look anywhere but at Michael, think about anything but his mouth. Her gaze ended up drifting back toward him. He was on the phone with someone about their demon, telling whoever it was everything they'd discovered.

He had full, midnight black brows that matched his hair. He needed a haircut, though she kind of liked it long and shaggy like he wore it. Lots of hair there for a woman to sift her fingers through during—

And there her mind wandered into very unfamiliar territory, setting off mental visuals that warmed her up considerably. Someone needed to turn the heat down. She shifted, turned on her side so she leaned against her hip, and laid her head against her hand, studying Michael as he turned his back to her.

He had a great ass. Narrow waist, muscular thighs, but not overly big like a lot of the guys she was used to. He was all lean muscle, really well built but not like a bodybuilder. She'd bet if she touched his body, he'd be solid.

Her gaze drifted up, and she realized he'd turned back around, was off the phone and staring at her, his expression that of bemused interest. Like he'd been checking her out the same way she'd been checking him out.

Oh, God. This was so embarrassing. Men as fellow demon hunters, fine. As her pseudo brothers, check. She had those relationships down pat. Men as...men, as sexual creatures, as potential partners...she had no clue how to handle that aspect of the male species.

"Mandy."

His voice had gone all low and sexy. She jumped off the sofa and ran her sweaty palms down the front of her pants. "I think I'll go check on our demon."

She nearly ran down the hall, hoping the breeze it created would quell the heat flaming her body. As she reached the interrogation chamber, she looked at her coat, then grimaced. She probably wouldn't even need it. The arctic temperatures inside the chamber were just what she needed to cool down her libido.

Bad time for her sex drive to decide to kick into high gear.

And with the wrong damn person. The absolutely wrong damn person.

CHAPTER TWELVE

Isabelle had found peace. A tenuous peace, anyway. Last night she'd slept in Dalton's arms, and the dreams had stayed away. If she'd known all it was going to take to keep the demons of her nightmares away was sleeping with Dalton, she'd have done that a long time ago.

This morning was the first time she hadn't woken in a haze, or with the remnants of her nightmares still with her. She'd woken with a gorgeous, sexy man slumbering next to her. Her body cradled against his, her butt nestled up against him, had been the most pleasant wake-up call, especially since Dalton woke up hard.

Morning sex was an amazing thing. Warm, half asleep, he'd roused her to full wakefulness by sliding inside her, stroking her breasts with one hand and her sex with the other until she cried out and arched against him in an amazing orgasm. They'd showered together afterward, had breakfast, then Dalton said he wanted to work with her out back on weapons and strength training.

All in all, it had been a damn fine day so far, even if Dalton was a bit quiet.

Men. Who could figure them out. She was happy and she wasn't about to start questioning every little thing. They worked companionably together, Dalton teaching her some basic moves. She was lithe and learned quickly. It wasn't like he intended to drop-kick her across the yard, so she came at him head-on, kicking like he taught her, though she couldn't imagine coming that close to a demon, or what possible use any martial arts training would be on a demon. But Dalton explained it had more to do with honing her physical and mental reaction skills. He didn't expect her to fight a demon one-on-one.

After they'd worked themselves into a decent sweat doing the physical stuff, they took a break, had a drink, and Dalton brought out the weapons. Lasers, sonic guns, rifles, swords—amazing things, from the ancient to the high-tech. She was riveted while he explained how everything worked.

The day wasn't even as hot. After the storm the night before last, the heat had lifted. Of course it was still hot as blazes, but not as humid, and there was even a breeze. Every little bit helped. She felt so much lighter now. Was it the weather or something else? She decided it was the weather. After the hellacious heat they'd battled the past few days, this weather seemed like fall and it made her happy.

But really, it was probably the sex. Isabelle smiled.

"You make me nervous when you smile at the weapons."

Her gaze lifted to his and her smile widened. "Actually, I was thinking about sex."

"Oh. In that case, keep smiling." He winked.

She laughed and he held out one of the lasers to her. "You have to be careful with these."

Her eyes widened. "It's loaded?"

"Yes. And the trigger is an easy pull. It doesn't take much to set it off. But I want you to get a feel for it because it's heavy and bulky."

He laid the rifle in her hands. He was right. It was heavy. She lifted it and, as Dalton showed her, she laid the butt against her shoulder and aimed for the trees at the back of the yard.

Shoot him.

She stilled, blinked, turned to Dalton. "Did you say something?"

"No."

She shook her head.

Kill him.

She closed her eyes as a wave of dizziness swept over her, a blanket of evil wrapping itself around her. It was like darkness cloaking her, touching her, fingers caressing her hand, willing her to do something she didn't want to do.

Pull the trigger. Kill him.

"No. I won't."

Dalton was right there in front of her. She wanted to scream at him to get out of the way, but her voice wouldn't work.

He's going to hurt you. Kill him before he can.

She refused to listen to Tase's voice. He was behind her. She could feel him, his presence so real she felt the heat coming off him. She shook her head, the tears in her eyes blinding her. She lifted the barrel of the laser, pivoted and pulled the trigger.

"Leave me alone, damn you."

A blue stream shot from the barrel of the rifle.

And right into Dalton.

No. No. That couldn't be. Dalton had been on the other side of her.

Dalton fell to the ground and Isabelle dropped the rifle.

Oh, God, what had she done?

She heard Tase's laughter in her ears, wanted to cover them to drown out the sound of his evil.

That's my girl.

No. She hadn't done this, had she?

But she had.

"Dalton!"

She smelled burning flesh and nausea rose into her throat. She forced it down, dropped to her knees in front of him. His eyes were closed, his shirt torn, a large dark hole in his stomach where she'd—

She'd shot him. With a laser. Dear God, he was dead. He had to be dead. No one could survive that. She looked for blood but there was nothing but a deep, dark hole in the middle of his stomach.

Frantic, her hands shaking, she touched two fingers to the side of his neck.

A pulse! She felt a pulse! Weak, but it was there.

She had to get help. She swept her hand over his forehead.

He looked so pale.

"I'm going to get help, Dalton. I'll be right back."

Don't die. Please don't die.

She didn't want to leave him there alone, afraid he'd die while she was gone. But she knew she couldn't help him. She pushed off the ground and sprinted to the main house so fast her lungs burned by the time she flew through the front door. Georgie must have known from the look on Isabelle's face that something was wrong. She grabbed a tapestry bag from the kitchen counter. "Don't talk. Let's go."

Fueled by panic and concern for Dalton, Isabelle nodded and they ran down the path back to the cabin. She was certain she was going to find Dalton already dead by the time they returned.

She'd shot him. How could she have done that?

Don't think about that now. Save him. Don't let him die.

She should have told Georgie to call 911. Dalton needed an ambulance, not a voodoo priestess with a carpetbag. Where were her brains?

She flew through the house and out the back door, skidding to a halt when she saw him.

Dalton not only wasn't dead, he was sitting up.

She dropped to her feet next to him. "You need to lie down."

"I'm fine."

"You are not fine." She reached for his middle, but he grasped her wrist.

"I said I was fine."

"Let me." Georgie moved in and Isabelle stood.

"I'm okay, really."

"What happened here?" Georgie asked.

"I shot him. With a laser."

Georgie lifted her gaze to Isabelle, then back at Dalton.

"It was an accident," Isabelle added. "I didn't mean to."

"It's okay," Dalton said, his voice calm and even. "I'm going to be fine."

Georgie turned to her. "I'm going to bring him in the house. Go grab a pot and boil me some water."

Isabelle nodded and ran inside to start filling the pot with water, the whole time lifting up on her toes to peer out the window to see what Georgie was doing. She had Dalton on his feet and was helping him to the door. Isabelle ran to open it. They came inside, and she was heading toward the bedroom when she noticed they weren't following.

"In the kitchen is fine," Georgie said.

She didn't understand this. The wound was the size of both her hands. He should be in the hospital having major surgery, not sitting at the kitchen table.

By the time Isabelle had dragged the pot out of the bottom cupboard, washed and rinsed it and filled it with water, then set it on the stove, Georgie had removed Dalton's shirt and was inspecting the wound.

"I need more light, Isabelle. Can you find me a lamp?"

"Sure." The kitchen only had an overhead light, so Isabelle pulled the lamp from the living room and set it on the table, plugging it into one of the floor outlets in the kitchen. Georgie was bent close over Dalton. Dalton was watching Isabelle. He actually looked pretty good, all things considered. He should have been in shock, and pale, but he looked dark. Tan. Normal. Completely different from how he'd looked before she'd run up to get Georgie.

The water was boiling, so Isabelle took the cloths

Georgie gave her and soaked them, pulled them out with tongs, and set them on the clean cutting board to cool a bit before handing them to Georgie.

"This isn't bad at all," Georgie said after washing Dalton's stomach.

"Are you serious? That hole was huge. It was a laser blast and he was only a foot away from me, Georgie. I had to have hit major organs."

Georgie looked up at her. "No, Isabelle. It's not that bad."

Georgie stood and went to the sink to wash her hands. Isabelle leaned over the table, then frowned as she examined the hole.

There . . . was no hole. It was closed, a small puckered wound the only evidence of what she'd done.

"You don't even need stitches," Georgie said to Dalton with a satisfied smile, then handed Isabelle a tube. "Keep it clean, put this antibiotic cream on it to ward infection away."

Still puzzled, Isabelle nodded, then lifted her gaze to Georgie. "I don't understand. It was much worse. Did you—"

Georgie laid her hand on Isabelle's arm. "No, *chère*. I didn't." Georgie looked over at Dalton.

Isabelle shook her head. She didn't understand this. Not at all.

Georgie gathered up her supplies and left, but before she did Isabelle saw the frown Georgie had cast at Dalton.

Throughout it all, Dalton had stayed quiet. After Isabelle saw Georgie to the door, she walked back into

the kitchen and pulled up a chair across the table from
Dalton. Less than an hour ago she'd blown a hole the size
of both her hands in his stomach. Dalton had looked
near death.

Now, the hole was closed and he looked plenty
healthy.

"You want to tell me what's going on?"

He shrugged. "I heal fast. I told you I was going to be
okay."

She cocked a brow. "You must think I'm really
stupid."

"No, Isabelle. I don't think you're stupid at all."

"Then do you want to tell me what happened out
there?"

He reached for her hand. "Maybe *you* should tell *me*
what happened."

Okay, fine. They'd go there first. She owed him that,
since she was the one who'd shot him. But then she
wanted answers. "I don't know. I had the rifle in my hands.
Then I heard Tase's voice. He told me to shoot you."

Dalton leaned back in the chair. "So you did?"

"No! I fought it off."

"Fought what off?"

"Him. The urges. His influence."

"What influence?"

She inhaled, sighed. "It's hard to explain unless
you're the one feeling it. But I'll try. It's like he crawled
inside my head and became part of me."

"Like he was controlling you?"

"Sort of. He kept talking to me, telling me to shoot

you, to kill you. That I shouldn't trust you, that you were going to hurt me."

Dalton frowned. "Then what happened?"

"I saw you step in front of me, right in front of the barrel of the rifle. And I heard Tase's voice behind me. I was so frustrated and so afraid I wanted to make him go away. So I turned around and fired. I thought I was aiming the laser at him."

"I was behind you."

She looked down at her hands, then swept her gaze back up to him. "I know that now. I didn't then. I saw you in front of me, not behind me."

"He manipulated you."

"I know."

"Tase wasn't really there. I didn't see him."

"He's in my head."

"And he's making you see things. He's messing with your mind."

"I guess I'm not getting stronger. I'm getting weaker." Defeat hung like a weight around her neck, making it hard to breathe. She was beginning to think she wasn't going to win this battle.

"He's a strong demon, Isabelle. He's hard to fight."

"And I'm not powerful enough."

"Between the two of us, we are."

"How can you say that? Look what he just did to me, what he made me do, how easily I fell under his spell. And he's not even here. What happens when he finds us, Dalton? It'll be just like Sicily all over again. He'll make me his." She stood and turned away, paced, her mind awash in things she didn't want to think about, but could no longer deny.

Dalton came up behind her and wrapped his arms around her. "I won't let that happen."

She pulled away and turned to him. "Oh, really. And how are you going to stop him? Tase is a demon, Dalton. So am I. You're only a human." She paused and stared at him.

"Or—are you human? Does a human recover from an injury like what you suffered today?" She reached out, traced her fingers along his stomach, where there was barely a visible scar now. "Even as we've been talking you've healed further. In another hour you won't even be able to see that wound." He didn't respond.

"Dalton. No one heals like that. I thought you were going to die."

He tilted his head and gave her a disbelieving look. "I think maybe you panicked. It wasn't that bad."

If there was one thing she hated, it was being patronized. "You had a huge hole in your middle. I could see inside it. You should have been unconscious. You needed major surgery."

"But as you can see, I'm fine."

"Yes, I see. It isn't right."

He smiled. "You don't want me to be fine?"

She pushed at him, fury and frustration making her entire body vibrate. "Goddammit! There's something not right about this and you know what I'm talking about. You almost died out there, Dalton! I saw it, you know what happened. My heart nearly stopped when I saw how deep that wound was. I'm not delusional. So don't blow smoke up my ass and tell me I didn't see what I did. I know what I saw then and what I see now. Nobody heals this fast. Nobody. Now explain it to me and quit treating me like I'm some simpleminded idiot that you can divert with pretty clouds and ridiculous explanations."

He looked at her, silent for a few moments before saying, "I can't."

She rested her hip against the counter and crossed her arms. "Bullshit. You mean you don't want to."

At least he had the good sense not to answer her. She was right.

"How the hell can you heal so fast, Dalton? And don't tell me it was Georgie's magic. She already said it wasn't her."

Dalton sat down and leaned back in the chair and tapped his fingers against the tabletop. Now he wouldn't look at her.

"Trying to come up with a plausible explanation?"

He continued to look away from her.

"You won't tell me, will you?"

He dragged his fingers through his hair. "Isabelle, I can't. This is complicated."

"All this bullshit about you wanting me to trust you. But you can't trust me with your secrets. And it must be some powerful secret for you to be able to recover like that." She pivoted and walked out of the room.

"Where are you going?"

"Out."

"You can't go out there by yourself."

"Watch me."

"I'll go with you."

She was out the door, slamming it behind her before he could finish the sentence. And then she ran, needing distance between them.

She didn't go up to the main house; instead, she deviated halfway and headed toward the dock. Dusk cast a gray cloak over the orange ball as it sank into the water. She sat on the old dock, feeling it sway under her body as she found a spot and watched the water undulate the boats anchored there.

Thankfully, he didn't follow.

But it was quiet here and she had time to clear her head and think about Dalton and what had happened. She felt safe here, no warning signals blaring in her head that she was in any kind of danger. And thankfully, no voices.

It was dark. Fireflies danced around her, over the water, flitting in and around the trees on the other side of the lake. Carefree, they twirled around and up into the sky, then zoomed back toward land again, their yellow blinkers lighting the way like a beacon in the night.

She could use a beacon because she felt like she was fumbling in the dark, when instead she wanted clarity, to be able to fly around without a care or a thought other than the breeze blowing through her hair.

Sadly, unlike the fireflies, she was grounded, her mind muddled with thoughts of Dalton. She was beginning to wonder exactly what kind of man he was. First that strange glow surrounding him when they made love, and now the almost Superman healing ability. Who was her supposed savior, anyway?

She'd followed him blindly because he'd saved her life in Sicily. But what did she really know about him? And what were his motives in sparing her? What was in it for him?

And what was happening to her? Tase seemed to be gaining a foothold in her mind more and more. She wanted to be strong, yet she felt like she was weakening. She didn't want to be weak. She didn't want to give in and become one of the demons again. She'd rather die.

She felt more isolated than ever, and no one here would give her answers. She massaged her temples, wishing she could talk to Angelique. She missed her sister. Angie would know what to say to make her feel better. She'd help her reason this out, and maybe come up with some logical explanations for what was going on here.

Then again, nothing had been logical in her life since she found out she was part demon. Why should this situation be any different? She already felt like an alien in this foreign body. Why not add a glowing, self-healing lover to the mix?

She sighed and stared across the water, realizing the fireflies weren't going to give her any answers. She was tired. But she couldn't face Dalton.

He didn't trust her. And now, after all this time, she no longer trusted him, either. He had a secret. A big one. And he refused to tell her what it was.

So where did that leave them? Where did that leave her?

Alone, as usual. Right back where she'd started.

Kill him.

She squeezed her eyes shut, refusing to acknowledge that voice. She was stronger than the specter trying to invade her mind.

You shouldn't trust him. You have to kill him before he kills you.

How long before Tase succeeded in making her do just that? She'd almost killed Dalton today. Maybe next time Dalton wouldn't be so lucky.

She might not trust him, but she cared about him, would never want to hurt him. He'd saved her life in Italy, and maybe she didn't know why, but she owed him for that.

She had to get away from here, away from Dalton, where she couldn't hurt him or anyone else.

She stood and headed down the walkway, careful to keep her gaze on the house. Dalton hadn't come out, but he might any minute. Once she moved past the house she ran like hell, figuring it was only a matter of time before he'd come looking for her and not be able to find her.

He'd come after her. She didn't want to be found. It wasn't safe for Dalton with her there. Not after what she'd done today. Things were out of her control, more so now than ever before. The demon in her was coming out, growing stronger, and it was dangerous.

She headed toward the swamp and the thick trees, hoping they would swallow her up. She pushed hard, running until her chest ached from the effort, until she was forced to slow, lean forward, and rest her hands above her knees to catch her breath.

She had no idea where she was, and didn't care. It was so dark outside she felt enveloped by it, yet found it strangely comforting; she was no longer frightened or appalled by the smells and sounds of the swamp. Maybe the demon side of her was growing, coming out, and that's why she didn't mind being here in the murky woods.

This place seemed suitable for a demon. It was dark, it was depressing, and it smelled bad.

Honestly, she didn't care, as long as wherever she ended up was away from Dalton.

She kept walking, heading deeper into the swamp. Wetness seeped into her shoes, and walking became more difficult as she stalked through the thick mud. She had no flashlight, no idea where she was going. After a while she realized she'd become hopelessly lost, and she didn't mind. Not this time. Not anymore. She was sick to her stomach. She found a thick fallen trunk and sat on it, figuring she was far enough into the woods now that maybe Dalton wouldn't find her. And she'd hear him if he came for her. She could run then. She'd have to.

She'd never hurt Dalton. The human part of her, anyway.

The demon? Now that part of her she didn't know at all. And it was obviously the demon that had taken over while she held that rifle. That was the side of her that Tase could so easily manipulate. But how could she let that happen? Why couldn't she tell the difference between what was real and what wasn't?

How could she make herself stronger so she could fight it?

What would have happened had Dalton not been able to heal so well?

She knew the answer to that. He'd be dead. And the demon would be in control now. The Isabelle she knew—the only part of herself she really understood—would be gone.

Tears filled her eyes and she used her hands to wipe them away. She had no right to feel sorry for herself. This wasn't about her. This was about what she was capable of doing, if not now, then eventually.

Dalton shouldn't have saved her back in Italy. He should have destroyed her like he'd been ordered to do. The Realm of Light was smart about those things. They knew.

She wasn't worth saving. Good God, there were children back there at the main house. What if she'd succeeded in killing Dalton? Would she have marched up there, laser rifle in hand, and done the same to Georgie, to the men, women, and children up there?

Tase would like that. Destroying the innocent. She'd have been damned for sure. That was what frightened her the most. She knew she could do that. Deep down in the most secret, horrible part of herself that she never wanted to face, but knew existed, she knew that she could kill, that she could take someone's life without hesitation.

And a part of her would enjoy it.

She clutched her head. "That's sick. So, so sick. What's wrong with me?" She tilted her head back and stared up at the low hanging cypress limbs, the mosslike tendrils of fingers reaching out to her. She wished they would take her away, drown her in the swamp.

"Dalton, why did you save me? Why would you do this to me?"

"Because I thought you were worth saving."

She hadn't even heard him. In this place filled with heavy roots, sticky muck, mud and water, no one should be able to get to her without her hearing them.

But Dalton had. And she wasn't at all surprised. She sighed, drew her knees up to her chest and laid her forehead on them.

Defeat settled over her like a heavy weight. She'd tried so hard to put distance between them, and even in that she'd failed. She couldn't even manage successfully to be noble.

"Go away, Dalton. Leave me alone."

He was behind her, probably about twenty-five feet or so from the sound of his voice. "The last thing you need right now is to be alone. What the hell were you thinking, coming out this far by yourself? Do you even have a flashlight?"

"No. Do you?"

"No. But I know the area."

"And I don't care."

"Let's go back."

"No." She lifted her head, peered ahead to see if she could figure out where she could run.

"Nowhere."

"What?"

"There's no place you can go that I couldn't find you. Don't even try it."

He was so smug about it, too. She'd just bet right now he was smiling, certain he'd won this battle. That a little reassurance and she'd be placated and ready to go back with him. Well, he was wrong. This time he wasn't going to win. She wasn't going back to endanger him and the rest of the people he held dear. She planted her feet and launched upright, shooting forward at a dead run. She didn't even bother to look back because she knew Dalton would be right on her heels. She flew across the water, hoping like hell it would continue to be only ankle deep, because she had no idea how to gauge its depth in this midnight dark bayou. She cleared her mind and focused on pushing one foot in front of the other, keeping her gaze on what was in front of her.

Don't think. Don't panic. Don't feel.

She wasn't prepared to be tackled and flung forward into the mud and water. She'd thought she was outrunning him—until his arms wrapped around her waist and they both went down.

She came up furious, kicking and scratching, tearing at him with all the fury she'd held inside. She was angry. Angry at her fate, because she couldn't eliminate this blood of evil inside her, angry at Dalton because he hadn't killed her when he should have. And angry at herself, because despite it all, she still cared enough to want to live, to want everything fixed, to want to throw her arms around Dalton and beg him to make it all right.

Dalton bore the brunt of Isabelle's attack, knowing she was striking out mainly in fear. He'd seen that fear today when she thought she'd hurt him. He knew it wasn't the human Isabelle who had fired that laser. She'd been manipulated. The human Isabelle had hesitated. The demon in her could have easily taken Tase's suggestion and fired. She didn't. Tase had to alter the game a bit so Isabelle shot him. Which meant she was fighting the demon inside her, and she was winning. Why couldn't she see that? Why did she run? He didn't want her to hurt herself, and she couldn't hurt him. Not like this. Now it was the human Isabelle attacking him, and he knew she had to let off some steam.

After several minutes of kicking and scratching, she began to wear down. He let her go at him for as long as it took. He knew what this was like—this pain, fear, and confusion, not knowing who or what you were or whether you could control your impulses.

Been there, done that.

He finally turned her around and pulled her back against his chest, crouching down so she could catch her breath. With his free hand he pulled her hair away from her face. She was dragging in air, shallow and fast.

"Slow down, Isabelle."

"I feel sick," she said, her voice hoarse as she wheezed in and out.

"You're breathing too fast. You need to bring it down." He breathed with her, loud enough so she could hear his rhythm. She sucked in air, then blew it out, taking it down a notch, trying to match him. "That's it. In and out, slow and easy."

When he had her calmed, he stood and lifted her out of the mud and carried her to the bank, then sat and placed her on his lap. She laid her head against his chest, her palm there, too. He felt his heart beating against her hand and closed his eyes, just . . . absorbing her.

What was he going to do with her? How was he going to help her?

"I can't do this, Dalton."

He stroked her mud covered hair. "Yeah, you can."

She pushed back and looked at him. Her face was a ragged mess of tears, caked mud, and agony. "You don't understand. You don't know what I did, what I could do."

"Yes, I do. And you won't."

She shook her head. There was a sadness in her eyes he wanted to obliterate, to make her realize she could change who and what she was.

If he could, anyone could. But he couldn't tell her that. Not yet. Not when she was so raw. She wouldn't believe him, wouldn't understand. And he wasn't ready.

"They're getting stronger." She pushed away, stood, and turned to face him. "I can't fight them if they take over when I'm sleeping. Or if the demon part of me does."

He didn't make a move, just sat on the hill watching her. "You didn't kill me, Isabelle."

"I could have."

"If the demon side of you was so strong, it would have latched on to Tase's suggestion, found me, and fired. But you fought him and he had to manipulate you to win. You know what that signals to me? Hesitation. Internal battle. The human side of you warring with the demon side. If the demon side of you had taken over, you'd have pointed that laser and fired without a second's hesitation."

She flinched at that.

"But you didn't. You held it there and did nothing until you thought you were hitting Tase with that laser. Your human side is winning this battle, Isabelle. Have any demons attacked since we've been here?"

"No."

"That's because they don't know where we are. They can't fix a signal on you because you won't let them. You're stronger than they are. You have more fight and determination in you than you think. Maybe it's time you start believing in yourself."

"I can't."

She looked so damned defeated, her chin tucked down on her chest, her arms wrapped tight around her middle. It was goddamned infuriating. "Why is it so hard? I believe in you. You're here because I believed you could be saved."

Her head snapped up. "Why? Why do you think that?"

He shrugged. "Because I know how strong you are. I saw it in Italy. Your determination, your refusal to quit despite insurmountable odds. Where did that Isabelle go?"

"I don't know."

He stood, went to her, lifted her chin so she was forced to look at him. "I want that Isabelle back. Fight for her."

"I don't know if I can. I'm afraid, Dalton. I've never been afraid before, and I hate this feeling. What if I lose myself? What if I hurt someone?"

"I won't let it happen."

"You can't guarantee that."

He could do more than she thought. "No, I can't, but I can help you if you let me. I won't let them get to you. I won't let the demon inside you take over. I won't lose you."

She grasped his arms, laid her forehead against his chest. "I don't want to lose you, either. I've never allowed myself to care about anyone before." She tilted her head back and looked at him, her eyes clear and guileless. "I care about you. I have all these feelings rolling around inside me, and they're all centered around you. I think that scares me most of all."

He sucked in a breath and held it. This was the worst thing that could have happened. He shouldn't want Isabelle to care for him. But he did. Because he had feelings for her, too. Feelings he had no business having. Not with what needed to happen between them.

Talk about lousy timing. The cosmos had a warped sense of humor sometimes. He tilted his head back and stared up into the heavens, wondering if after all this time he'd found love, only to have to make the biggest sacrifice of all.

He looked down at Isabelle, and everything else went away. He didn't care that they stood in the middle of the swamp, that it was night, that he should get them both back to the house.

"I don't ever want you to be afraid to care about me." He pulled her against him and pressed his lips to hers.

She let out a soft sigh, her lips opening under his. He tasted mud, and smiled against her mouth as he pressed more firmly, sliding his tongue inside to lick against hers. He wanted—no, demanded that she be his. He wouldn't take anything less.

Something about Isabelle always called to the more dominant, darker side of himself. He stopped questioning it, stopped fighting it, and let it take over.

This bayou, where secrets hid and darkness lived, was the perfect place. He held her and dropped down on the mossy bank, pulling her on top of him, needing to feel the full length of her body stretched out over his. She moaned against him, splayed her hands over his chest as she wriggled into position on top of him, then pulled her mouth from his to stare down at him.

She had the face of an angel, and when her lips curled, the smile of the devil himself. Wicked, tempting him to want things he knew he shouldn't.

He wanted them anyway.

"I'm covered in mud," she said, rocking her pelvis against his cock.

"I don't care. Undress."

She cocked a brow. "Demanding, aren't you?"

He tightened his fingers around her hips. "Not much patience. Do it."

She pushed up into a sitting position, smiling down at him. "You sure change personalities in a hurry, Dalton." She teased him by taking her time, reaching for the bottom of her tank top and slowly baring her stomach as she lifted it. "Sweet and oh, so gentle one minute, harsh and gruff the next."

His fingers bit into the fabric of her shorts as he waited, fast losing tolerance. "You gonna do it or am I going to have to do it for you?"

She had started to lift the shirt, but she paused. "Are

you sure you wouldn't like it slower, more like a strip-
tease?"

"I'm warning you, Isabelle."

She laughed, the darkness of it so erotic he felt it in
his balls, tightening them as if she had squeezed them
with her hands. He lifted, arching up against her.

Her eyes darkened. "Okay then, faster it is."

She pulled off her top and tossed it onto the hill. Her
breasts were bare and he reached for them, sliding his
palms over her nipples. The feel of the metal piercing her
nipples never failed to excite him. Her nipples were hot
to the touch and already hard as she leaned into his hands
and whimpered.

"Yes. More. I want more of that. Touch me."

Her words didn't help his patience. Nor did her
hands as they crept over his body, lifting his shirt and
smoothing over the bare expanse of his stomach and
chest, claiming him in ways that defied explanation. Even
with mud clinging to her skin and hair, she was beautiful,
his angel with the devil inside. He arched up and pulled
her down to him, needing the touch of her lips against
his, the smoky fire that churned inside him whenever
they connected mouth to mouth.

He pushed at her shorts, wanting her naked, no bar-
riers between them. She wriggled out of them, stretching flat over his body as she kicked them off, then set to
work unsnapping his pants and pulling them down his
legs while he drew his shirt off. When she spread her
body over his again, he hissed at the heated contact of
skin to skin. Her body was always hot, as if she had a
fever.

"You're nothing like a demon. Demons are cold to the touch. You're like fire."

Her eyes glazed with a golden shimmer as she took a deep breath, her breasts pillowed against his chest. She pushed against him, sliding her sex along his shaft. "You make me melt inside. Feel me."

She grasped him with her hand, guiding his cock inside her wet sheath, surrounding him with that molten heat that threatened to make him explode all too soon. He fought the sensation, gritting his teeth as she gripped him in a tight vise of pleasure, then began to rock against him.

His world narrowed to just this woman. It didn't matter where they were. They could be in a lush bed, sunlight streaming in on their bodies, or this dark marsh, covered in mud, and he still would see only Isabelle, her body over him, her breasts moving as she rode him, her thighs clamped tightly to his, her head tilted back as she sought her own pleasure and gave him the greatest he'd ever experienced.

And as she tilted her head forward and her gaze met his, he realized that with Isabelle it was different because it was much more than physical. He felt her in so many more ways than just being inside her. He was with her, feeling her; he knew her like he'd never known another woman. With her it was easy like it had never been easy before, as if he'd been created to be with this one woman. Where she was dark, he was light. Where he was midnight, she was his dawn.

She smiled down at him, smoothed her hand over his face and hair. "You're doing it again."

"What?"

"Glowing."

He stilled, frowned, not knowing how to stop it. Not when he had all these feelings pouring out of him.

"Don't." She caressed his bottom lip with her fingers, then bent down to slide her lips across his. She whispered against his mouth. "Don't make it stop." She clenched her fingers against his shoulders and lifted, then slid down his shaft in a way that made him forget about the light pouring from him, made him forget everything but making love to her, taking her to that place where she'd forget, too. He gripped her hips and lifted her, set the rhythm as madness took over.

Isabelle gasped as he held her tight against him and lifted into her with a hard thrust. She rocked back and forth, clutched his arms, and whimpered, her sheath tightening around him. He watched as she came apart and then he couldn't hold back, going with her. And then he saw it, too: light bursting all around them as he poured forth everything he had. He lifted up to wrap his arms around Isabelle, taking her mouth in a kiss that spoke of everything he wanted to say, but couldn't.

He held her like that for a long time, both of them sitting up, wrapped around each other. It seemed like neither of them wanted to let go, but he knew they had to.

"We need to get back," he said, murmuring against her neck, kissing the soft column of her throat. He was still inside her, still throbbing with the aftereffects, and more than ready for round two.

"I don't want to go back."

"You going to live out here as a marsh rat?"

She giggled. "Maybe. I do know how to fish."

"So do the alligators."

She shuddered. "Dirty trick. Now we'll *have* to get dressed and leave."

"Hot shower. Food. Warm bed," he said.

"Oh, now you're upping the ante. That's not fair."

"Just stating the facts, babe."

She sighed. "Okay. I guess we have to."

They untangled themselves and dressed, then walked back to the cabin where the hot shower felt pretty damn good, especially since this time they took it together. And it took a long time to finish that shower, since washing each other led to touching, and touching led to tasting.

By the time they fell into bed, the sun had started to peek up over the horizon. Dalton growled, rose from the bed, and yanked down the shades. They needed at least a little bit of sleep.

"Dalton," Isabelle said, snuggling against him.

"Yeah."

"We need to talk. About you."

He inhaled. "Okay. We'll sleep for a while. Then we'll talk first thing tomorrow."

"Okay," she said with a yawn. "I'm holding you to that. Tomorrow."

He had to think. What was he going to tell her? Or rather, not tell her?

Things were changing between Isabelle and him. He wasn't sure all those changes were for the better.

CHAPTER THIRTEEN

Mandy looked through the glass at James—the de-mon. He—it—looked so human, so normal, lying on the table like that. Who knew that inside lurked a de-mon? No one would know if they hadn't seen what Mandy and Michael had seen.

"Why wouldn't freezing have worked to save Lou?" she asked, turning to Michael who had walked up be-side her.

"Huh?"

"That demon can't do a thing in the cold room. Couldn't we have done the same thing to Lou? And to Isabelle? Frozen them until we figured out what to do to . . . fix them?"

Michael shook his head. "This demon is a unique species, Mandy. It would be like trying to treat a human and a shark the same way. Even demons can be biologi-cally distinct from one another. This demon is nothing like the demon that was inside Lou, or Isabelle. Just like half demons and hybrid demons are different from one another. And like the Sons of Darkness are different from every other demon."

She scratched her nose and frowned. "Genetics and evolution?"

"Yes. They're constantly changing the demons, mixing up genetics and producing something new. And we have to keep up with them so we know how to fight them. Because every demon species is unique. How we treat them, how we fight them, is unique."

"So freezing Lou like we freeze this demon would have done no good."

She saw the sadness in his eyes. "No. It wouldn't. I'm sorry."

She had to ask. She had to know if there was some way that Lou could have been saved. She should have known there wasn't.

She followed Michael into the weapons room. "So do we really get to battle it?"

The Realm scientists had run tests on the demon for two days now, while Mandy had paced and waited, biding her time, keeping watch over James to see how it reacted, what it did. It did nothing but stare at the walls, at the glass, as if it knew she was on the other side, watching.

Maybe it was waiting for its opportunity to do battle with her. She hoped so.

"We're going to test it, see what it reacts to," Michael said. "We know from Ryder battling the disappearing-in-the-mist type of demon that anything silver makes it dematerialize. Assuming that this is the same type of demon, we don't want it heading back to the Sons of Darkness to report on where it's been. And we don't know if the silver just weakens it enough to make it disappear with its tail between its legs, or if the silver can kill it."

"Which means what exactly?"

"Which means we're going to have to try out different methods under a more controlled atmosphere. We'll test several silver weapons."

Ugh. That meant the cold room again. "It's going to be really hard to wield weapons in that arctic chamber."

"I'm not going to chance it getting away. That's a risk I'm unwilling to take. But we do have new weaponry. It would give us a chance to try it out on this demon."

"And I'll be the one to do that, right?"

He stopped, looked at her. "I don't want you to get hurt."

She cocked her head to the side and grinned. "Aww, Mike. You care about me. You really do."

"Of course I do. You're a valuable demon hunter. Losing you would put a huge hole in our team. Do you know how long it takes to find and train new hunters?"

She laughed. "I'm touched. Really. I'm near tears at the depth of your caring."

He rolled his eyes. "What I'm trying to tell you is that I'll be going in with you."

She frowned. "That takes all the fun out of it."

"I'm sorry you won't be able to fight the demon on your own, but you need backup. And we'll have our tech team on alert in case we need to take it down in any other way."

"Meaning?"

"Knock it out if it gets out of control, or to a point where we both can't handle the situation. The last thing I want is that demon getting past us, escaping and killing our techs and scientists, then dematerializing. Or worse, taking you with it to wherever the hell it goes."

There was no point in objecting. Michael was right. They had to have fail-safes in place to protect everyone in the center. "Okay. But I still want to be the one to battle it."

Michael's lips curled in a wry smile. "I'll do my best to stay out of your way."

"So what do we have in the way of weapons?" she asked, turning to the toys laid out on the tables.

The weapons room was her favorite place. It was like the mall of her dreams. Racks of lasers, guns, swords, and all the high-tech weaponry and accessories she could ever want. Lots of new things, too, all spread out on a few tables in front of them.

"We've converted a few of the standard ultraviolet lasers that we've used in the past on the other demons." He picked up one of the rifles that looked like the ones they used to fill with the blue liquid that shot out UV light and melted demons down to nothing but gelatinous matter. "Now, instead of UV light, this will inject bullets of liquid nitrogen."

Mandy picked up the rifle, examining the cartridges filled with silver liquid instead of blue. "Wicked. So the bullet will explode inside the demon—and then what happens?"

"Freezes it from the inside out. Putting the ice in its bloodstream and attacking its internal organs with a shot of liquid nitrogen should stop it dead in its tracks."

"But will that kill it?"

Michael shrugged. "Don't know. That's what we'll have to find out."

"Cool."

"We also have coated swords with pure silver. We know stabbing demons makes them dematerialize, but we don't know if that means they're dead, or if they just disappear to go lick their wounds. However, we do know that beheading the Sons of Darkness is pretty effective."

Mandy lifted the lightweight sword, standing back from Michael to swing it in a few wide arcs. "I like this. If you lop its head off, surely it won't grow another one."

"Yeah, I'm thinking that would probably do the job, too. But not handy on the street, so I'd like to keep that option as a last resort."

"Good point. We can't really walk around beheading people in the downtown business district, can we?"

"Uh, no." He led her over to another table. "Similar to the rifles, these are more compact guns with the same kind of liquid nitrogen bullets. Easier to conceal inside a coat or jacket. You can choose any size and weight and we can manufacture bullets sized to accommodate the weapon, plus add a silencer."

Mandy nodded. "This is really impressive." She chose a forty-five caliber. "Got bullets made up for this one?"

"Already loaded up with an extra clip to the side. There's a holster next to it if you need it."

"I won't."

She was admiring the weaponry when lights flashed and alarms sounded. She jerked, instantly on alert, and started grabbing weapons.

Michael picked up his comm, listened, then frowned.

"Drop the temp in the entire compound. Secure the area. Now!"

He turned to her. "Demon has escaped the cold room. Killed a tech and two guards."

Mandy didn't say a word, just tucked extra clips into the side pocket of her camos, then shouldered the rifle by the strap and ran like hell out of the room and down the hallway, Michael right on her heels.

"You take the north. I'll come around on the south side," Michael said.

Mandy nodded, not even stopping in her dead run down the hall toward the room where the demon had been held.

When she got there, she grimaced at the bodies on the floor, the blood, the guards standing over them holding their weapons, then she was off around the corner, shivering at the rapid drop in temperature as the compound went to subzero in an effort to keep the demon from dematerializing.

That bastard was not going to get away.

She tried doors along her way. They were all secure, the compound having gone into lockdown as soon as the alarm was set off.

By the time she made a complete circle and ran into Michael, she was utterly out of breath, sucking in frozen oxygen and confused as hell. Where was the demon?

"Emergency exit door," Michael said, turning on his heel. She followed right behind him, hitting the stairs two at a time as they punched through the exit door and up the stairs to the second level.

"What's up here?" she whispered over Michael's shoulder.

"Nothing. Storage. All the rooms should be secure."

"I'll take the south end."

He nodded and she pivoted, lifting her weapon and moving as fast as she could despite the extreme chill making her shiver all over. But if the subzero temp slowed her down, it would slow the demon down, too.

As she rounded the corner, she saw a flash of... something. She sucked in a breath and ran, hard, sliding around the corner.

The demon crashed into her and slammed her against the wall, knocking the breath from her. She lost the gun, watching it slide down the hall and just out of her reach.

Shit.

But she still had her rifle. Unfortunately she couldn't pull it over her shoulder because the demon had her pinned to the wall.

Fury thawed her frozen body out, gave her some strength. And James was weakened by the cold that affected the demon more than her, allowing her to give it a good, hard thrust and make some space between them. When she did, she lifted her foot and planted a boot in its midsection, shoving it away.

James landed on the floor and she went for her rifle.

Stunned or winded, she didn't know which, the demon lay there, unmoving, staring at her.

She aimed, her finger on the trigger.

The demon scrambled to get up, then froze as she got it in her sights.

"You're dead," she said, her finger hovering on the trigger.

But as soon as she started to pull, the demon's face disappeared. She was transported back to that awful night in Italy, when they'd stood in front of Lou and were forced to fire on him, kill him.

She blinked, trying to obliterate the vision from her mind. She lifted her head for a second, clearing the sight, then refocused, but all she could see was Lou, fighting the demon inside him, begging them to destroy him.

She wasn't going to let this happen. She wasn't weak. She'd recovered from Lou's death. It was in the past.

Michael pulled up behind her. "Pull the damn trigger, Mandy."

She blinked and leveled the laser, but the demon leaped and came at her, knocking both her and Michael to the ground. Too late to fire, she swung the butt at the demon's head, knocking it off balance. Her rifle went flying.

Shit. She scrambled for her gun, grabbed it with her fingertips, and turned around, aiming for the demon as it grabbed her feet. She aimed, and there it was again.

Lou's face. Not the demon's.

What the hell was wrong with her?

"No," she whispered, pulling back from the sight.

It was Lou. Not the demon. She held her hand out in front of her, trying to banish the visual. "No, I can't."

"Mandy!"

She heard Michael's voice, but it was as if it came from a tunnel, far away. All she could see was Lou in front of her, coming toward her, his hands outstretched, reaching for her.

God, she missed him. Tears filled her eyes. She leaned up toward him. "Lou."

Her world tipped when Michael shoved her out of the way. Shocked back into reality, her vision cleared just in time to see the demon leap over her and lunge at Michael.

Oh, God, what had she done? She'd utterly lost it. It hadn't been Lou reaching for her, it had been the demon. And now Michael was being attacked by the demon, who'd landed on top of him. She tried to get up, but her legs felt like rubber, unable to support her. All she could do was stare in horror as the demon wrapped its fingers around Michael's throat.

Mandy held her breath, feeling what Michael felt as the demon squeezed.

But Michael wedged his gun between his body and the demon's and fired, slamming the demon off him.

James looked down at its chest and then back up at them, smiling.

"You can't stop me with bullets."

But then its smile died, its eyes widening as the liquid nitrogen began to work. The demon started to jerk wildly, falling to the ground like it was having some kind of neurological attack, then stilled completely. After waiting a minute, Michael leaned over the demon, still holding the pistol trained on its chest.

Michael punched his comm. "Security and tech, we're on second level and demon is contained. Get up here."

Within a minute a security team and three technicians showed up. The security team inspected the demon first, then pronounced it dead so tech could remove it.

"Restrain it and keep watch. I want to see if it comes to."

They nodded and removed the demon. Michael holstered his pistol and went to Mandy, bending down to help her up.

She pulled away from him and pushed herself to a standing position, hating the weakness that still made her legs feel wobbly. "I'm fine."

Michael took a step back and nodded. "Let's go to debriefing."

Mandy followed Michael silently, not understanding what had happened.

For someone so grounded in the here and now, what had gone down had been really fucked up. She'd always been able to do her job.

So what the hell had happened to her?

Michael led her into the office and waited while she stepped in, then closed the door behind him. Mandy laid her weapons on the table, took a seat and stared down at the floor.

She knew what was coming. This wasn't going to be fun.

Michael pulled a chair across from her.

"Want to tell me what happened in there?"

No. "I froze."

"So I noticed. Literally or figuratively?"

"Both, I guess." She leaned forward and laid her head

in her hands. "I don't know what the hell happened to me. I was ready to kill that thing. I really was."

"Maybe this is too much for you too soon."

She snapped her gaze to his. "No, it isn't."

"You couldn't pull the trigger, Mandy. You had the demon in your sights, your finger on the trigger, and you couldn't get it done. That demon could have killed you."

Or it could have killed Michael. And that would have been her fault. Just like Lou was her fault. Perfect. Another death of one of the Realm's Keepers on her head.

"Tell me what you're thinking," Michael said.

She shrugged, leaned back. "I'm not thinking anything."

"Bullshit. You either come clean with me or I'm pulling you off active duty."

Her eyes widened. "Are you serious? I had one second of hesitation and now you think I can't do my job?"

"It wasn't one second. Something happened up there. Something that wasn't normal for you. You could have died. I could have died. We need to talk about it."

She hated that he presumed to know all about her. He knew nothing about what was "normal" for her. "We don't need to talk about anything."

He cocked his head in disbelief, then pushed the chair back. "We're done here."

"What does that mean?"

"It means until you're ready to talk to me, or to someone else, about what really happened up there, you're no longer a hunter."

She shot out of the chair. "What? You can't do that."

"Yeah, I can." He started to walk away but she grabbed his arm and forced him to turn to her.

"Who made you judge and jury over me? Who put you in charge?"

His gaze never wavered as he said, "Lou did. The Realm did. You report to me now, Mandy. Lou is gone."

"I know that. Don't you think I know that?" All too well, unfortunately. She couldn't begin to explain to Michael what had happened. Not when she didn't understand it herself. And no way would she reveal anything that could be considered a weakness. Especially not to her Keeper. He'd ground her for sure. Permanently. "Look, there was just something not right about the situation. It just didn't feel right."

Michael shook his head. "That's not it and you know it. And if you can't be straight with me, then this isn't going to work. I said you're off duty and I meant it."

Fury filled her. She fisted her hands at her sides, but knew striking out at Michael would seal her fate. He looked down at her hands as if he knew what she felt. She saw only compassion in his eyes.

Goddammit. She didn't want his compassion. She didn't want anything from him, especially not the caring she saw reflected in his gorgeous baby blues.

He turned and left the room.

This time, Mandy didn't try to stop him.

She had nothing left to say. Nothing at all.

CHAPTER FOURTEEN

Dalton was drinking coffee when Georgie came around the side of the cabin and into the backyard. He smiled at her.

"What are you doing down here?" he asked.

"I came to check on you."

He'd pulled on jeans this morning, careful not to wake Isabelle. Without his shirt on, Georgie could see his stomach.

"I can't even tell where you were injured, Dalton. Pretty impressive."

"Yeah, well, I heal quick," he said, lowering his voice.

"You haven't told her, have you?"

"No."

"Why not?"

He glanced at the back door, turned to Georgie. "I've told her all I can."

Georgie crossed her arms. "If you haven't told her everything, then it's not enough. How can you hope to succeed in what you plan to do if she doesn't know the entire story? Until she knows all, I won't be able to help her, and neither will you."

He was hoping it wouldn't come to that. "Georgie, no one knows except your family."

"Knowledge is power. Isabelle will need all the power she can wield in order to make it through this trial by fire you have in mind for her."

"Shit." He dragged his hand through his hair.

"You don't trust her?"

"Yes. No. I don't know. I do trust her. I think."

Georgie let out a soft laugh. "Well, that's definite."

"Yeah, well, I guess I'm not a hundred percent sure. And you can imagine what this kind of information could do in the wrong hands."

"But she trusts you with her secret."

"She had no choice."

"Neither do you. Not if you want this to succeed."

"I know what I need to do. I'm just not ready."

"What's holding you back?"

"I need to be able to trust Isabelle to tell her everything. But I'm not sure the demon side of her won't somehow use it against me."

"Trust is a two-way street, Dalton. I hate to be trite, but it's the truth."

He nodded. "I realize that."

"She's put her life in your hands. You might have to do the same with her."

"I still haven't figured out what kind of hold the Sons of Darkness really have over Isabelle, how much control they wield over her. She shot me yesterday."

"Do you think that was her intent?"

"No. But still, the Sons of Darkness have a hold on her."

"You don't think she's fully in charge of herself."

"No."

Georgie sighed. "Then you're not ready."

So not what he wanted to hear. "I wish I believed one hundred percent in Isabelle, enough to tell her who I am—enough to trust her fully. But I don't trust the Sons of Darkness. They could be using her. And if they're using her, they could use me. I can't let that happen. We'll both suffer."

It was at that moment he caught sight of Isabelle, leaning against the back screen door. Close enough to have heard them. But how much had she heard?

She pushed open the door and came toward them, stopping in front of him. He didn't need her to say a word to know she'd heard everything. The hurt and anger on her face said enough.

"Things are so much clearer now."

"Isabelle, before you start—"

"Oh, no," she said, holding out her hand. "You've had your say and I heard it all. Now you let me talk."

He nodded, knowing he deserved whatever she had to say.

"I always felt you were holding back with me, but I just couldn't figure out why. Now I know. All those times you told me you believed in me, you trusted me. All bullshit."

"Isabelle—"

"Not that I can blame you," she continued, ignoring him. "I don't trust myself, so how can I expect you to have faith in me? I'm not angry at you, Dalton. Just... disappointed, I guess. I thought we were past hiding secrets about how we felt. I've been pretty straight with you and I thought you had been with me. I was wrong."

She laughed. "I'm always wrong about men."

She turned and walked back in the house.

Well, fuck. Dalton turned to Georgie.

"Don't look at me, *cher*. You dug this grave. Now crawl out yourself."

After Georgie walked away, Dalton felt more alone than ever. Goddammit, every time he thought he was making the right decision, it turned out to be the wrong one. By not telling her what he was, he was trying to protect her. Was that wrong? Had he failed her by keeping secrets?

He was going to have to fix this, which meant doing something he really didn't want to do. He went inside the house.

He saw her silhouette on the sofa, her legs pulled up to her chest, her chin resting on her knees.

He went to her, deciding it was probably best to sit in the chair across from the sofa.

Now that he faced her, he didn't know where to start.

"Is this going to be another chat where you feed me a line of bullshit until you think I'm placated, then I fall into your arms and we have sex?"

He smiled at that. "Well, that'd be nice, but I don't think it's going to happen."

"You're right. It's not. You're wasting your time here, Dalton. I'm through with trusting you."

He let out a long breath, knowing that the only way to get through to her was just to get to the truth.

"I brought you here for several reasons. One, because it's safe here. I know this place. I can defend it. No one can get to you. Second, it's a magical place where we can all work together to help you. You, Georgie, and me. In order for Georgie to help you, I have to take part."

She lifted her head. "In what way?"

"It's kind of complicated, and I'll get to that in a bit. What I'm trying to tell you is that my involvement requires full trust."

"I don't understand. I mean I get that you don't trust me. I really do. Like I said outside, I wouldn't, either. But what part could you possibly have in eliminating, or lessening, this demon side of me?"

"Georgie will merge the two of us together."

"What?"

"The darkness in you with the light in me. Our goal is to have my light battle with your darkness, and hopefully my light will vanquish the hold the demons have on you so that the human part of you becomes stronger, the demon side of you weaker. Or at least something you can manage."

Isabelle untangled her legs and sat straight. "Um, okay, but what the hell are you talking about? Dalton, I believe that you're a good man. Honestly, I do. But you're just that—a man. Or at least I used to think that. Now, I'm not so sure. So maybe you need to clarify what you could do to help someone like me who has demon blood?"

Revelation time. He didn't know why he'd waited so long to tell her. The truth was going to have to come out eventually. And he did trust Isabelle. The human side of her would never betray him. Not consciously, anyway. He had to believe that part of her was stronger. It had been so far.

"Isabelle, I'm not human."

She frowned. "You're not?"

"No, I'm not. I look like a human, I've lived like a human for hundreds of years. But I'm not human."

"Then what are you?"

"I'm an angel."

Isabelle was dumbstruck. Her mouth hung open, yet no words came out.

She laughed. "No, you're not."

He didn't laugh back. "Yes, I am."

Was he serious? Did he expect her to believe it? "Dalton. An angel? Really? Come on. Angels don't exist."

"Demons do. Why is it so easy to believe in their existence, but not in the existence of angels?"

"Because I *am* a demon."

"And I'm an angel."

She stared at him, waiting for him to . . . to what? Transform or something? That wasn't going to happen. She had to accept what he said. Why would he lie about something like this?

Angel? Dalton was an angel? What did that even mean?

She swallowed. "You're serious, aren't you?"

"It's not like I'd bullshit about something like that," he said, his lips quirking in a wry smile.

"I can't imagine you would. But, an angel?" Then it hit her. "The light. The white light around you. The way you healed."

"Yes."

She frowned. "This is what you refused to tell me?"

"Yes."

"Oh, my God." It was true. Chills broke out on her skin. She stood and moved away from him, suddenly feeling as if she shouldn't even be in the same room with him.

He frowned. "Isabelle."

"Do you know what this means?"

He shook his head. "No. What does it mean?"

"We're diametrical opposites. I'm a demon. You're an angel." She wrapped her arms around herself. Talk about a major screwup. Could she pick 'em or what?

"Yes. That's true."

Her gaze shot to his. "How can you be so blasé about this? You and me . . . for God's sake, Dalton. I made love to an angel. Is that even allowed?"

He laughed. "Typically, no. But . . . this is kind of complicated."

Complicated? Understatement. "I'm listening."

"Okay. I'm a fallen angel."

Eyes wide, she said, "I'm having this rush of memories. Statues I've seen and folklore I've heard about fallen angels."

"It's not like that."

"Then I think you have a lot to tell me."

"I guess I do."

Dalton could almost have been amused by the enraptured look on Isabelle's face, if the subject matter wasn't so serious. He just wasn't sure where to begin. And maybe this is what had caused his hesitation in coming clean with her before. It wasn't like he was proud of what he'd done.

"Dalton, trust me, please. I know it may seem like I

can't control the part of me that's demon. But I'd rather hurt myself than hurt you. Especially knowing what you are now."

He smiled at her. "I know that. The human part of you fights every minute of every day. That's what I admire most about you. Your spirit and your generous nature are admirable qualities, Isabelle. You don't really want to hurt anyone."

"I don't know if I believe that. Well, I do believe I don't want to hurt anyone. But it seems that's all I end up doing. I need to make it stop. I'm trying to fix it."

"You're not as bad as you think you are."

She cocked her head to the side. "Maybe not. But I could be. And that's what we have to fix."

It was at that moment—listening to her, watching her as she came to grips with that revelation about herself—he knew he was in love with her. She had a warm, generous heart, and a willingness for self-sacrifice that even she was unaware of yet. He had great hope for Isabelle. He'd do anything to save her.

"I was once an angel, one of the Guardians. Our job was to patrol the earth, to protect humans, to make sure no harm came to them from the evil ones."

"Like a guardian angel?"

"Not really. We were there to keep evil out, to prevent them from gaining a toehold on humanity. There are rules."

"Really? What kind of rules?"

"Just as we were forbidden to interfere, so was the other side."

"The other side, meaning demons, or the dark side."

"Yes."

"How did that work?"

"The Guardians were here to help keep the balance, to keep the demons from interfering in the outcome of human decision-making."

"Of course. Because the other side doesn't play fair."

"No, they don't."

"You said you were a fallen angel. What happened?"

"I interfered. I broke the cardinal rule."

"How?"

"The reason I brought you to this place is that this is where it happened. In the latter part of the nineteenth century, Georgie's family owned this land. There was a rival landowner who not only wanted to take over the land, but coveted Georgie's great-grandmother, Celine.

"Celine was fifteen, the oldest child of four children. She was flawless. Beautiful, bright, innocent, but she was in love with someone else and they were going to be married.

"This older guy—Ratineau—owned the neighboring land. He bid for Celine's hand but her father said no, that she was promised to another. Ratineau was furious. He wanted Celine and the Labeau land and he'd stop at nothing to get both."

"Did you think this Ratineau was being influenced by the other side?"

Dalton nodded. "I was convinced of it. Celine was perfectly beautiful, possessed of magic, with a serene, ethereal quality about her. What man wouldn't fall in love with her?"

Isabelle's lips quirked. "Including you?"

Dalton's gaze lifted to hers. "I wasn't a man. I was an angel. I was supposed to be above those human emotions."

"But you weren't, were you?"

"No, I wasn't. I fell in love with Celine. And it clouded my judgment."

"In what way?"

"I was convinced Ratineau was possessed by darkness. And then he did the unthinkable. He killed Celine's parents and her brothers, and kidnapped Celine. He chained her up in his cellar and told her she was going to agree to marry him. She cried, brokenhearted over her family. She refused and told him she'd rather die than have anything to do with a murderer. He was so angry at her. He tortured her, raped her. Over and over again. He told her he'd keep her there until she died, but she'd be his and so would her land."

Isabelle covered her mouth. "Oh, God. No."

Dalton nodded. "For the first time in my existence I felt fury. Hatred. The need for revenge. I had to save her. So I used my power to strike him down."

Isabelle's eyes widened. "How?"

Dalton hesitated, remembering the moment as if it had just happened yesterday instead of over a century ago. "I used my sword and ran him through."

"You killed him?"

"Yes."

"Oh, Dalton. But what choice did you have if he was possessed?"

"Well, you see, that's where I failed. He wasn't possessed. Not by demons, anyway. Mad with desire, power-hungry, evil in his own right, yes. But the other side hadn't taken control of him. And in my hazy, lovesick mind, I failed to see it. I only saw him hurting my beloved Celine and I had to save her. I was the one who decided that he had to have been taken over by darkness. I broke the rule."

"But you loved her. And you saved her. Who knows what he would have done to her if you hadn't. I'm so sorry, Dalton." Isabelle crawled onto his lap, curled her fingers into the front of his shirt and held tight.

When she lifted her head, her eyes glistened with tears.

"I'm sorry," he said.

"You have nothing to be sorry for." She swept her hand across his face. "I love you." She leaned in, pressing her lips to his in a gentle kiss that made him ache inside. "I always knew there was something special about you."

He smiled. "I'm not special, Isabelle. I'm damned. I broke the cardinal law of the Guardians. I interfered. I took human life."

"It was deserved."

"That wasn't my call to make. Only the Creator can do that."

She shook her head. "So unfair. You did the right thing."

He shrugged. "I had reached my limit. It was my weakness. Because I couldn't stand to see those innocents murdered, even if it meant my own damnation. The guy deserved what I gave him. So even though I was punished for what I'd done, I was able to save Celine.

That was good enough for me and well worth my punishment."

"What was your punishment?"

"I was cast out as a Guardian, forced to live in darkness for one hundred years."

"In darkness? What does that mean?"

"I served the Sons of Darkness."

She leaned back, a look of horror on her face. "Oh, no. Oh, Dalton, I'm so sorry. From heaven into hell."

"Something like that."

"You spent a hundred years with demons? As a demon?"

"Yes."

"So you're . . . intimately familiar with the Sons of Darkness."

"Yes."

"How did you end up back here? Couldn't you return to your life as an angel once you served your punishment?"

He shook his head. "Once I had served my time, I was doomed to live as an immortal, in neither light nor darkness, until the day I find redemption."

She smoothed her hand over his chest. "So after all those years of living hell, you couldn't go home."

"No."

"Wow. They take punishment pretty seriously, don't they?"

"They take the rules seriously. Otherwise, there would be chaos, as you can imagine."

"It must have been so hard for you all this time.

Living as a human. But still, you're not really a human, are you?"

"Yes and no. I don't age or get sick and I can't be killed."

"Which is why when I shot you with the laser, you recovered so fast."

"They want to make sure I serve out my sentence. Death is easy, you know."

"What a lonely existence. Hard to make friends, since you can't get too close to anyone."

"Yeah, it can be difficult."

"But you found the Realm of Light."

He smiled. "I did. So now I can battle those I used to serve."

"Is that your redemption?"

His smile died. "No, Isabelle, it isn't."

"What is, then?"

"I once took a life. I'll be redeemed when I can save a life."

She frowned. "But don't you do that as one of the hunters? Don't you save lives every time you kill a demon?"

"Indirectly."

"So what is it going to take for you to earn your redemption?"

Her brows knit together as she pondered what he had said.

Come on, Isabelle. You're smart. You'll put it together.

He felt her tension as soon as she connected the dots. "Me. You mean me."

"Yes."

———

Isabelle slid off Dalton's lap and backed away from him. Too much information to soak in all at once. First finding out he was an angel, putting all the pieces together about the white light she'd seen, the miraculous healing after his injury. Then hearing the story of his heroic deed, how he became damned, the terrible and beautiful sacrifice he'd made, and the unfairness of it all. And the hideous punishment he'd suffered because of it.

And now, to discover that he meant to obtain his redemption through her? Had he always felt that way, from the first moment he'd discovered she was a demon?

She stared at him, not knowing what to say. She wasn't even certain what she felt.

"Tell me what you're thinking."

He hadn't moved from his spot on the chair. Part of her wanted to crawl back in his lap and give him comfort. What it must have cost him to tell her his story, the pain that had to be gutting him inside, the horrible memories his tale had dredged up.

The other part of her was afraid—because she realized she might be nothing more than a means to an end for Dalton, that he was quite possibly using her to obtain his own redemption, to once again become the angel he used to be.

She thought he felt something for her. That maybe he loved her, like she loved him. When she told him she loved him, she meant it.

Was she a fool?

"I'm thinking a lot of things," she admitted.

He came to her, grasped her hands. Warm. Alive. Human. But he wasn't, was he?

"Talk to me. Don't let the questions eat you up inside."

She let him lead her to the sofa and sat next to him, needing the comfort of his body next to hers. Weak, she knew, but right now he was all she had, even if his motives were suspect.

"How do you know I'm the one you need?"

"The life I save has to mean something. Saving you from the Sons of Darkness...stealing you from their grasp...that's meaningful."

"Okay. That makes sense." So was she his target? Had she been since that night in Sicily? Maybe he *was* using her. Then again, maybe she was using him, too. Maybe she needed this redemption as much as he did. But could you build a love based on ulterior motives? Did that even matter anymore? How could they even have something together now, knowing what she knew about him? And what happened...

"What happens if I am your redemption? If this works and you...save me?" she asked. "Do you become an angel again and disappear forever?"

He looked at her for a while before answering. That meant she wasn't going to like what he had to say.

"Ideally, yes. When I redeem myself, I become a Guardian once again, and everything that entails. It means I'm invisible to the human realm."

She would not cry. It wouldn't be the first time she lost someone she loved. She'd get over it. She'd be human again. Or at least human enough that she'd have control over the demon inside her. That's all she wanted, right? "I see."

"No, you don't see." He picked up her hand, squeezed it. "I hadn't counted on any of this when we started."

"What?"

"Falling in love with you. I love you, Isabelle. I don't want to leave you. But it may be the only way to save you. So what do I do? Let myself love you and let the Sons of Darkness have you? That would be the ultimate selfish act, and it would only allow us to be together a short period of time."

Damn. He loved her. Or maybe he was just saying that to get her to agree to all this. Why couldn't she believe in him, or in herself?

"You don't believe me," he said.

She almost laughed at the look of shock on his face. "I do. I mean I'd like to. Oh, hell, Dalton, it's not like I get declarations of love every day."

He pulled her against him, swept her hair away from her face. "You should. Goddammit, you should."

He kissed her, and she sensed his anguish, his uncertainty, and all his regret. It equaled everything she felt, which somehow eased her. She leaned into him, wrapped her arms around him, needing to lose herself in something that had nothing to do with what was going to happen between them in the future, and everything to do with right now.

All she wanted, all she could handle, was this moment. She no longer wanted to think about the future. The future didn't seem full of hope and promise, or full

of anything to fear. It was simply a place she didn't want
to go—not if that future was without Dalton.

She loved him. No matter what his reasons for being
with her, for saving her, for bringing her here for whatever kind of otherworldly merger he had concocted with
Georgie, she loved him. That wasn't going to change.
And if the demon inside her could give him his redemption, she'd make that sacrifice. For him.

As she moved against him, touching him, memorizing every part of his body under her hands, she was filled
with a sense of wonder.

So this was love, this all-encompassing sensation of
being filled to bursting with so much emotion she felt she
couldn't contain it all. She felt like she could explode, like
she couldn't sit still, yet there was nowhere else she
wanted to be but right here next to Dalton.

They spoke no words, just pulled at each other's
clothes. Isabelle wanted only skin against her, his heat
touching hers. Consumed by a sense of urgency, she
wanted access to his body. Who knew how little time
they had left? The clock ticked, the sound echoing in her
mind.

When he stood and dropped his shorts, she scooted
in front of him, rolling her palms over the angled planes
of his hips and buttocks.

"I should have known you weren't human," she said,
her voice a whisper in the darkness. "No man is this beautiful, this perfect."

There wasn't a single mark on him, nothing to mar
the perfection of his body. The wound on his stomach
was gone, as if it had never happened. She'd never

noticed before that he didn't even have scars on his body. He really was perfect. Ideal coloring, ideal body shape, and as she encircled his shaft and it slid into her hand, pulsing with life, she smiled.

"Yes. Perfect."

She stroked him with both hands, deriving the greatest pleasure at watching his head roll back, his lips part and a wild groan escape his lips. And when she took him between her lips, he focused on her with a fierce gaze of utter possession, his hand cupping the back of her neck to guide her movements. He was like satin over steel, the softest skin over hard stone. She cupped the sac that hung between his legs, squeezing him gently while she rolled her tongue over his shaft.

Dalton muttered an oath and pulled away, knelt down and pressed her against the sofa, then spread her legs with his shoulder. He kissed her inner thighs, his silky hair tickling the skin there.

But she didn't laugh. Not when his warm breath caressed her sex, not when his mouth covered her. She gasped, arching upward against all that wet, hot delight, reaching for more of that sweet pleasure. He held her hips and licked her, his tongue loving every part of her until she was shaking, hanging on a ragged edge. And when he slid his finger inside her, she rolled over that edge, gripped his wrists, and bucked against him, completely out of control.

Dalton didn't let her regain an ounce of that control. He flipped her over on her knees, her face against the sofa, and slid inside her with one swift thrust. She tilted her head back, embedded in sensation as he rolled his hips to give her the perfect angle.

He bent over her, his chest pressed to her back, and nibbled her ear.

"I love you, Isabelle."

The words whispered were dark, inviting, his fingers threaded through her hair and pulling as he pushed.

"You're mine. No matter what happens, you're mine."

Thrilled by his possession of her, she couldn't speak, could only react with her body, pushing back against him with every move he made. Every time he sank into her, he drove his meaning home.

She was his. She would always be his, body, heart, and soul.

"Yes," was all she could manage as he licked the column of her throat, his fingers tight in her hair, refusing to let her budge, possessing her in every way possible. He lifted her up and one hand covered her breast, surrounding her nipple and tweaking it with soft, measured strokes until she cried out with delight. He moved his hand down, over her ribs, her belly, stroking her hip and moving inward to cup her sex, rolling over the taut bud to massage the burgeoning ache that threatened to devour her from the inside out.

Gripping, swelling, she was only pleasure now. Whatever Dalton wanted from her she would gladly give. Lost in sensation, she was mindless against the assault of his body, his mouth, his teeth grazing her shoulder as his hand worked its magic along with the rhythmic strokes of his shaft. It was too much; unintelligible words spilled from her lips as she catapulted into orgasm.

Dalton pressed tight against her and shuddered, going with her over that wave as they held together in a wild ride where nothing existed but the two of them.

When they collapsed against the sofa and the white light surrounded them, she felt no shock. This time, she was at peace with the knowledge that this man was something incredibly special.

And he was hers.

For as long as it lasted.

CHAPTER FIFTEEN

Mandy sat in the corner of the seedy bar appropriately named The Bomb, scanning the activity around her, soaking in a bottle of beer and the atmosphere, and trying to avoid her own muddled thoughts.

Grounded. Banned from work. Michael thought she was frozen with fear and unable to pull the trigger.

Ha! Bullshit. She'd show Michael she could get the job done. All she had to do was find a demon. And what better place for a demon to hunt for victims than a bar that catered to the drunk and senseless? Easy to take them down when they weaved their way out of the club and into the parking lot.

She'd scouted all the hot spots over the past couple days. Nothing better to do, since Michael wouldn't let her work—though she'd kept her eyes and ears on the pulse of Realm activity, so she knew what was going on. Through their investigations the hunters had discovered some strange attacks that could denote demon activity, both in this area and in others. Fortunately not yet as widespread as they'd feared, but definitely growing. Mandy had feigned disinterest, but oh, she'd been listening, especially when the report zeroed in to this area specifically. One body had been found a block from here, the corpse seemingly emaciated, as if it had been drained of every liquid. And finger marks were noted on the victim's throat. Cause of death was listed as strangulation, but the Realm knew better. Mandy had snuck in and studied the files when Michael wasn't around. It appeared another victim had turned up a few blocks away, right behind The Bomb's sister club, The Shelter.

She rolled her eyes at the irony of the name. Hadn't provided much shelter for the poor dead victim, had it? Autopsy reports indicated hard-pressed impressions of fingers on the throat, including puncture wounds, which the police surmised were caused by some kind of small tool like an ice pick.

Or a demon's sharp claws, but the coroner hadn't guessed that, unsurprisingly.

So there she sat in her perfect spot in the darkened corner, her gaze pouring over every table, every patron seated at the long, scarred bar, searching out anyone who just might fit a demon's profile. She picked out what she thought might be a few suspicious characters, and kept an eye on them. Tall, dark, and handsome types who seemed cold and aloof, with the kinds of smiles that didn't quite reach their eyes. Then again, that could be just a normal guy thing. How would she know? Still, worth a try anyway. She did her best to throw off signals that made herself approachable, but not too easy. And she made it appear as if she'd been drinking. A lot.

Which in the eyes of a demon looking for food made her prey.

When one of those types approached her, she leaned

back in the booth and propped one of her booted feet up on the threadbare vinyl seat.

"You alone?" he asked.

"You blind?" She shot it back dripping with sarcasm, not wanting to appear too available.

Not at all deterred by her attitude, he slid into the booth alongside her and held out his hand. "I'm John."

How nondescript. She slid her hand in his, noting the icy cold fingers barely touching hers before he pulled away. *Bingo.* "I'm Mandy."

"So what are you doing here tonight, Mandy?"

She decided she'd play it like a woman who'd just gotten dumped and was looking to rebound in a hurry with some anonymous guy. She gave him a half smile. "Getting drunk, John. What about you?"

He lifted his beer. "Same. Not much action, though."

She gazed around the bar. "It's a slow night. Are you looking for some action?" She made a point of giving him the once-over, hoping she could fake some glimmer of attraction.

"Who wouldn't be? You're gorgeous."

She took a drink of her beer to hide her grimace, then forced a smile afterward. "Thanks. You're not so bad looking yourself."

"You wanna dance?" he asked.

Someone must have pumped a couple quarters in the jukebox, because there seemed to be music playing. Really lousy music.

"Uh, sure." She stood and followed him across the floor, stomping on cracked peanut shells on the way. He held out his hands and she stepped into his arms, trying not to shudder in revulsion when he touched her.

God, he was cold. And it was like ninety degrees outside, not much cooler in the bar. These demons were going to have to do a better job of masking the chill factor.

He laid his cheek against hers. "You smell really nice. Like vanilla."

"Thanks."

"Your skin is soft, too."

Is this what went on between the opposite sexes, this lame search for something romantic or sexy to say? If it was, she realized she hadn't been missing a damn thing all these years.

"I bathe regularly. Glad to know it's effective." Really, she was at a loss here. All she wanted to do was kill this thing, not make a date.

The killing part took front and center when he grabbed her ass and pulled her against what appeared to be a rather sizeable erection.

Now he really was going to have to die.

Plastering on what she hoped was her sexiest smile, she leaned back. "Got something in mind?"

"I think you know I do."

Gag. She lowered her voice in an attempt to sound sexy. "Then let's get out of here. My car's in back. I've got a nice big SUV." *With weapons in the backseat.*

"Sounds great. Let me go pay the tab and I'll be right behind you."

She let her lips brush his. "I'm counting the seconds." *Until you're dead.*

She turned on her heel and went out the door, stalking

to her car, shuddering off the effects of that thing touching her. She clicked the remote on the SUV and went straight for the backseat, climbed in and left the door open. She grabbed the pistol and slid it behind her back, then scooted into the far corner. Silence was on, safety was off. She was ready for him.

For *it*.

While she waited, she reminded herself this thing wasn't human.

And it wasn't Lou. It was okay to kill it.

As the demon approached her vehicle in the deserted, dark alley, she caught the telltale glow of his pale blue eyes and knew with full certainty that she'd found the right target. She grinned as he ducked his head inside the SUV.

"Ready for me?" he asked.

"More than. Come on in and shut the door behind you."

His teeth gleamed white as he pulled the door closed and slid across the bench seat until their thighs touched.

She had to force herself to stay put and not move away, especially when he loomed over her, his intent more than obvious. He was going to kiss her.

Okay, she could handle this. It would make her job easier.

"You are so beautiful."

The demon needed some original lines. Did women fall for this shit? He leaned in, his eyes glowing an unnatural blue as he pressed cold lips to hers. She fought to keep her lips moving, trying to act like she was into it while she moved her arm from around her back, insinuating the gun between them. In a lightning quick moment she pressed the barrel of the pistol against the demon's middle.

He had no time to react, and Mandy didn't give herself time to think or to focus on his face. She pulled the trigger, the force of the blast catapulting the demon off her and across the vehicle. It slammed against the door, blood spraying everywhere. She fired again, once, twice, three times. Again and again she pulled the trigger, emptying the clip containing the liquid nitrogen. The demon had long ago stopped moving, the clip was empty, but she kept pulling the trigger. Sweat poured from her body, soaking through her clothes. She wasn't even seeing the creature anymore.

All she saw was Lou's face swimming in front of her, the sadness in his eyes as he crumpled to the ground. He knew the price of what he'd asked of them, but he'd asked it anyway. She'd see his face every day, every night, until she died. She'd relive the horror of what she'd done, just as she was doing right now.

Then she couldn't see anything at all, her vision distorted by tears.

"I'm sorry," she whispered, continuing to press down on the trigger. "I'm so, so sorry."

What seemed like hours later, Mandy was still in the backseat, staring at the dead demon. Her fingers had long ago gone numb, still wrapped around that pistol, still in full press on the trigger.

She swiped at her eyes. How long had she been there frozen in some cosmic funk, sitting in the car with a dead demon?

She was going to have to move, and soon. The bar would be closing. People would come. They'd probably notice the dead body slumped against the back window, the splotches of blood on the windows. She was surprised someone hadn't come along and seen them.

God, she was such a mess. Stiff, sore, wrung out.

But she'd managed to kill the demon—at least, she figured it was dead. She raised her boot and gave it a hard kick between the legs. No reaction.

Okay, it was dead. She grabbed it by the collar and pulled it facedown onto the floor of the backseat, then crawled into the driver's seat and started up the engine, cranking up the heater. Despite the sweltering humidity outside, she was shivering cold. She drove to the compound, her mind on autopilot, refusing to think about anything that had happened. When she reached the compound, she pressed the remote to the security gate and announced her arrival, then indicated on her comm that she was coming in with a dead demon.

She backed in and techs were there waiting to unload the carcass. She slid out the door and tossed the keys to the waiting tech. "It's in the backseat," she said, then scooted by a waiting Michael. She felt his stare on her as she walked into the center and down the long hallway. She made it into the elevator, hoping Michael would want to see the demon, but he stepped into the elevator with her. She pushed the button for the second floor.

Michael didn't say a word. Neither did she. When the doors opened, she hung a right, stopping at her room to key in her code. She pulled the door open and turned around to face him.

"Do you mind?"

"Yes, I do." He stepped in and closed the door behind him.

She rolled her eyes and moved into the room, unbuckled her belt, and pulled clips of ammo out of the pockets of her camos. She lifted the tight shirt off and threw that on the little sofa, then toed off her boots.

Clad in only her tank top, camo pants, and socks, she glared at Michael. "I'd like to take a shower. I have blood all over me."

"Did you have a good time tonight?"

"Yeah. I killed a demon. You should go check it out."

"You look destroyed, Mandy."

She dragged her hand through her hair. She'd purposely left it down and loose tonight to look more attractive. Normally she had it pulled up or braided. Now it was a tangled mess. "I need to brush my hair. Sorry if I don't look my best."

"That's not what I'm talking about. There are dark circles under your eyes. You're pale as death. You look ragged. Have you slept?"

Sleep? What's that? "Of course. I'm fine. Did you hear me say I shot a demon? Are you at all interested in my report?"

"Eventually. I'm more interested in you. Something happened in that cold room the other day with the demon."

She waved her hand in a dismissive gesture. "It was nothing. I'm over it. Did you hear what I said? I killed a demon tonight, Michael." She needed him to hear her. She needed to get back in the field. She really needed a shower. The smell of demon blood was making her dizzy, nauseous. Michael's face began to swim before her eyes. Shit.

"It wasn't nothing. You look pale. Oh, Christ, Mandy, put your head down."

All she heard was his voice buzzing in her ears. He reached behind her and grabbed the nape of her neck, shoving her head down between her knees.

"Stay there. Don't move."

It wasn't like she could sit upright. Not with the room spinning. Her whole body began to shake. This wasn't good. What the hell was happening to her? Some kind of delayed stress reaction or something?

The last thing she wanted was to fall apart.

Correction: The last thing she wanted was to fall apart with Michael in here. She'd held it together just fine the whole way back here. Why did he have to follow her to her room?

"Get out, Michael." She was going to throw up. She had to . . . oh, man, this sucked. She pressed her fingers to her temples. She was hot, cold, sweaty. What was happening to her?

Michael came back a few seconds later and swept her hair away from her nape. Something cold and wet pressed to the back of her neck. It felt good, helped to stem the nausea some.

He squatted down in front of her, stroked her hair while he held the washcloth against her neck. "Better?"

"Yeah."

"Let's get you up."

Get up? No way. "I'll be fine here. You can go now."

"You're covered in blood, Mandy. It's all over your hands and your face."

She wrinkled her nose. "Ick."

If she kept her eyes closed, the dizziness wasn't so bad. She could just stay like this. But suddenly hands slid under her arms.

"Come on. We need to get you cleaned up."

She didn't want to get up. She wanted to go to sleep, to shut everything off, to stop thinking and feeling for a while. "No."

"Yes."

She was lifted, cradled against Michael's chest. Really, she wanted to protest. She wasn't a little thing, not petite like many women. She was almost six feet tall and not at all a lightweight, yet Michael carried her effortlessly into the bathroom. She heard the sound of water turning on. The shower.

He set her on her feet, leaning her against the cool tile wall, then she felt hands at the button on her camos. Her eyes shot open.

"I don't think so."

"Can you do it on your own?" He took a step back, only an inch or so. Her fingers fumbled at the buttons, her legs rubbery and unsteady as she began to slide down the wall.

Fuck. "No." She fell back against the wall, helpless.

"You want me to get one of the female techs to come in and help you?"

"Oh, hell, no." That would be just what she needed, some twit, gossipy female whispering about her. At least she could trust Michael not to blab about her failures. "Just do it."

Michael undid the button and zipper on her pants, let them drop to the floor, then wrapped his arm around her while he lifted her tank top above her head. As she stood in her bathroom with the shower running, clad only in her bra and panties, she realized that no man had ever seen her in this little clothing.

And it was about to get worse than that.

"Hold on, Mandy."

"Uh-huh."

He bent down and she felt his hands on her hips as he dropped to the floor.

"Lift your foot so I can get your socks off."

She cooperated to the extent she was able, her gaze drifting down to see Michael's head against her thigh. She laid her hand on top of it. Soft, silky hair, just as she'd imagined. Too bad she was too dizzy, too sick, to really enjoy this, because Michael was a hot guy.

He stood and gazed down at her, something unfathomable in the depths of his blue eyes. "Can you get in there on your own?"

"Um. Sure."

"Okay. I'll let you take it from here, then."

He let go. She wobbled and her knees buckled.

"Shit," Michael said, grabbing her around the waist.

"My thoughts exactly."

"Hold on to this." He grabbed her hand and pulled the shower door closed, putting her hand on the towel rail outside the door. "Don't let go. I'll be right back."

"Uh-huh." Like she could go anywhere. Between the wall and the rack, she was good right here.

But Michael didn't leave. He took a couple steps back and started undressing.

"What the hell are you doing?"

"Taking off my clothes." He kicked off his boots, then dropped his pants—oh, my God, he went commando. He did want her still standing, didn't he? Why was he torturing her like this? And then he pulled his T-shirt off, revealing one tight, expanded chest with a smattering of dark hair.

She might be dizzy and sick, but by all that was holy, she wasn't dead. Her mouth watered at the sight of all that male flesh. Dark, tanned, delicious. She couldn't come up with enough adjectives to adequately describe the body being revealed in front of her. Really, she was weak enough already. This was agony. She had no experience with men. Especially naked men. Tall, well-built naked men. Damn.

And then he moved in, swept his arm around her and pressed his naked body against hers. She couldn't breathe.

"Your body is hot to the touch, Mandy."

Yeah, she was hot all right. This wasn't helping any. "I think I can probably handle it on my own."

He cocked a brow. "Really."

She managed a short nod. "Yeah." She palmed his chest. Oh, man she really wanted to touch him, let her hands wander down his sculpted abs to that dark hair below, and points further south. "Let me give it a shot."

"Okay." He pulled the shower door open. She turned

and her legs buckled. Michael was right there to catch her, his arm sweeping under her breasts to pick her up and brace her back against his chest. "I think I'll just step in here with you."

His deep voice reverberated against her back, his warm breath ruffling her hair. "Fine." She gritted her teeth, figuring she had to get this blood off. And she was too dizzy, weak, and sick to do anything about him being naked, so she figured this was going to be completely innocent.

Michael walked her slowly into the shower and under the spray. And oh, sweet heaven, it felt so good, the hot water cascading down over her face. She closed her eyes and let it cleanse her. She could already feel the demon's blood washing away. She needed it to go away. She needed all of it to go away, especially the memories. Maybe those could slither down the drain, too.

Michael kept his arm firmly around her, and she had to admit, it helped. So did the water, offering her some clarity. He took a step back and grabbed the shampoo, poured it over her head.

"Lean against me," he said.

"Like I have a choice?" She did, and he washed her hair. The act was so painfully intimate because no one had ever done it for her before—not that she could remember, anyway—and because no man had ever touched her this way. Hell, no man had ever touched her. The guys in the Realm would never let anyone close, and she hadn't exactly lived a normal life. She wasn't used to this kind of intimacy. Even though she knew Michael was just being kind. It wasn't like he was interested or anything.

He dipped her head forward, rinsed her hair, applied conditioner and rinsed again. Then he grabbed the bar of soap and began to run it over her body. All. Over. Her. Body. Her arms, her back, sliding his soapy hands down her spine, stopping just short of her butt. And even though she wore bra and panties, this was delicious.

And he was, after all, naked.

She so wanted to explore that. She wanted to be naked, too.

Clearly she was starting to feel better. A lot better. So much better that the shock of awareness slid through her senses, overpowering everything but the man behind her. She shivered, goose bumps prickling her flesh, which had nothing to do with the soap and everything to do with his hands on her. He smoothed his hands over her hips, digging his fingers in and stalling.

"Turn around so you can rinse your back under the water."

His voice had changed, dropped an octave and had an added edge to it. She took it easy as she turned, then tilted her head back and opened her eyes.

His eyes looked like a coming storm, dark and intense. He reached for her shoulders and helped her take a step back under the water as she rinsed.

Then she made a fatal error. She looked down, casually glancing over his body.

Unaffected? She thought him uninterested? Um, no. He was most definitely interested. Her gaze snapped up to his face. His lips curled in the most devastating smile a man could give a woman.

"Sorry. I can't help it," he said, as if he had to apologize for being hard, for being so utterly masculine he took her breath away?

For the first time in her life, Mandy realized that she was, in fact, a woman. Before, when she'd been with the guys, they were...family, or fellow hunters. There had never been a man/woman thing between her and any of the guys. Hell, she'd *been* one of the guys.

But she stood almost naked in the shower with Michael, and for the very first time she felt like a woman. Dizzy and nauseous with whatever this thing was that gripped her from the inside out, but even that couldn't stop the rush of her sexual awakening. Despite how she felt, she wanted to explore. She was twenty-three years old, sick, disgusted, and she might never get another chance.

She placed her hands on Michael's shoulders.

He lifted his hands, rubbed the soap, and gently washed her face. "You still had a few spots of blood there."

He seemed to have trouble speaking, like his voice was hoarse. She tilted her head back and rinsed her face, then shook the water droplets off and opened her eyes to look at him again. "Thanks."

"How do you feel?"

Hot, shivery, turned on, weak. She felt so many things at once she couldn't begin to describe them all, not when most of it made no sense to her. "I'm okay."

"You ready to get out of here?"

"No." Not yet, not while she still had a chance... "This hot water feels really good, Michael. I'm still a little shook up. Please stay in here with me."

The way he looked at her—she wished she could ask him what he was thinking.

"Okay."

She smoothed her hands over his shoulders, then down his arms. Soft skin over such incredible strength. His muscles flexed under her questing hands.

"What are you doing, Mandy?"

She didn't—couldn't—look at his eyes. "I'm touching you."

"Why?"

"Because I've never done this before."

She felt that tension increase.

"What?"

She swept her gaze up to his face, figuring she owed him the truth. "I've never had an opportunity to touch a man before, Michael. Please don't stop me."

Michael held his breath, a thousand thoughts running through his head, most of them screaming at him to get out of the shower, *now*.

He'd done this to help Mandy, to clean her up, to try to get her warm. Her skin had been icy cold despite the sweltering heat outside. She'd been pale, obviously in shock, and God only knows what else had been going on in her head. Covered in blood, she'd sauntered in spouting off and so sure of herself, but the haunted look in her eyes told him she'd been teetering near the edge—and about to drop.

He'd been right.

But now? High color fused her cheeks a dark pink.

Her hair streamed like raven rain down her back and over her shoulders, barely covering her full, upturned breasts. Her bra, soaked through, revealed everything, as did the tiny panties resting on her his. Dark brown nipples peaked and hardened against his chest.

His cock stood rigid betwen them, throbbing with a mind of its own. It was telling him to take her, to lift her leg over his hip, push her against the tile wall and slide inside her. She'd be hot, gripping, pulsing. She could ease both their aches.

He had no right thinking that.

And now, if what she was telling him was true . . .

"Mandy, are you a virgin?"

She lifted her fingers to his lips, stroked his bottom lip in awe. "So soft. How can a man's mouth be so soft?"

She looked at him with such wonder and curiosity, tearing his resolve into ragged pieces. He'd never had a woman look at him like that.

"Answer me, Mandy. Are you a virgin?"

She lifted her gaze to his. "I've lived with the Realm since I was a kid, since Lou rescued me. I've been sheltered by demon hunters. I never had a normal life. I never dated. I've never had a boyfriend. I've never even been kissed, Michael. I missed everything. I'm twenty-three years old and I've missed everything."

Christ. So tough on the outside, such a warrior, and yet such unbelievable innocence. How had this happened? Mandy was on equal footing with the mightiest of the demon hunters. He hadn't expected this. He wasn't prepared for this, not this incredibly beautiful, vulnerable woman standing naked in his arms.

"I want a kiss, Michael." Tears filled her eyes. "Would you at least kiss me?"

The mutinous, buck-the-rules Mandy, the one he fought with daily—he could handle her. This one? Soft, vulnerable, desirable—he had no idea what to do with her.

He was a Keeper, her Keeper. Her superior. He had no business touching her, being with her like this. This was a line he shouldn't cross.

He'd already crossed it in spades.

And he wanted more.

He cupped the back of her neck and drew her mouth to his, pressed his lips against hers in a kiss so featherlight it made him ache inside.

She let out a little sigh against his mouth, then leaned forward, her breasts pillowed against his chest. Oh, man, he liked the way she felt against him. He deepened the kiss, sliding his lips along the seam of hers. Her bottom lip trembled. He was going to have to take this slow. She was weak, sick, and he felt like an asshole for doing this when she was in this condition, but God, how could she have never been kissed? That wasn't right.

And you're making excuses for doing something you shouldn't be doing.

Yeah, he was. He didn't care. Mandy whimpered against his mouth and his balls tightened in response. He let his hands roam along her back, traveled down to the dip where her lower back ended and her phenomenally great ass began. He cupped the globes, drawing her forward against his cock, rubbing her slick heat against the rock-hard part of him that ached to show her what it could be like between a man and a woman.

He separated her lips with his tongue and she parted for him, letting him slide inside to taste her. Hot, soft, he wrapped his tongue around hers, showed her what it was like to play, to lick, to enjoy the touch and taste of another.

She inhaled deeply, her fingers digging into his arms. He knew this was sensory overload for someone so inexperienced, was awed that he could give this to her, and knew he should slow things down. She might not be a young teenager in the throes of her first journey into passion, but Mandy was still new at all of this. And she had other things going on in her head, things she was no doubt trying to push away. What a great way to forget.

Sex was always a great way to forget. He knew that better than anyone.

Was he helping her by doing this, or hurting her?

As her Keeper, he should force her to face reality. As a man, he couldn't care less what her motivations were. He wanted to make love to her.

Talk about conflicted.

He pulled his mouth away from hers, leaned around her, and turned the shower off.

"Water's getting cool," he said.

"But—"

"Wait," he said. He pulled open the door and stepped out, leading Mandy. He grabbed the big towel and threw it around her so she wouldn't get chilled.

"I'm not cold."

He dried her body, her hair, then took another towel to dry himself.

"Michael."

He cupped his palms around her face. Damn she was beautiful. Innocent and sultry, provocative and naïve.

He wanted her. The hell with protocol and doing what was right. He was going to have her. But not in the shower.

"Michael, please."

"Shut up, Mandy." He scooped her up in his arms and carried her to the bedroom, deposited her next to the bed, holding tight to the towel around her. "How do you feel?"

"I feel fine."

"Good." He let her towel drop, then swept her damp hair away from her neck so he could press his lips there. Her pulse beat fast, her skin was hot, but she was standing on her own now, so at least he didn't have to worry about her collapsing on him.

He threaded his arms around her, needing to touch her. Her wet bra pressed against his chest and he lifted to look at her. "Let's take this off."

She nodded, no hesitation on her face. He released the clasp and pulled the straps down her arms, then drew the bra away from her breasts, revealing dark nipples that puckered to hard peaks under his gaze. His cock lurched to attention, and Mandy looked down, then back at him, offering up a tremulous smile.

She was always so hyperconfident in everything she did. Except this. Now she looked unsure of herself. He kind of figured her bravado was an act she put on, and seeing her now proved that. Underneath her swagger was a woman very unsure of herself. For that he was going to take his time and make this special for her.

He crouched down and reached for her panties, slid them over her hips and down her legs. She stepped out of them and he grasped her ankles, then smoothed his hands over her calves, the backs of her knees, her thighs. She truly was a beautifully made woman. Not thin, but well muscled. He loved that she had flesh on her body, something to touch and grab on to.

And her scent—fresh from her shower, and yet the musky scent of arousal drew him to her. He pressed a kiss to her inner thigh, then lifted her leg and positioned it over his shoulder. Her legs trembled and he looked up at her.

"You okay?"

She nodded, bit down on her lower lip, watching him.

He pressed his nose against her sweet flesh, inhaled her scent, then swept his tongue along her sex, feeling her body quiver in response. He reached up and she took his hand, grasped it tight as he latched on to the tight bud there and sucked. He heard her gasp, felt her response, which fueled his eagerness to please her. She tasted like warm honey and he captured it with his tongue, slid inside her to taste more of her, then tucked a finger inside her tight folds, feeling her clench around him in response.

He heard her, every sound she made, from whimpers to moans to the steady increasing of each breath. Only this time it wasn't shock that drove her breaths, it was pleasure. He took her there with every lick, every swirl of his tongue around her clit, every thrust of his finger inside her, until he felt her convulse around him, her leg squeezing against his shoulder.

"Michael." She moaned his name in a low throaty whisper as she came, thrusting her sex against him as an offering that he took gladly, lapping up her gift with a hunger that drove his own desire to a wild fever.

When she settled, he stood, reaching behind her to cup the globes of her ass and bring her against him, shuddering at the contact of their bodies. He wanted this as much as she did. He'd tried to hide behind his job, but from the moment he'd met her he'd felt the sparks between them, had known there was . . . something. But he'd denied it, deprived himself of this expression of passion that he needed as much as she did.

And now he was torn between wanting to take his time, take hours, to explore this with her, and needing to make her his right now, as fast as he could. Because he didn't want to wait to be inside her. But everything—all of this—was new to her. And he had to take it slow.

He swept his hands over her buttocks, the small of her back, and upward, just feeling the softness of her skin. She leaned into him, following his movements, caressing him the way he had done to her. She laid her hands on his shoulders, then swept down his arms, slid her arms around his waist to palm his back. Every move she made was tentative, watching for his reaction.

"Touch me," he said. "I like it."

She pushed back, looked at him, and oh, man, did her bold appraisal of his body turn him on. It made patience that much harder. Among other things.

When her gaze swept over his shaft, then up at him, he nodded. She circled him with a light grasp.

"Harder."

She did, her grip strong. He sucked in a breath of pure pleasure. "Oh, yeah. That's good. Now move your hand."

She did, stroking him light and easy at first, then with a firm grasp and steadier movements. He clenched his jaw and held on, letting her explore, learn the feel of him, but God help him it was hard to hold back when all he wanted to do was let go.

Finally, he grasped her wrist. "I don't want to finish before we start."

She lifted her gaze to him and quirked a smile. And still, the look on her face was so innocent, it tore him to pieces. He took her mouth, drinking in the taste of her because it had been so damn long since he'd been anywhere near anything so pure.

He held her tight, crushed against him, afraid he was hurting her. But the feelings inside him were so intense he felt like he was losing control. And it was important that he be in control. He pulled away, took a step back.

"What's wrong?"

He shook his head. "Just need to take a breath. Being with you . . . I kind of lost it there."

She moved back in. "Quit worrying about whether or not I'll break, Michael. I'm strong. And I need this. Just love me."

He nodded, jerked her against him and fell onto his back on the bed, pulling her with him. Not wanting to scare her, he rolled to the side so she faced him, but she surprised him by pulling him on top of her.

"I want to feel your weight on me when you're inside me."

Mandy always surprised him. Maybe that's what attracted him to her. He'd never met a woman like her before.

She braced her hands on his chest, and widened her legs so he could settle between them.

"Now, Michael. I'm tired of waiting. I've already waited a lifetime."

Yeah, she had. And what he was about to do would irrevocably change their relationship.

But right now he couldn't muster up a single objection to why he shouldn't, even though there were hundreds. Not when this lush, beautiful woman lay underneath him, lifting her hips in silent invitation.

He positioned himself at her entrance, and thrust. Mandy tilted her head back and gasped, and he stilled, feeling the heat and wetness of her surrounding him, the sensations of her body convulsing around him. He cupped her cheek.

"Mandy. Look at me."

She opened her eyes, and he closed the gap between them, kissing her deeply, sliding his tongue between her parted lips, forcing her attention on their mouths, his tongue. Soon, her tension melted away and he began to move against her, slow and easy until he felt her responding.

He'd never felt anything so perfect, from the way their bodies fit together to the way it felt to be inside her. And Mandy lifted her hips, asking for more, giving him what he needed—more than he ever expected.

Because the look in her eyes was magical, luring him in much more than physically. She drew him closer, with her midnight hair and lush body, and he rocked against her, never wanting this to end. He wanted to stay like this—inside her—a part of her forever. Where there were no demons and no war, only pleasure and kissing and sharing this incredible experience with a woman he felt closer to after such a short period of time than anyone he'd ever known.

Was that even possible?

It had to be, because he felt it, their fingers entwined, their bodies joined, moving in unison as they climbed together. He waited, grinding against her, taking her there again, and when she fell, this time crying out and trembling against him, he went with her, and the orgasm was so powerful the intensity of it shocked him, pouring out of him from every nerve ending, leaving him spent. He collapsed on top of her, breathing so heavily it left him light-headed.

Soaked with sweat, their bodies still tightly strung together, Michael didn't want to move. Especially since Mandy stroked his hair, one leg slung over his back.

"It would be okay if we ran off together and pretended the rest of the world didn't exist, right?"

She'd read his mind. "Oh, sure."

Her laugh rumbled against his chest. "I knew you'd see it my way."

He finally managed to lift his head. Her lips were too much for him to resist, so he kissed her again, what he thought would be a short peck turning into something deeper, something that made his blood run hot and made him grow hard again.

"We both need another shower," he said.

Mandy arched a brow. "Time for lesson number two."

He grinned and got up, pulling her into the bathroom with him, then turned on the shower.

Then his phone went off. He pulled away, staring down at the pile of clothes they'd left on the bathroom floor.

She grasped his wrists. "Don't."

The shock of his phone ringing was like a slap of reality. "I have to." He bent down, fished the phone out of his pocket, frowned at the number. He stood and flipped the phone open.

"Yeah."

He listened, mentally cursing as Derek filled him on what he'd found.

"We'll be on the road in an hour. We'll meet you there tomorrow." He closed the phone, turned to Mandy.

"We've got to go," she said.

With a sigh, he touched his forehead to hers. "Derek's found Dalton. He's in Louisiana."

She inhaled, let it out on a shaky sigh. "Well, this is damned inconvenient."

Yes and no. He had been so caught up in her, he had almost forgotten his mission. Men should never lead with their dicks. He should have known better.

"Mandy. You have no idea how much I want to... linger here with you. But you and I both know this can never be."

The soft, dreamy look in her eyes died. She pushed away from him. "Oh, of course. How convenient for you to figure that out now. I get it. Thanks. You can go now."

He knew he was going to hurt her, that she was going to take this wrong. "Mandy."

She skirted around him. "Get out of my bathroom, Michael. I need to shower and pack."

"Are you feeling all right?"

"I'm fine now."

He didn't believe her. Nothing about this was fine.

And if he was a lot less honorable, he'd take a few extra minutes—or an hour or two—and finish what they'd barely started. Because he wasn't finished with Mandy. Not by a long shot.

But he was right. Where was this leading? He was a Keeper. Keepers that had...mates, put those mates in danger. The Sons of Darkness didn't want Keepers to continue the line.

Being with Mandy would put her at risk and he refused to do that to her.

He couldn't lead her if he allowed anything to happen between them. He couldn't help her if he got too close to her. And helping her, making a good hunter out of her—that part was his job.

Wasn't it?

Hell.

He grabbed his clothes and dressed, then went to his room, took a quick shower, and packed up. By the time he went back into her room, she'd already showered, her damp hair pulled up into a ponytail. She was dressed and jamming things in her bag, her back turned to him. He wanted to go to her, to kiss her, to taste her again, touch her skin, breathe her in, to spend hours—days—hanging out with her. He craved being with her, felt cheated because they'd only just started. But what he wanted and what he had to do were two different things.

Just like always.

"I'll be downstairs in a few minutes," she said.

"Fine."

He left the room, hoping she'd understand, that they could talk on the road, but he had a feeling that what had just happened had driven a wedge between them.

And just when they'd started to make progress. Now he had to figure out what happened to her tonight, what was going on in her head. Yeah, she'd killed a demon, but it had cost her.

Too much to talk about. Nothing resolved. Mandy's issues, these new demons they'd discovered, not to mention the biggest issue of all: the two of them.

Now everything would have to be put on hold, because they had to go find Dalton and deal with him.

Shit.

CHAPTER SIXTEEN

Dalton sipped the steaming cup of black coffee and stared out the window at the gathering storm clouds marring the normally blue and orange sunrise. Thunder rolled from a distance. There'd be no doing anything outside today. He gave it an hour, max, before the storm arrived. The clouds were an angry gray, tumbling over one another, seemingly in a hurry to get wherever they were headed. They gradually obliterated the morning light and cast a dismal pall over the cheerful morning.

How freakin' appropriate.

He opened the front door and stepped out, barefoot, wearing only the jeans he hadn't bothered to finish buttoning. He hadn't put a shirt on; the morning humidity was overbearing, another curse of the coming storm.

The weather suited his mood. Ominous, angry, expectant.

A lot had happened last night. Everything had changed. He couldn't go back. Isabelle knew so much now. Did it even matter?

Loving her would change nothing, in fact would likely make things worse. Every decision he made from here on out would be affected by his love for her, and knowing how she felt about him.

And doing this alone, without the help of the Realm, of his friends, sucked. Last night as he lay awake in bed, he had actually thought about picking up the phone and calling Derek.

But in the end, he hadn't been able to make the call, because a part of him wasn't sure Derek would take his side, and he wouldn't take that chance and risk Isabelle's life.

It didn't matter anyway, because the Realm was coming. It was only a matter of time. He sensed them drawing closer—both a comfort and something else to ratchet up the sense of urgency. His time was running out. Which meant he could either wait and hopefully enlist their aid, using the demon hunters to help him with Isabelle, or hurry it along without them so it would be done before they got here.

Part of him wanted it to be over.

A larger part of him wanted to drag his feet. He'd just found Isabelle. He wasn't ready to lose her yet. And if this worked, he *would* lose her. Forever.

But wouldn't he have what he'd waited all this time for? Redemption.

He'd be what he was meant to be.

Because he wasn't a human. He wasn't supposed to be here, living this life, loving the woman sleeping in the house. He was stealing love from her, love he wasn't entitled to. They had no future together; there was no tomorrow for them. Individually, there was a promise for a better life for each of them. But not together.

He heard her behind him, her soft bare feet padding on the dock.

"What are you doing out here?" She came up next to him, cup of coffee in her hand. Her hair was sleep-tousled, her eyes had a dreamy quality about them... and something else.

He put his arm around her. "Watching the storm come in." He kissed the top of her head. "You okay?"

She nodded and leaned into him. "Had a nightmare. Nothing new there."

He frowned, not liking that she still wasn't settled. He smelled the tinge of rain in the air and the wind had picked up, whipping her loose hair against his chest. He steered them back toward the house, not wanting to end up caught outside in a storm again.

Once inside the house, they refilled their coffee cups and sat at the kitchen table.

"Tell me about your nightmare."

She shrugged. "It was nothing, really."

"You're starting to remember them now, aren't you?"

She lifted her gaze to his. "Yes."

So her mental progress was moving along, which was good. "Okay, so talk to me about it."

She inhaled, lifting her shoulders, then rolled her head from side to side, but she sipped her coffee and didn't say anything. That meant the dream disturbed her. Or else he was in it, it was bad, and she didn't want to tell him about it.

"Isabelle, you can tell me anything. I can handle it. It's just a dream."

"The demon in me felt like it was in control while I was asleep. It went to the Sons of Darkness. I saw all of them. Tase was surrounded by flames."

She wrinkled her nose as if she found the mention of Tase unpleasant. He knew the feeling. He didn't like dredging up the memories, but since his life had been all about dealing with the Sons of Darkness, he'd learned to live with facing his demons, both metaphorically and in the physical form.

"The others stayed away from him. For some reason, in my dream I didn't avoid him. I went to him and he hugged me. I remember heat surrounding me, so strong it felt like I was burning alive. And yet I welcomed it. It's what I wanted." She rubbed her arms with her hands, as if she was trying to cool down her skin.

"Tase told me that you were using me. He said you were going to kill me as a way to gain your redemption, that I had to save myself and I shouldn't trust you."

His lips lifted. "Not bad advice, actually."

She frowned and crossed her arms. "That's not funny."

"It has to be partly your own subconscious giving you these dreams, Isabelle."

"Is it?"

"Do you think they're somehow tuning in to what's happening between the two of us, then giving you advice in your dreams? Don't you think some of what you're hearing has to come from your own misgivings? About where you are, what's happened to you? About how you've felt about me?"

"I do trust you, Dalton."

"But up until now you've known very little about me. You had no reason to trust me. Sure, the Sons of Darkness might be prodding you. But I think some of it comes from you, too."

She leaned forward, laid her head against the palm of her hand, and took a sip of coffee. "I don't know anymore. These dreams are so vivid, unlike any dreams I've had before. It's like as soon as I fall asleep I'm transported, like I'm really with them. Every sense comes alive. I can feel everything—the heat, the crisp cut of their clothes when I touch them. I smell the acrid burning odor when Tase enfolds me in his arms. I shiver when I step away from him and am surrounded by the others, because they are completely the opposite of him—ice cold. It's all so clear, no dreamlike quality to it."

"I slept next to you last night, Isabelle. Or I should say I lay next to you all night, because I didn't sleep. Trust me—you were there the entire time."

She sighed. "I don't claim to understand it, Dalton. You probably would better than me. I just know it feels so real. Like I'm there."

"Are you thinking the Sons of Darkness have some kind of control over your soul—that they're actually transporting you, just not physically?"

She shrugged. "Maybe. I don't know. Is that even possible?"

"No. Trust me when I tell you that all of you was here last night. Just like when they come to you during the daytime, all of you is still here. They're screwing with your head, making you doubt yourself—and me."

She nodded. "The logical part of me understands that. But it's so easy to believe in the darkness."

He reached out, stroked his palm across her cheek. "Maybe it's time you start believing in the light."

"What if I don't think I'm deserving of it?"

"Try harder. I believe in you. I believe we can take that darkness within you and make it manageable, so that you can control it and live a normal life."

She smiled. "I'll try harder."

"That's my girl."

Thunder cracked and lightning lit up the dark sky. Isabelle jumped at the sound and Dalton held her tighter. He knew she was skittish, no doubt frightened, and probably confused as hell. The weather wasn't helping, especially since the sky took that moment to open and dump its contents in a hellacious downpour, accompanied by nonstop arcing lightning and thunder so loud it hurt the ears.

"Let me show you something," he said, backing away from her, but still holding on to her hand.

Dalton led her into the second bedroom, the one he'd taken as his own when they'd first arrived. He motioned for her to sit on the bed, then he went into the closet and dragged something out of the back, wrapped in an old, worn cloth.

"What's that?"

He laid it on the bed and began to unwrap it, the cloth falling apart as he did.

Isabelle gasped as Dalton unveiled a sword, about a foot and a half long, gleaming bright in the semidarkness of the bedroom. The intricate scrolling pattern on the scabbard was like nothing she'd seen before, as was the writing on the blade.

"May I?" she asked.

He nodded, and she lifted the blade, which seemed so light, not heavy as she thought it would be. "This metal seems so unfamiliar. What is it?"

"Nothing that's made on earth."

Her gaze snapped to his and she laid the sword back on the bed. "What is that, Dalton?"

"It used to be mine. A long, long time ago. It's the sword of the Guardians, a weapon we used to fight the darkness."

She stared at it in awe. "To fight demons."

"Yes."

"Where did it come from?"

"It's always been here. It was left behind when I was banished. And when I returned, I left it here."

"When was the last time you used it?"

"That night I killed Ratineau."

"So you used this sword to kill a human."

He picked it up, his fingers curling lightly over the scabbard. "The sword lost its power that night, too, just like I did. But I'm hoping we can rectify that."

"How?"

"With your blood. And mine."

Isabelle tried not to let the tiny leap of fear show on her face. She meant what she said when she told Dalton she trusted him. She'd come this far with him. He knew what he was doing, and she was putting her life in his hands. She wouldn't still be alive if it wasn't for him, anyway.

"Okay. Do you want to explain how?"

"Georgie will help us. She'll conduct a voodoo

ceremony. During the ceremony, you and I will use the
sword, slice into our hands, mingle our blood. And we
will call upon the spirits to give you back your strength,
your humanity, so you can fight the Sons of Darkness.
Our request will be to empower you so that the human
side of you becomes stronger than the demon side."

"Georgie has that kind of power?"

"Alone? No. But with my help, yes."

Isabelle leaned back against the bed, staring at him in
wonder. "Every time we talk, I learn so many more of
your secrets, and I'm just so amazed by you."

He laid the sword down and reached for her hand,
kissed her palm, tucked it between both of his. "I'm not a
knight in shining armor, Isabelle. I'm a fallen angel. I've
made more mistakes than I've done good. Don't put
me up on a pedestal because I'm more likely to disap-
point you."

Her bottom lip trembled and tears filled her eyes. "I
think you're too hard on yourself." She raised up and
kissed him, the brush of her lips so tender it made him
ache inside. "I love you. You love me. There's strength in
that. We'll figure this out together."

That made the ache even more painful. This love,
this human thing that he never quite understood, was becoming all too clear to him.

Losing it was going to kill him.

"The Realm will be here soon."

She stilled, pulled back. "What? How do you know?"

"Logic. I worked with them long enough to know
that after my call to Derek, it's only a matter of time before they zero in our location and find us."

Dalton saw the fear in her eyes, wished he hadn't been the one to put it there, but he wasn't going to hold back information any longer.

"So what does that mean? Should we pack up and go?"

He shook his head. "No. We stay. I'll convince them that I had a good reason for what I did."

"Will you explain that to them before or after they kill me?"

"I'm not going to let them kill you."

"You'll be using your amazing angel superpowers to prevent that, then."

He smiled. "No. But they're reasonable. They're not going to come in with lasers blazing. Trust me, they'll listen."

"Uh-huh. I'd feel a lot better about that if we could do this whole ceremony thing before they got here." She stood and began to pace in front of the bed, rubbing her temples as she walked. "Well, maybe. Maybe not." She paused, turned to him. "Because if we do it, and it actually works, then you'll leave. Shit. This sucks."

He understood her feelings of ambiguity. He wanted it to work, too. And part of him didn't because he wanted things to stay just as they were. "I know, babe." He stood and grasped her arms, rubbed them. "I have to stay, to explain. I can't be gone when they get here. I think we should wait."

She tilted her head back, searched his face. "Oh, that's right. Otherwise they'd only have my word. They'd never believe me."

"I didn't say that. If Lou were still alive, I think you'd

have a really good shot at making him understand. He had an uncanny ability to sense things. He'd...know.

"But Lou is gone now. Given that, I think I'd rather stay and explain my reasoning. I'm the one who defied orders. I need to stand and face that. I need to make sure you're protected."

After he told the hunters all they needed to know, he and Isabelle would do the ceremony, which would hopefully work. Isabelle wouldn't have to worry about not being able to handle her demon side. He'd at least be able to leave with some peace of mind about that. She'd be okay, be reunited with her sister. The Realm would take care of her. They'd have to, because he'd be gone, back where he belonged.

It's what he'd wanted for so long, and it was within reach.

So why was he so damned miserable?

Michael sat with Derek, Gina, Ryder, and Angelique at a truck stop restaurant on the outskirts of Louisiana. He focused his attention on listening to Derek's report, glad to have something to occupy his mind other than the sullen woman sitting next to him—the one who hadn't said much to him all through the night.

When they left Florida, she'd tossed her gear in the SUV and tilted her seat back, promptly cutting off any conversation between them by going to sleep. Michael knew she needed the rest, considering what she'd been through, so he hadn't bothered her.

Unfortunately, that left him alone with his thoughts.

none of them good, most of them dealing with the master clusterfuck he'd started by having sex with one of his own team members. It got worse from there.

He'd stolen occasional glances at Mandy throughout the twelve-hour drive, but she hadn't budged other than during the few stops they'd made to refuel, use the bathroom, and grab coffee.

Then she'd curled up and gone back to sleep. Or at least she'd feigned sleep. As restless as she'd seemed, Michael figured that was the excuse she used to keep from having a conversation with him.

They were going to have to talk—eventually. But for now, they had other things to deal with. Michael had given the rest of the team a full report on the demons they'd found in Florida, the testing, what the demon had told them, and how they'd killed it. Now it was on to another crisis: Dalton and Isabelle.

Derek had found Dalton. After Dalton called him, Derek had set to work with the Realm's help tracing the call. It hadn't been easy, but they'd pinpointed the call to Louisiana. After that, they'd relied on Angelique, who had finally been able to pick up her sister's connection. Isabelle must have finally started opening up so Angelique could get psychic impulses, or whatever it was the twins exchanged. Between the two of them, Derek and Angelique had followed the trail into Louisiana with Gina and Ryder, confirming Dalton's and Isabelle's arrival in a small bayou town. So far the fugitives hadn't left.

"So what's our plan?" Gina asked.

They'd eaten breakfast and now sat drinking coffee while a vicious storm blew through, leaving gray clouds and wet roads in its wake. The sun had finally started to break through in pinhole points. There might be hope for the day after all.

"We're heading straight to the house where they're holed up," he said.

Angelique frowned, worry etching her features. "We're going to talk to them, right?"

"Yes, Angelique. Don't worry. We're not going in with lasers pointing at your sister. Dalton needs to explain why he took Isabelle there. I'm sure he had a good reason for it."

"Any clue what that might be?" Ryder asked, stroking Angelique's back.

Michael knew that Ryder was looking for assurances, for Angelique's benefit. He had none to give her. "I have no idea, other than he wanted to keep Isabelle alive."

"He believes in her, in the goodness in her," Angelique said. "So do I."

He supposed it would do no good to say that Angelique would believe in anything to save her sister. And that would only piss off Mandy even more. Not that it mattered whether she was angry at him or not. He should be used to that by now.

Still silent, Mandy cupped the ceramic mug in both hands and stared into it like it held tea leaves that would reveal her future.

"You're quiet," Gina said to Mandy.

Mandy lifted her gaze and attempted a smile. "Sorry. Tired."

Gina arched a brow. "Evasive, too."

Mandy shrugged. "It's been a long few weeks."

Derek slung his arm around Mandy's shoulder. "We all miss Lou, honey."

Her gaze shifted to the mug again. "Yeah. Sometimes I forget that there were other people who knew him as well as I did." She turned her gaze to Derek, lifted her lips in a smile, then laid her head on Derek's shoulder.

Derek had been with Lou for a long time. He was tight with Mandy, like a big brother. They had all been close, like family. And devastated when Lou had been killed.

Which only served to remind Michael why getting close to Mandy would be a colossal mistake.

Of course it was a little late for that, wasn't it? He'd already gotten close, closer than he'd ever expected to. Throughout all the arguing, all the bullshit, he'd discovered something about her—about himself.

He could feel again. And not just physically. The short period of time he'd been with Mandy, he felt more alive than he'd felt in years.

So why couldn't they continue what they'd started?

Besides him being her boss—and that was a serious enough conflict right there.

Attraction could be deterred. He'd channel her energies in different directions. She had a natural talent for demon hunting, a zeal for adventure.

She also needed a life outside demon hunting, a chance to develop relationships with men, to explore her sexuality . . .

But the thought of that burned him inside with a rage that shocked him. He'd just had his hands all over Mandy last night. He'd been inside her.

He'd had her first.

The thought of anyone else touching her was out of the question.

And none of his business, considering the conversation he planned to have with her.

"Do you need a nap? Should we plan this surprise on Dalton without you?"

Mandy's not-so-subtle elbow in his side nudged him out of his thoughts.

"Sorry. My mind was elsewhere." He sidled a glance in Mandy's direction. She quickly looked away, but not before he caught the tinge of pink darkening her cheeks. He turned to the others, dragging a hand through his hair. "I drove all night so I didn't sleep. I'm a little fuzzy."

"You need to catch a little shut-eye before we confront Dalton," Ryder said. "We all need to be sharp for this. I'll drive your vehicle when we take off."

Michael nodded. Based on the map they'd laid out, they had about four hours before they'd arrive at Dalton's hideout. He could use a little sleep.

"I call shotgun," Mandy said.

Michael smiled. "You can have it. I'll stretch out in the back. I'm dead tired."

More so than he thought. He was out cold before Ryder backed the SUV out of the truck stop parking lot, and didn't wake until they pulled into a gas station about twenty minutes from their destination. He went inside to grab a soda, needing the caffeine to clear his head. Derek met him in there.

"What bug crawled up Mandy's ass?" Derek asked. "She was grumpy and quiet the whole way."

Michael took a long swallow of the soda. "That's different for Mandy?"

Derek laughed. "Okay, so she's normally moody. But there's something off about her."

"She froze when she tried to kill the demon in Florida. Couldn't pull the trigger. It really messed her up. She had some kind of meltdown over it."

Derek's brows lifted. "That's weird. She's usually right on the front line and eager to be the first on a kill."

"Yeah, I know. I read her file. But something's going on with her, Derek. She went out after that and hunted down another, made a kill, but it screwed with her head. She came back a wreck."

"Physically?"

Michael shook his head. "Physically and emotionally. My guess is she's still pretty messed up over Lou's death and the part she was forced to play in it."

"You talk to her about that?"

No. He got her naked and made love to her. "I've tried."

"Do you want me to talk to her?"

"I'll handle it. I'm her Keeper and in charge of her. She needs a cooling-off period right now."

Derek nodded. "Your call. If you need me, let me know. In the meantime, I'll make sure we all have her back. She's family."

To them she was family. To him she was . . . something entirely different.

"Okay. Thanks. Look, I know I'm not Lou and I'll never try to be, but I have all your best interests in mind with this. My job is to protect you. If you can't do your jobs, I'll pull you. Any of you. That's what I told Mandy."

Derek's lips lifted. "I'll bet she hated that. And you for doing it."

Michael leaned against the counter and waited for the store clerk to make change, grinning back at Derek. "Uh, yeah, you could say she was a little unhappy with me."

Derek looked Michael over from head to foot.

"What are you doing?" Michael asked.

"Searching for wounds. Frankly, I'm surprised you're still walking."

Michael laughed. At that moment, Mandy walked in and they both stared at her. She stopped, looked at both of them, then glared.

"What?"

"Nothing," Derek said.

Her gaze narrowed. She had to know they'd been discussing her. She cast a look at Michael, then moved on to the back of the store.

"Yeah, she's pissed," Derek said.

"I'll handle her. But first we need to get through this situation with Dalton and Isabelle. One crisis at a time."

"Do you think there'll be a problem when we get there?"

Michael took the change from the clerk and they walked outside. He shrugged. "No idea. You know Dalton better than I do."

"Yeah, I do. But what he did wasn't like him. He's always been pretty much by the book. So I have no idea what we'll find."

Great. Michael hated surprises. Then again, in their line of work, every damn day was a surprise.

"I do know one thing, though," Derek added.

"Yeah? What's that?"

"Dalton's a good guy. We need to give him the benefit of the doubt."

Michael shrugged. "Why? Just because he's a 'good guy' doesn't mean he gets a pass. But I'm not going to go up to him and shoot him, either. I'll listen to what he has to say." And then decide what to do.

The last thing he wanted was more bloodshed, more death. Especially of one of their own. Michael would do anything to avoid that.

Frankly, he didn't think Mandy could handle it if it came to having to take drastic measures against Dalton. Not that Mandy's feelings were his concern, or his primary consideration when tackling an issue.

Or at least they shouldn't be. But part of his decision-making in this situation did take her feelings into account. Mandy was on the edge, teetering on the cliff. One gentle push and she'd go over. It wasn't his personal feelings for Mandy—or that's what he told himself—he just didn't want to lose another team member.

Yeah, he'd be handling Dalton with care.

At least until he found out what the hell was going on.

CHAPTER SEVENTEEN

By late afternoon the puddles had mostly cleared and the sun was out, doing its best to dry the rain-soaked area. Frankly, all the sun was doing was making it even more hellishly humid. It was damned near unbearable outside, but Dalton couldn't stand being cooped up in the house. The sense of expectation had become intolerable.

Isabelle seemed to feel it, too. She'd been quiet since he told her about the Realm coming. He could only wonder about what she was thinking and having to deal with: everything he'd told her about himself, plus her realistic dreams about the Sons of Darkness—now she also had to worry about what would happen when the Realm showed up.

He'd protect her. Nothing bad would happen. He wouldn't let it. They'd come too far to fail now.

He was out back when he heard the sounds of car engines approaching along the main road. It would take the hunters a bit to maneuver their way to the main house, then figure out where Isabelle and he were. Abandoning his work, he grabbed a towel to wipe the mud off his hands and headed inside to clean up. Isabelle was standing at the front window, her arms crossed. A light breeze blew the curtains inward.

"I heard cars," she said, not turning to look at him.

"Yeah. It's probably the hunters."

She nodded. Even without touching her, he felt her tension.

"It's going to be okay."

She turned to him. "Is it? How do you know?"

"You're right. I don't know. But I'll make it okay. We haven't come this far for me to let them strike you down. And I know the Realm, Isabelle. They don't operate that way."

She tilted her head back, her hair picking up sunlight and shining like golden fire. "They ordered you to kill me once, and you defied them. They may just decide to kill me now and *then* talk to you. Or kill us both."

He shook his head. "It's not going to happen that way." He swept his knuckles across her cheek. "Please, just trust that I will do whatever it takes to protect you."

She nodded. "You always have, haven't you?"

"Yes. And I don't intend to stop."

She inhaled and let it out on an audible sigh. "I'll be fine."

He wanted to go to her, hold her, tell her to relax. But he knew it wouldn't help. She wasn't going to be calm. Not until this was over.

He washed up, threw on jeans and a sleeveless shirt, and came back out. Isabelle was still standing at the window. He walked up behind her and wrapped his arms around her.

"My sister is with them," she said. "I've felt my connection to her growing lately."

"That's a good thing, right?"

She shrugged. "I don't know. I guess so. But I can't help but wonder: If Angie broke through long enough to help the Realm locate me, maybe the Sons of Darkness can find me, too."

"Isabelle, it was only a matter of time before the Realm picked up our trail. Angelique may have had nothing to do with it."

"Maybe. But I feel her. I know she feels me, too."

"Isn't it possible you let her in? That you can distinguish between light and darkness?"

"True enough. I do need her."

"It'll be good for you to see your sister again."

She laid her head back against his chest. "I liked being alone with you."

He liked it, too; he wasn't ready for the intrusion of reality. But there was nothing either of them could do about it. It was time. "We'll get through it." He took her hand in his. "Come on, let's go outside and greet them."

She looked up at him in disbelief. "Couldn't we hide in the closet instead?"

He laughed. "Nice try. But some things have to be faced. And it's better if they see us waiting for them than if they have to come hunt for us."

He watched the hunters come down the path from the main house and toward the cabin. A bunch of them, making Dalton wish he had a weapon by his side. But holding a weapon in front of him and Isabelle behind him wouldn't be a show of good faith, no matter how exposed he felt.

He spotted Derek in the lead, and relaxed a little. He wasn't sure who would be there, but he knew he had at least one friend. If only Lou were here . . .

Derek walked with Gina on one side, Michael on the other.

Dalton frowned. What was Michael doing here? Dalton held tight to Isabelle's hand.

Michael, Mandy, Derek and Gina, Ryder and Angelique—they were all there.

"Hey," Dalton said, offering up a casual smile. They all smiled back. That was a good sign.

"Hell of a time for you to take a vacation," Derek said, stepping forward for a quick embrace and a clap on the back.

Gina hugged him, Ryder shook his hand. Angelique flew forward to embrace her sister. Dalton let go of Isabelle's hand—reluctantly, but she needed this time.

Dalton looked to Michael. "Why are you here?"

Michael frowned. "We need to talk. Dalton, if we could go someplace private."

Dalton shook his head. "I'd rather keep this public if you don't mind. Besides, I don't want any secrets. Isabelle needs to hear it all."

"Isabelle doesn't need to be privy to Realm business."

Dalton crossed his arms. "I've already told her a lot. More than you all know, probably."

"What does that mean?" Angelique asked, searching Isabelle's face.

Isabelle shook her head. "That's for Dalton to say, not me."

Michael shook his head. "If that's the way you want it."

Georgie had showed up and stood next to Dalton. Michael turned to her. "Do you mind if we use your house?"

"Of course not." She led them all to the main house. They went in the back way and toward Georgie's sitting room. It was dark and cool in there.

"I'll leave you all to your talk."

"Georgie, stay," Dalton said. "You're going to be in this shortly anyway."

She paused, then sat, smoothing her voluminous skirt down as she did. "All right."

At Michael's frown, Dalton said, "Georgie knows all about the Realm. About the Sons of Darkness and demons."

Michael shook his head again. "So much for confidentiality."

Dalton chose one of the two-person chaises, smiling when Isabelle sat next to him and grasped his hand.

"I guess you need to start by explaining why you're here, Dalton," Michael said.

At least Michael was giving him the opportunity to explain. He should be grateful for that. But something about Michael's tone irked him.

"Why are *you* here, Michael?" It made no sense for a Keeper in charge of one of the European factions to be all the way over in Louisiana.

"Derek said he told you about Lou."

Dalton gave a short nod.

"I'm sorry. I know how devastating it must have been for you to hear that. But the Realm has put me in charge of your group. I'm your—their—Keeper now."

Dalton sucked in a breath, feeling raw inside. "This just sucks. I've been thinking about Lou the whole time I've been here, wishing I could talk to him about all this. If only I'd been there. If I'd stayed . . ."

"It wouldn't have made a difference," Mandy said, her voice tinged with equal parts pain and anger. "You would have been forced to do what we did. It's better you left. At least you're spared this guilt we all feel."

Derek smoothed his hand over Mandy's hair. "You have nothing to feel guilty over. You did what was asked of you."

"We could have walked away."

"And what? Let the demon consume him? Let the Sons of Darkness take him over? Trust me, Lou wouldn't have wanted to live like that. He'd have taken his own life before he allowed that to happen."

"That's true," Derek said. "We saved him."

Mandy snorted. "Some saving."

Isabelle squeezed Dalton's hand with a fierce grip and refused to let go. He appreciated her strength, the fact that she stayed by his side, more than he could tell her right now.

He couldn't imagine what they'd all been through, but what he saw on their faces gave him a pretty good idea.

"I'm sorry I wan't there." He felt like he'd missed out on so much.

"You made that choice when you took Isabelle and left."

Michael's tone told him everything he needed to know. He wasn't out of the woods yet. Neither was Isabelle.

"I know. But I had a reason for it."

"You were given instructions."

"To kill her. She knows."

Angelique gasped and grasped Isabelle's other hand. "You can all be so coldhearted sometimes. This is a human being we're talking about here. My sister."

"At the time she was neither," Michael reminded them. "She was a full demon and about to become one of the Sons of Darkness. She almost killed you. What would you have had us do with her?"

"I don't know. But to give that order without thinking it through..."

"In this business we don't have the luxury of time to think. Lou and I made that decision based on the evidence given at the moment. Isabelle exhibited no humanity in the cemetery in Sicily. She had to be destroyed." Michael look to Dalton. "Obviously Dalton thought differently."

"I did. Because I saw humanity in her that night. And I felt she could be saved. As you can see looking at her now, there's nothing demonic about her."

"And since Sicily?"

Dalton shook his head. "Nothing."

"That's not true," Isabelle said, interrupting him. "I've had dreams where Tase comes for me and takes me with him. And even during the day I've felt his presence, heard his voice. He manipulates me on a subconscious level." She looked to Dalton. "I tried to kill Dalton with a laser."

Michael stood. So did Angelique, and Ryder moved in front of both of them.

"Is this true?" Michael asked, looking at Dalton.

"Not the way she explains it."

"It is, too."

"You're not helping, Isabelle," Dalton said.

"I'm trying to be honest. You only want to see the good in me."

"And you only want to see the bad."

"There's both in Isabelle." Georgie, who'd sat behind them all, finally stood and came to the front of the room. "And that's why Dalton came here. This is his home. There's magic here. Magic that can help Isabelle." She turned to Michael. "Maybe at the time you saw her you saw only the darkness within her. Dalton has the capability to see much more than that. That's why she still lives, because he feels she can be saved."

"I don't mean to be disrespectful, ma'am," Michael said, "but are you some kind of expert?"

Georgie lifted her lips. "I'm an expert in no things. But I do know some things. And this child has humanity and light within her. Enough to attempt to save her. You would do well to listen to Dalton. He knows what he's talking about."

Isabelle smiled at Georgie. "Thank you."

Georgie nodded and stepped back.

Michael blew out a breath and turned his attention back to Dalton. "I assume you have a plan?"

"Yes."

"Then why don't you fill us in?"

Dalton knew better than to assume all was forgiven. For now, maybe they had a reprieve. And that would have to be good enough. He inhaled, exhaled, knowing the time had come for him to come clean. About everything.

"Back at the graveyard in Sicily, when Isabelle and Angelique had their altercation, there was a moment when Isabelle became human again. A fraction of a second when I saw the desperate, pleading human side of her, crying out for help. I knew then that I couldn't destroy her, no matter what my orders were."

"Why didn't you say something to me or to Lou?" Michael asked.

"We were all kind of busy at the time. There was a battle going on. The Sons of Darkness were there. Hardly a moment to call a meeting to discuss Isabelle's future. I made an executive decision, but honestly even I wasn't sure at that moment it was the right one. I wanted some time alone with her, to see if I'd made the right choice."

"And if you hadn't?" Angelique asked.

He knew what she wanted to know. "If she never came back human, if the demon side of her resurfaced with a vengeance, I'd have killed her."

Isabelle didn't even flinch. Instead, she scooted closer to him, squeezed his hand.

"It's what I would have wanted. I don't want to be a demon," Isabelle said. "I'm human. I have demon blood inside me, but that...creature you saw in Italy—that wasn't me. I don't want it to be me. Ever."

"We're going to take steps to make sure it doesn't become her again. That's why I brought Isabelle here to Louisiana, to Georgie. She's a voodoo priestess, and she can help transform Isabelle."

"How?" Angelique asked, her gaze incredulous.

Dalton couldn't blame her. The rest of the story was going to blow their minds.

CHAPTER EIGHTEEN

Isabelle sat back and patiently watched while Dalton explained everything to the wide-eyed group. They, too, had a difficult time believing that he was a fallen angel, especially since they hadn't been around during the episodes she had witnessed. They didn't have proof, and it wasn't like Dalton could sprout white wings and hover near the ceiling.

Her lips lifted. She'd kind of like to see that. Dalton would look sexy with wings. With his face and body... yeah, he could be art on the wall of any chapel.

She was probably going to hell just for thinking that. *Bad Isabelle.*

"Did Lou know about this?" Michael finally asked.

Dalton shook his head. "No one knew. It wasn't necessary for anyone to know."

Michael arched a brow. "Any one of our hunters who possesses otherworldly skills is kind of an important information tool, Dalton. You should have reported it."

Dalton shrugged. "It was personal, and it's not like I can levitate. I'm not psychic. I'm basically human in all respects, so I have no advantage over any of the rest of you, other than the immortal thing."

"That is kind of cool," Gina said.

"Handy when fighting demons," Derek added with a quirk of his lips. "You go into a fight knowing you can't die. If we'd known that, we'd have made sure you were always in the front."

Dalton snorted. "Sorry. Maybe I should have told you."

"Does the fact that you're an angel come into play where Isabelle is concerned?" Michael asked.

Dalton nodded.

"Okay." Michael turned to Isabelle. "We're here and we'll see this through. You may think the Realm wants to do you harm, but we want the same thing you and Dalton do: to make sure that the Sons of Darkness don't get their claws in you again."

Dalton tugged Isabelle's hand and drew her up alongside him. "We're not going to let that happen."

"Care to share the plan with us?" Derek asked.

"Yeah. It requires Georgie's skills as a voodoo priestess. She's going to merge Isabelle's darkness with my light."

"How?"

"Georgie will conduct a ceremony, drawing our souls together via blood and a sword that I once held when I was a Guardian. She'll bring out Isabelle's demon side, and the angel within me. The two will do battle."

"So you're saying she's going to tap into your angel side, and it's going to somehow fight her demon?"

"More like a merger."

"That should be interesting. And dangerous. What happens to you when this . . . merger occurs?" Angelique asked, concern evident on her face.

Dalton started to answer, but Isabelle moved in. "If

all goes well and the strength of the demon within me vanishes, Dalton will be redeemed and become a full-fledged angel again."

Michael whipped his gaze from Isabelle to Dalton. "Are you serious?"

"Pretty much, yeah."

"And you really think this is going to work?"

Dalton shrugged. "Yeah, I do."

Michael inhaled and blew it out. "This is pretty unorthodox."

Dalton cocked his head to the side. "Michael. Everything we do is unorthodox."

"True enough. So when are you planning to do this?"

Dalton slanted his gaze to Isabelle. "Soon."

Isabelle wanted to know the answer to that question, too. "When is soon, Dalton? Are we putting it off for any specific reason? I know you wanted to wait for the Realm to get here, but they're here now. Shouldn't we get started?"

There was a sadness in his smile that pained her. "Eager to get rid of me?"

Oh, God. If this worked, Dalton would leave her. She kept conveniently pushing that oh-so-important part of the equation right out of her head, refusing to face it. She leaned into him, whispering in his ear, her palms warm against his chest. "No. Not eager at all." She tilted her head back to search his face. "We don't have to do this."

He grasped her hands in his. "Yeah, we do. You know we do. There's no other choice. Sooner or later the Sons of Darkness will come for you. They'll take you over and you won't be able to fight them—we won't be able to fight them."

She laid her head on his shoulder, feeling the clock ticking. Too fast. Way too fast. She wasn't ready to let him go.

Dalton kissed the top of her head. "It's going to be all right, Isabelle."

No, it wouldn't. She could already feel him slipping away. Either way this went down, she was going to lose him. If they were unsuccessful, it would only be a matter of time until the Sons of Darkness broke through Isabelle's defenses and came for her, returning her to the awful demon she had been in Sicily. She couldn't—wouldn't—live like that, and if the Realm didn't destroy her of their own accord, she'd beg them to. Or she'd make sure to ask Angelique to see that it was done. The thought of living as a demon repulsed her.

And if it did work, Dalton would disappear from her life forever.

This sucked. She wanted to grab Dalton and run away, refuse to face it.

Was this her punishment for all her years of being bad? To find the man of her dreams, the one person who accepted her with all her flaws, who loved her unconditionally, only to realize he could never be hers?

It wasn't until Michael cleared his throat that Dalton gently pulled away. Isabelle sucked in a breath and turned to her sister, who held out her hand and squeezed Isabelle's.

"Are you all right?" Angelique asked.

Isabelle nodded, hated seeing the worry in her sister's

face. Angelique had always watched over her. Maybe soon she wouldn't have to anymore. "I'm going to be fine. Everything's going to be fine. I promise."

"The Realm will allow you and Isabelle to attempt this transformation," Michael said. "But if it fails, we're going to take over."

Isabelle looked up at Dalton. "What does that mean?"

"It means if it fails and your demon comes up, the Realm will deal with it."

"Deal with *me*, you mean."

"I don't think I like that," Angelique interrupted. "You can't just make a decision about my sister's life without knowing what's going to happen."

"That's not what I meant, Angelique," Michael said.

"It's what you implied." For the first time in a long time, Mandy had actually spoken. She seemed angry. "It's just like the last time. You think you already know what's going to happen. Look at Isabelle. You ordered her death, and look at her. She's human now, not demon. Maybe if we'd waited, Lou would still be alive. Maybe he could have fought the demon inside him, too."

"Mandy," Derek warned. "There was nothing we could do."

"Wasn't there? We don't know that. We had to make a judgment just like that," she said, snapping her fingers. "What if we'd waited? Maybe we could have gotten the demon out of him somehow."

"Mandy," Michael said, his voice soft as he looked at her.

Mandy stared at him, anger lacing her features at

first, then Isabelle saw tears well in her eyes. She turned and walked out of the room, Michael watching her.

Georgie cleared her throat. "We can begin tonight, if you're ready."

Dalton focused only on Isabelle. "Are you ready?"

No. She'd never be ready. But she could no longer put it off. She could already feel herself weakening. The Sons of Darkness were knocking on the door, and soon she'd be too tired to keep them from busting through it.

"As ready as I'll ever be. Let's do it."

CHAPTER NINETEEN

Michael excused himself as soon as he could and went in search of Mandy. She'd walked away from the main house, but he couldn't find her until one of the kids said he'd seen her heading toward the boathouse on the east side of the dock.

The boathouse was a good-sized wooden building where boats were stored during winter and storms. Michael opened the door into darkness, the only light streaming in through small windows high above.

"Mandy?"

No answer.

"I know you're in here. Why don't you save me several bruises and just tell me where you are."

Silence, then, "Over here."

He turned and headed in the direction of her voice, found her sitting near the back door on a bench, farthest away from the light.

"I'd really like to be alone, Michael."

He sat next to her on the bench. "Wouldn't we all. But we need to talk."

She sighed. "I'm not the touchy-feely type that needs to rehash everything, okay? So if you're feeling guilty about the sex, don't be."

"I'm not feeling guilty about the sex. You wanted it. Why should there be any guilt?"

Okay, that was stretching the truth a bit since he did have guilt, but not for making love to her.

"We need to talk about these residual feelings you're having about Lou."

"Doesn't the Realm have counselors?"

"Yeah. You want to set up a talk with one?"

"No. But you're not one, so you're hardly equipped to hand out advice."

God, she was difficult. "True enough, but I am your Keeper and in charge of determining whether you're fit for duty or not. So I'm the first one you need to talk to."

"I killed a demon. I can handle my job."

"We've been over this before. You fell apart afterward. You went into shock. And don't bother trying to deny it, because I was there to pick you up when it happened."

She stared at the wall on the other side of the room. "It won't happen again."

"Yes, it will. Until you face your demons—sorry—it will. And no amount of trying to handle this on your own—not even sex—will make this go away."

She closed her eyes, and though it was dark in there, he saw the tear slip down her cheek.

"I loved him. He was all I had." When she opened her eyes again, she turned her head to face Michael, her lashes spiked with tears. "Why do I keep losing people I love?"

"I don't have an answer for that."

"He was my family after I lost my family. He was my

father after my father was killed by demons. And I had to kill him."

"No, you had to kill a demon."

"I killed Lou, Michael. You were there."

"I know. I know how hard it was for you."

"Do you? How do you know? How could you possibly know how it felt?"

"Because I had to kill my father."

Her eyes widened. "What?"

He hated reliving it, but it was important she understand that she wasn't the only one. "The Sons of Darkness had already killed my mother. They took my father and turned him into . . . one of them, their intent to have me killed."

"Because you were a descendant, and they want to kill all the Keepers."

He nodded. "So my father disappeared, and then came back. But it wasn't him. I knew it wasn't him. My father was warm, and this . . . thing was cold. He'd warned me once, told me what I had to do if there was ever a sudden change in him."

"So you killed him?"

Michael nodded, trying to block out the visuals of that night, but the pain soared back, nearly doubling him over. He stood, walked to the other end of the boathouse. "I got one of the old swords out, and when his back was turned I beheaded him."

"Oh, God." Mandy stood, went to him. "Michael, I'm sorry, I didn't know."

"No one knows, other than the Keepers."

She wrapped her arms around him and laid her head

on his shoulder. "And here I've been whining about how I feel, never knowing that you felt the same way."

"You didn't need to know this. I'm just trying to give you perspective."

Her hold on him tightened. "How do you deal with it?"

"I just remind myself that the man I knew as my father was already dead, and that's what he would have wanted." He drew her away so he could look at her. "And that's what you have to remember. Lou was already gone. You didn't kill Lou. You killed that demon. Lou would be proud of you."

"You and I are so much alike. I never saw it."

He slid his fingers under her chin. "I did. And maybe that's part of why I said what I did back in Florida."

"What do you mean?"

"Keepers' mates are vulnerable, Mandy."

Her eyes widened. "You thought . . . oh."

"Yeah."

"I can take care of myself, Michael. You don't have to worry about that. I'm not a housewife who's going to be slaughtered while you're off fighting demons."

He closed his eyes and dropped his chin to his chest. Stupid, he knew, because his mind had gone there.

"Oh, my God. You thought that, didn't you? About you and me."

"Maybe."

"That's a pretty broad jump. From sex to forever."

"Is it? In our line of work, hello to forever could be just days. We never know how long we have. I don't like to waste time."

She blew out a breath. "You scare me sometimes, Mike."

"You infuriate me sometimes, Mandy. But you intrigue me, and you excite me, and I really like being with you." And he knew now why he found her so irresistible. Beyond her beauty and her courage, she was just as lost as he was. He pressed his lips to hers, drawing strength from the way she kissed him back, moved into him to draw closer.

He'd prided himself on remaining aloof for years. Like Mandy, he'd lost so much.

But maybe it was time to fight back against the Sons of Darkness, and to take solace in someone else.

Maybe strength came in unity, not solitude.

He deepened the kiss, for the first time in years feeling that strength filling him. With Mandy at his side, he felt more powerful than ever.

They only had a few short hours until night fell. Isabelle felt the clock ticking even louder, the pounding echoing in her heart, tightening her throat like a noose. She tried to stay busy at the cabin as she watched the time click down to the zero hour, grateful at least that Dalton had brought her back here after telling Michael and the others that she needed a few hours' rest before the big event. She needed to be away from the main house, felt claustrophobic around the sympathetic looks and gestures of Dalton's friends and even her own sister. She couldn't handle it.

Before they'd left the others, they'd gone over the

ceremony with Georgie, outlining every possible scenario, though they realized that no one could predict what might really happen once things got under way. And playing the "what if" game with Isabelle's destiny—with her and Dalton's lives—had only ratcheted up her tension to the nth degree. By the time Dalton had called a halt to things and dragged her out of there, she'd been ready to explode.

She stared out the front window and watched the sun move over the water, every inch of its descent reminding her that time grew closer for tonight's event. She dreaded it, didn't look forward to it at all, wanted to just be a normal woman in love with a normal man.

She hated having no control over her own destiny, being unable to make her own choices regarding her future and what she wanted. She wanted Dalton in her life, and that wasn't going to happen.

So unfair. She closed her eyes, and for the first time in a very long time, she whispered a prayer for his safety. If she couldn't have him, she could only wish that he got what he wanted. No matter how things turned out for her, it was about time that she thought about someone else's needs. Dalton had paid a severe price over so many years for doing something so incredibly noble.

His time for redemption had come. She could only hope she was the catalyst. Maybe after all the bad things she'd done in her life, all the selfish ways she'd tried to serve herself and her own desires, she could finally do something good for someone else.

When Dalton's hands came around to encircle her waist, she melted into him, needing this more than she needed to breathe. His touch, being near him, was a balm to her psyche. She leaned against him, resting her head against his chest, wishing she could freeze this moment in time. She'd be perfectly content to stay like this, with Dalton's hands around her, the feel of his heart beating against her back, his chin resting on the top of her head. She'd never felt so relaxed.

"Our time is running out, Dalton."

He turned her around to face him. "Then let's not waste a minute of it." He kissed her, his lips barely a feather brush against hers. She sighed in utter bliss, swept off her feet from the sheer romance of his mouth sliding against hers. She poured everything she had into touching him, tasting him, knowing this would be the last time she would ever be close to him.

He led her into the bedroom and took his time removing her clothes. She was torn between wanting to hurry up and taking each moment in slow motion, wishing she could capture every second in her memories so she'd never forget. As he peeled away her shirt he pressed his lips to her neck, her shoulder, the touch of his lips so reverent it brought tears to her eyes. She sensed this moment was as special to him as it was to her, that he knew as well as she did that they would only have this time together, and then it would be gone.

He turned her around and drew her hair to the side, placing his lips against the nape of her neck. She shivered, goose bumps prickling her skin. He tilted her head up and pulled against him so he could reach around her to touch her breasts, sliding his thumbs over the piercings, tugging them with gentle pulls that made her whimper. She felt the sensation between her legs. So incredible, so erotic, he knew her body like he owned it.

He did.

How would she ever live without him?

Don't think. Don't waste a moment of this. Just feel.

She did—everything. His touch, his hands on her nipples, the ecstasy of his familiarity with her, the way his body felt against hers after he pulled off his shirt. The smoothness of his chest against her back, the heat, the possessiveness as he drew her shorts down and pressed a soft kiss to her right hip, then turned her around and claimed her sex with his mouth. She widened her legs and let him take her, threading her fingers through his hair, watching him while absorbing every wild sensation and committing it to memory. He loved her slowly, sliding his tongue in tantalizing fashion over her until she lost the ability to think coherently. She gripped his hair and held him to her while she rode the crest and fell, rocking against him in unabashed frenzy.

He rose and took her mouth again in a tart kiss that told her she belonged to him and only him.

As if she could ever hope to experience this with anyone else again. She was his, always would be, no matter if they were separated.

When he lifted her and carried her to the bed, she wrapped her arms around his neck, staring at his face, sliding her fingertips along his jaw. There was so much she wanted to say, but she said nothing. Neither did he. She understood.

There was nothing they could say to each other now.

They could only show, without words, the depth of their feelings.

He rolled her to her side to face him, lifted her leg over his hip and slid inside her. Slow and easy, he rocked in and out, letting her feel every inch of him. Her body gripped him in utter pleasure, and now it was her turn to claim him, to tell him that he was hers, and always would be.

She watched the tension on his face, the way he clamped his lips together and concentrated on their bodies gliding back and forth as one. She pulled up and kissed him, rimming his lips with her tongue. He opened for her and she found his tongue, sucked it, and he groaned, curling her toes at the extreme pleasure of his response. He tunneled his fingers in her hair and gripped tight, tilting her head back to kiss her hard as he quickened his movements with harder thrusts.

As he ground against her she lost control, bit his lip, tasting his blood in her mouth, but she didn't care. It was just more of him that became a part of her. She wrapped her leg around him, digging her heel in his buttocks to drive him harder. And when her climax washed over her, she didn't bother to hold back the tears that told him how much she'd miss him, how much she loved him. He buried his face in her neck, his teeth grazing her skin as he groaned and shuddered against her.

He held her tight and stroked her back, her shoulders, her hip. And still, neither of them spoke.

They'd both just said all there was to say.

They loved each other.

But it was over.

———

For some reason Isabelle thought the ceremony would take place in the house, but that's not how it was going to happen. She stood outside along with Dalton and the other hunters, as well as Georgie and several of her family and coworkers. The women wore long cotton dresses, the men knee-cropped pants and vests, no shirts. Even children came along. Georgie had told her that young children were groomed in the way of voodoo at an early age, many to take over as *mambo* or *houngan*—the female or male voodoo priestess or priest—when they came of age.

They'd all taken a walk deep into the woods, staying parallel to the bayou. The night was sultry, the moon full, the sounds of birds and God only knew what other kinds of creatures keeping them company as they trekked single-file along a narrow pathway carved into the dense woods. Alone with her thoughts, Isabelle had stayed in step, Derek in front of her, Dalton behind her, all of the hunters fully armed in case the Sons of Darkness decided to make an impromptu appearance while all of this went down tonight.

Great. Another thing to worry about, though Dalton assured her she'd done a fine job so far of keeping their location from the Sons of Darkness. But who knew what would happen during the ceremony? Maybe she'd weaken when her demon went to war with Dalton's angel. She still couldn't wrap her mind about how this was going to take place, and didn't even want to try.

She was tired—bone weary and exhausted. Whether

it was from fighting off the Sons of Darkness' constant attempts to reach her, the lack of sleep, or the utter emptiness she felt inside knowing she was going to lose Dalton tonight, she didn't know. She'd rather be asleep curled up in Dalton's arms than go through this. But she'd agreed, it was going to happen, and moaning about it wasn't going to do any good.

The group finally arrived at what appeared to be a man-made clearing carved out of the dense foliage, a huge circle surrounded by low-hanging cypress trees that seemed to bow down to them in reverence. Water moved behind them on one side, and there was nothing but woods the rest of the way.

Off to one side stood an altar made of wood, with several shelves. On the shelves were varied items—strange stuff. Candles were already lit, their flames wavering in the slight balmy breeze. There were also framed pictures of what looked to be Georgie's ancestors, beaded necklaces, amulets, cloth voodoo dolls, trinkets of every sort, bottles of rum, some full, some half full. There was even money scattered along the shelves. A crazy assortment, like what you'd find at a flea market, yet absolutely fascinating. In front of the altar was a circle of dirt, none of the lush green grass that surrounded the rest of the area. Behind the circle lay a wooden pole and a stone bench stained with some kind of dark, rusty-looking material. Isabelle crinkled her nose and hoped that wasn't where some kind of bizarre blood sacrifices had occurred.

Georgie had dressed the part tonight, in a white flowing cotton dress, sleeveless but covering the rest of her body down to her ankles, one of which bore a braided anklet. She was barefoot and wore a multicolored turban on her head. She'd provided Isabelle with a similar type of dress, only Isabelle's was all colorful. She'd told Isabelle not to wear shoes, either.

"Georgie, what is all this stuff?" Isabelle asked.

"It is the altar where we pay homage to the gods. We make our offerings here. The altar is the passageway between this world and the next. The place where the immortal spirits make their home."

Dalton laid his sword on the stone bench and Isabelle swallowed, her throat scratchy and dry. She'd have given anything for a glass of water right now.

Georgie faced the crowd gathered around her. "We will make an offering to Loa, the spirits that gather here. Isabelle will chant with me, protected within the divine circle. She will shed the blood of sacrifice, and be inhabited by those who shelter her from harm."

Isabelle's gaze snapped to Dalton, who raised his hand as if to tell her everything would be all right.

"None of you may interfere. To do so will anger the gods. Please be aware that we practice white magic here. There will be no evil, only purity. Our goal is to cleanse Isabelle, to rid her of the demons possessing her. No harm will come to her as long as you do not disrupt the ceremony."

Isabelle inhaled and blew it out, forcing the shaking fear back. She had to trust in Dalton. They were in it—deep in it, now. She had no choice.

Returning her attention to Georgie, she nodded, and

Georgie bent down on the ground and opened a container with some type of yellow granules.

"This is cornmeal," she said. "We use it to create the Vévé, the symbol for the spirits we call. It is our homage to them. These spirits will embody us and guide us on our journey to the other side."

Isabelle was mesmerized as Georgie painstakingly created an amazing geometric design in the dirt from simple cornmeal, a series of triangles, spheres, and dots with connecting lines that formed the shape of some unidentifiable creature. It resembled the kind of drawing a child might make, only much more intricate.

"Don't leave my side for any reason. Within this area you will be protected. Outside it I cannot help you. Do as I say, everything I say, even if it sounds strange to you."

Isabelle nodded. Georgie turned to the others. "Ready?"

No one said anything, so Georgie pivoted, bent her head, and began to chant in French. Fortunately, Isabelle understood and could follow, though little of it made sense. Georgie made a prayer to the gods, both dark and light, calling them forth, offering what stood on the altar as gifts, and asking for their blessings and protections. She called out the names Petro and Rada, darkness and benevolence, and the Ghede, the powers of the dead.

Georgie kneeled, eyes closed, moving her hand over the Vévé and continuing to chant.

When Georgie mentioned Dalton's name along with Isabelle's, then said the *gros-bon-ange,* which meant great good angel, Isabelle's gaze shifted to Dalton. His lips curled in an encouraging smile.

But then Georgie explained that the *tis-bon-ange* wandered, that a soul was lost, captured by evil, and must be caught and put to rest.

Was Georgie talking about Dalton? Or her? Isabelle so wanted to ask, but Georgie chanted nonstop, her hands moving, her body undulating. And behind her, people pounded drums in a slow, soft rhythm, other people chanted, even sang in soft, melodic tones to music unfamiliar to her. It was lovely, really. Was it part of the ceremony? Did it have some kind of profound effect on what would happen?

Because so far she felt nothing. Though she was relaxed, and enjoying the symbolism of the ceremony, nothing was happening to her.

There was, however, something apparently happening with Georgie. Her body moved like it was made of rubber, and her eyes rolled back in her head. She began to dance, her feet digging up a cloud of dust around her. She lifted her hands in the air, her hips moving in a seductive rhythm. She picked up a black top hat from the makeshift altar, lit two cigarettes, smoked them simultaneously, and grabbed an open bottle of rum, taking several deep swigs. She picked up another bottle, moved toward Isabelle, a wicked smile on her face.

"Drink."

It looked like rum in there. But was it?

Georgie thrust the bottle at her again. "Drink!"

Isabelle tipped the bottle and took a sip. It burned, the alcohol strong.

"Drink more."

She did, taking several swallows of the hot liquid, then handed the bottle back to Georgie.

"You are the demon," Georgie said, her voice lower.

Georgie didn't seem to be herself any longer, but appeared to be channeling someone else.

Isabelle nodded. "Who are you?"

"I am Ghede. I am god of the dead. Why are you here? What do you want?"

Isabelle didn't know how to answer.

"I'm Isabelle. I have half demon blood. The demon inside me controls me. I want that to change."

"You wish to eliminate the darkness?"

Thankfully the entity asked leading questions. "Yes."

"Are you worthy, Isabelle?"

Was she? She didn't know how to answer that.

"She is."

Dalton had moved beside her and laid his arm around her. She breathed in his scent, absorbed his strength, relaxing the tension that had crept into her body.

Georgie examined Dalton. "You have fallen. You walk the edge between light and darkness."

"Yes."

"This one will need you. And you will need her. But first, we dance!" Georgie, or Ghede, tilted her head back and laughed, taking the bottle of rum with her and emptying it in several swallows. Then she tossed the bottle and grabbed her skirts as the drums picked up the beat, and swirled around the circle, dancing madly.

"Come. Dance. Celebrate," Georgie bid. "Nothing happens until you do."

Isabelle looked at Dalton.

"Do what she says."

They held hands and moved together to the music.

"Everyone must dance. Feel the music. Let it enter your bodies until it lives inside you."

The singing and drumming grew louder as Georgie's family threw themselves into the dance. Even the hunters joined in, and soon they were all moving around the fire in a circle.

The music was infectious, the drums equaling Isabelle's pounding heart as she stomped her feet in the dirt and circled Dalton, sliding her body against his. Sweat poured between her breasts, the heat from the fire adding to the nearly unbearable temperature of the night, but she didn't care. Lost in the music, in the magic of the night, she felt wild, free, totally without care. She slid against Dalton, reaching up on her toes to press her lips against his.

"I love you," she whispered against his ear. "I always will."

He circled her waist with his hand and drew her into a deeper kiss, his body moving against hers in time to the music.

"No, no." Georgie pulled them apart. "Dance."

Laughing, Isabelle moved away, filled with joy, her heart lighter now than it had been in ages. Was it the rum doing this to her?

Suddenly she was spun around and she grinned, certain it was Dalton again, ready to pull her into another kiss.

It wasn't. It was Georgie. Dalton was right next to her.

Before Isabelle could even blink, Georgie had reached out and grabbed Isabelle's and Dalton's wrists in a tight hold. She felt the power flowing from Georgie to her, then realized it wasn't Georgie after all, but some kind of phenomenal force.

Georgie held Dalton's sword in her hand.

"Now the darkness begins."

Isabelle stilled, then tried to jerk away. She wasn't ready yet, but Georgie's hold was strong.

"Isabelle."

Dalton's voice was a soothing balm, calming her tension. "Don't fight this. It has to happen." Dalton held out his hand to Georgie, palm up.

She nodded and did the same, trying to show no fear. Inside, she was quaking so hard she could barely stand, her heart pumping so loud it was all she could hear.

Georgie took Dalton's hand and slid the sword across it, scoring his palm lightly. A crimson line appeared. She took Isabelle's hand and did the same. Isabelle bit down on her lip at the pain, but it was only momentary.

Georgie laid the sword down.

"Your blood will mingle and light shall find the darkness." Georgie grasped their wrists and pressed their hands together, mixing their blood.

"Close your eyes, child," Georgie said. "Let it wash over you. Do not fear. We are here to protect you. Release the demon."

Isabelle shook her head, too afraid to let it go. She'd held it inside for so long, fighting it, fighting the Sons of Darkness and her own weakness. How could she release it? How could she give it free rein to do whatever it wanted?

"Isabelle, I'm here with you," Dalton said. "You're not alone. I won't let anything hurt you. Never again."

She believed him. But God, how could she do this? In theory it had sounded fine, but now, the demon inside her licked its lips in anticipation of freedom. She felt it banging against her soul, demanding its liberation. She knew how destructive that side of her was, how utterly evil.

"I won't let you hurt anyone."

She felt Dalton next to her, his hand entwined with hers, his warm breath ruffling her hair. His voice soothed her, gave her confidence.

"You know you can beat it. And you have me."

"All right." She sucked in a courage-inducing breath, and did what Dalton instructed her to do. She exhaled, closed her eyes, and gave herself up to the darkness. She let the demon inside her free.

As soon as she did, she realized something was terribly wrong. She no longer felt safe, no longer felt close to Dalton. It was as if a chasm had opened between them, tearing her away from him, away from everyone.

Now she was completely alone, lost in a void of darkness. Her eyes shot open and all she could see was blackness around her. No Dalton, no Georgie or her sister, no hunters. She had no idea where she was.

The demon within her was freed.

Dalton jerked next to her. She felt him, but couldn't see him. She didn't understand any of this. It was like she was suspended somewhere, with no ability to snap out of it and return to reality.

"Dalton?" She could still feel him next to her, his hand entwined with hers. She could feel the tension in his body, knew something had gone wrong, but she didn't know what.

Then she heard it, faint at first, but growing stronger.

Laughter. A deep, rumbling sound that grew like the soft roll of thunder as it approached, growing louder until it became deafening. She shuddered at the malevolence in the tone.

"Welcome home, Dalton."

She recognized that voice, and it sent a cold chill skittering down her spine. She'd heard it before, in Italy. Memories washed over her. She'd seen him in that room after she'd been kidnapped, and then again after she'd embraced the power of the black diamond.

Tase. Leader of the Sons of Darkness.

What did he mean by welcoming Dalton?

Then it hit her. Oh, God, no. The demon side of her celebrated. She watched it as if it wasn't even a part of her any longer. And yet it was. It was her, joining in with the Sons of Darkness in rejoicing.

She'd been used.

They didn't want her at all. Well, they did, but she hadn't been the Sons of Darkness' prime target.

They'd wanted Dalton, to lure him through her in order to bring him closer to the Sons of Darkness again.

She had to stop this. Somehow, she had to pull away from him, to end this now, before it was too late. Because if Dalton fell again, he would fail, he would be forever damned, and there would never be redemption for him.

Isabelle wouldn't allow it.

CHAPTER TWENTY

Dalton knew the instant Isabelle let go of the strangle-hold she'd held on her demon side. He felt the surge of energy inside her exploding outward, and inched closer to give her the strength she needed to fight this battle.

But something else came with it—something he'd feared might happen but had hoped wouldn't surface: the Sons of Darkness. As soon as Isabelle's dark side was free, the demon world sucked him into a vortex that he couldn't battle, dragging him down into hellish remembrances alongside Isabelle, bringing him face-to-face with memories he'd vowed to forget, but never could.

"We've missed you in our world, Dalton. So glad to see you again. We knew someday you would come back to us."

The sound of Tase's voice evoked his hundred years in hell, a place he never wanted to revisit. Tase's laughter was a slap of reality, a change in the game. Cold realization washed over him. This was a trap, a means to trick Isabelle into dragging him into this, too. The Sons of Darkness wanted it all. Which meant he had to think fast, before he lost Isabelle—and himself—forever.

"Come closer," Tase said. "Let's discuss how this will play out."

Tase approached, and the remembered heat, the melting flesh, the years of terror, all came rushing back. Dalton pushed aside the horror to focus on a strategy. The most important thing was getting Isabelle away from Tase, making sure they didn't reclaim her. She might be tied to them, but with the exchange of blood she was also tied to him now. And he had to hold tight to that bond with her, hope it would be enough—along with Georgie's magic—to pull her away.

"What's going on here? Why has everything stopped?"

Dalton could hear Michael's voice, but could do nothing to reach back into reality to answer. He could feel Isabelle but couldn't see her. Tase and the Sons of Darkness he could see all too clearly. It was like being suspended in a black void. They only let him see and feel what they wanted him to.

And he really hated them having the upper hand.

"You cannot interfere," Georgie said. "The Realm cannot help Dalton now."

"Dalton?" Michael asked. "You mean Isabelle."

"This is Dalton's ordeal," Georgie explained. "He must stand this test alone."

Georgie knew. Had she always known that this was his trial by fire? Would have been nice if she'd let him in on it. He would like to have been a little more prepared.

"You knew about this?" Michael asked.

"It's not my place to interfere in what will be," Georgie said. "I can only see it through, just as you will. I can protect you all from the dark forces. Dalton walked through fire before, and came through it. Perhaps he will again. I will offer my strength to him to aid him in what will come. He can draw from that if he needs it."

Dalton would need it. Because he already knew what he'd have to do. He couldn't live with himself if he chose his life over the woman he loved. He'd give up everything to save Isabelle. The Sons of Darkness could win. They'd capture his soul once again and heaven would be out of his reach. As long as Isabelle was saved, he could live with that outcome.

"Dalton?" Isabelle squeezed his hand. "Why can't I see you?"

"Oh, the lovers wish to reunite?" Tase's voice teased. "Yes, you two need to see each other, to see what's about to happen."

In an instant, Dalton could see Isabelle as well as touch her. He could see everyone. He and Isabelle still stood in the circle of dirt, but now there was a ring of flame around them, and everyone else stood outside. Anger and concern etched their faces. Weapons were drawn, but he knew it would do no good. He couldn't worry about them right now, anyway. There was too much at stake.

Isabelle flew into his arms and he held her tight, burying his face in her neck. He closed his eyes and breathed her in. "We don't have much time."

She refused to let him go. "The demon side of me is out. I'm fighting it."

"Don't," he said, prying his body away from her tight hold on him. "You need to let me have that part of you."

She frowned. "I don't understand."

He tried a smile, needing to make certain he could reassure her. "I know you don't. But you will. I'll take care of it."

"Ever the angelic one, aren't you, Dalton? Making the supreme sacrifice for the one you love. You know it won't help you. It won't save Isabelle, either. We will have you both."

Tase walked a circle around them. It was like being in the center of a bonfire. Dalton shored up his defenses, sending out cooling light to protect Isabelle and him. He would use whatever strength he had for however long he had it. Tase would have his fun soon enough. But not before Dalton freed Isabelle.

"What is he talking about?" Isabelle asked.

"It's a game for him. He likes to mind-fuck. Don't pay attention." He held Isabelle's face in the palm of his hands. "Focus only on me. On what I say, on what I ask you to do. Trust me."

"Dalton, they're using you."

"I know."

"You know they want you."

"Yes."

"We have to fight this."

He shook his head, took her hands. "We can't. There are limited choices here and I've already made mine."

"Well, I haven't made mine. I don't want this. I refuse to let you give up your soul to save me. I won't be used by them that way."

He had nothing to say to her that hadn't already been said, refused to let her argue with him about a decision he'd already made. It had been a long damn time since he'd summoned up his power, but he concentrated, pulling it forth to grab hold of the part of Isabelle that was dark. The evil hovered over her like a protective cloak, daring anyone to come near and snatch it away.

He dared back, coming toward it with light. The darkness reared back, fearing, cowering, but angered at the audacity of anyone challenging it. Isabelle blanched.

"Dalton, what are you doing?"

He didn't answer, his concentration pouring into the task at hand. He threw a net of light against the darkness, then held on while it tried to break free. Sweat dripped down his body from the heat and the evil battling him.

"Dalton, please, don't do this."

He hated that she cried for him, but it wouldn't deter him from doing what he had to do.

She moved into him, spread her arms around him, her lips hovering at his ear. "Let me go, Dalton. This is my chance to do something right. To save you. Please, do this for me."

The demon inside her hated the words she spoke, fought in a mad struggle against the thought of perishing with her. It was all Dalton could do to keep the net of light surrounding it. He lifted one hand to stroke the softness of her cheek. "I love you enough to die for you."

His strength began to ebb, but he was winning. He would win. He'd pull the darkness from her and take it with him to hell.

He felt it creeping closer to him now, embracing him, thinking it was going to overpower him. It probably would. And when it did, Tase would win and take him down. The Sons of Darkness would lose Isabelle, but they'd gain an angel, a much bigger prize.

"Oh, this is so touching," Tase said. "The two of you so willing to sacrifice for the other. It rather makes me kind of ill."

The heat from Tase overwhelmed Dalton. He struggled against it, forcing every ounce of light he possessed around Isabelle and himself.

"But Dalton, don't you know I can have you both?" Tase moved now. Dalton felt Tase's presence behind him. "I'll take you first; then, when you're gone, Isabelle won't have the strength left to fight, and she'll be ours."

Dalton's gaze shot to Isabelle.

"I'm not going to let that happen," he said to her.

She nodded.

"Do you trust me, Isabelle?"

"Always."

He pulled the sword from his side and lifted it behind Isabelle.

Tase's burning fingers pressed against Dalton's shoulders, his fiery breath burning his neck as he leaned in and whispered in Dalton's ear. "Kill her and you're damned forever, Dalton."

Tase leaned in so close now that Dalton's clothes began to burn.

Perfect. That's exactly where he wanted the bastard.

Dalton pressed his lips to Isabelle. "I love you."

He lifted the sword, then sliced it into Isabelle's back, impaling her, himself, and Tase.

The pain burned more than Tase's heat, riddling his spine with white hot fire. Isabelle jerked, then stilled, no sound coming from her open mouth, her face frozen with wide-eyed shock. The only sound came from Tase, whose unholy scream shattered the air around them, and then the demon went silent.

Then nothingness. Death, Dalton supposed. And yet his consciousness remained. Dalton felt as if he were floating, weightless . . . somewhere. But where?

A burst of blinding brightness hit him. Dalton shielded his hands over his eyes. And then her felt her—Isabelle—right next to him.

"Where are we?" she asked.

"I don't know."

"What's the bright light?" She lifted her hand to shield her eyes.

"Not sure."

He knew one thing, though. The heat was gone. The evil had disappeared, too. He didn't sense Tase around them.

He felt embraced in healing power and a sense of goodness. He recognized immediately the presence of the heavens.

"Well, Dalton. That was an interesting solution to a no-win situation."

Dalton's lips lifted. The Archangel.

"Oh, my," Isabelle said. "He's beautiful."

"Shh, don't tell him that. He already has a huge ego."

The Archangel laughed and Isabelle shivered.

Yeah, he had that kind of effect. Supreme angels always did.

"I haven't seen you in a long time," Dalton said.

"And whose fault is that?" The Archangel did, as

usual, a fine job of looking imposing, towering above him all in white, his wings spread in impossible width behind him.

"It was my fault. My choice. Just like the choice I just made."

"Dalton has not won."

Dalton frowned. Tase's voice. "He's not destroyed."

"No. But you did a fine job of banishing him back to his own realm. We're . . . communicating."

"Like a conference call?" Isabelle asked.

The Archangel's lips quirked. "Yes."

"Suicide makes him mine," Tase said.

"You don't get to make the decision here." The Archangel's voice boomed in anger, silencing Tase. "This is my call. Dalton used *his* sword. And that, my old friend, changes all the rules. As I'm sure Dalton was aware."

Dalton couldn't help but smile.

"What's he talking about?" Isabelle asked. "You stabbed me. And yourself."

"Yes."

"Are we dead?"

"No."

Isabelle wrinkled her nose. "I'm confused."

"Dalton used the sword of a Guardian. Not a human," the Archangel explained.

"And?"

"It merely brought you here."

"Where is here, exactly?"

"The other plane."

Isabelle turned to Dalton. "I'm still confused. We're

not dead, but we're no longer standing in the middle of the circle on Georgie's property. Where are we?"

"Right now we're nowhere. Time is suspended."

Her eyes widened. "Really?"

"Yes. Until the Archangel makes a decision." Dalton turned back to him.

The Archangel asked, "You love this human?"

"I do."

"It's a limited future for you, Dalton."

"She's worth it."

"The blood of the evil one runs within her."

"I was working to rectify that. And her heart is pure. She didn't ask to be cursed."

"You cannot wholly remove it from her."

"I'm aware of that."

"I, however, can completely eliminate the demon blood from your Isabelle."

Dalton figured there'd be a catch in this. There had to be a reason the Archangel had appeared. "Okay. And at what price?"

"You agree to trade places with her. You absorb the demon blood she's carried within her, and you become what she has been."

"No!"

Dalton was shocked at Isabelle's outburst. She glared at the Archangel, who merely cocked a brow in her direction.

"You cannot sacrifice yourself for me." She turned to the Archangel. "And you people are supposed to be kind and benevolent, yet you're asking him to become a demon in my place? This is my curse, not his. How dare you ask him to give up his soul for me. What kind of people are you?"

Dalton was speechless. His gaze shot to the Archangel, whose lips twitched.

"'You people'? Outspoken, isn't she?"

"You have no idea."

"Dalton, how could you expect to me to live happily ever after, knowing I brought you damnation with the Sons of Darkness? Do you think I'd be content just because you took the demon blood away from me? I'd be miserable. I'd rather be dead or living with the demon inside me than know you suffered because of me." She turned her gaze to the Archangel. "Please, don't let this happen. I love him. He's deserving of redemption. He's already paid the price for his sins. Don't make him do it twice."

The Archangel grinned. "You made a very wise choice, Dalton. One hell of a hard road to earn your redemption, though."

He vanished in another burst of brilliant white.

Dalton smiled. The Archangel always loved those dramatic exits. He turned to Isabelle, pulled her into his arms. "I will always love you. Don't ever forget that." He pressed his lips to hers, then felt the world spinning out of control. He could no longer feel Isabelle's body. Or his own, for that matter.

He saw the panic in her wide eyes, saw her arms reaching out for him, but he was no longer there.

I'm sorry, Isabelle.

His world went dark. He closed his eyes and he awaited his punishment, awaited the heat, the flames.

Awaited his eternity in hell.

As long as Isabelle was safe, he was content.

Panic sent Isabelle into a tailspin. Dalton had vanished right in front of her. First the Archangel, then Dalton. What did it mean? The flames no longer surrounded her; Tase was gone. Everything had gone back to normal except that Dalton wasn't there.

Her gaze shot to Georgie. "Tell me what happened here."

"It's done," Georgie said. "But nothing was as we thought."

"What the hell does that mean? Where is Dalton?"

Even Georgie looked confused. "I don't know. He disappeared."

"You all saw that, didn't you?" she asked, turning around to all the hunters. "You saw him vanish."

Michael nodded, looking somber. "Yes."

"Did you see the Archangel?"

Michael frowned. "Who?"

"The Archangel. The angel. Flowing raven hair, dressed all in white, wings a mile wide?"

Georgie shook her head. "We saw no angel. You did?"

"Yes. How could you not see him?"

"It doesn't matter that we didn't. You did. He spoke to you and Dalton?"

Frustrated, Isabelle sighed. "He took Dalton. I know he did. He gave Dalton what he wanted."

"Redemption?" Georgie asked.

Tears burned Isabelle's eyes, choked her as she fought for the words, hating that she had to say them out loud. "No. Damnation."

Her legs refused to support her and she sank to the ground, shaking. Georgie was the first one there to wrap her arms around her.

"Isabelle, stand."

"I can't." The splash of hot tears rolled down Isabelle's cheeks in rivulets she didn't even try to hide. He was gone. Vanished. Had the Archangel given Dalton what he'd asked for? The demon inside her had gone, too. She no longer struggled against it, trying to keep it from surfacing.

Instead, the worst form of emptiness she'd ever felt wrapped itself around her. Where had Dalton gone?

Angelique knelt down beside her, stroked her hair. "I'm sorry. I'm so sorry."

Isabelle tilted her head back to stare up at Angelique. "He did this for me. I'm not worth it, Angie. How could he have sacrificed so much for me?"

"Because he loved you, baby. He really loved you that much."

Her sister understood. She knew what had happened. Isabelle was free of her demon, but she'd lost the one thing, the only thing that was important to her. She couldn't survive this. It hurt too much.

She bent forward, pressed her head against her knees, and sobbed. Her heart was torn in two. She never thought she could feel this much pain, never thought anything could hurt this much.

She cried until there was nothing left, until she felt

sick. Then hands reached underneath her and lifted her. Through swollen lids she recognized Michael, who picked her up and started toward the main house.

"No. Wait. I want to go to the cabin."

Michael shook his head. "You can't be there alone."

"Yes, I can. I'll be fine. It's just up the road from the main house. You can leave someone there with me if you want. I need to be where Dalton was." She clutched his shirt. "Please."

He relented and carried her toward the cabin, laid her down on the bed, and covered her.

Angie was there a minute later, pressing a cool, wet washcloth over her face. It felt good, washing away some of the grit and the tears.

"You want me to stay with you?" she asked.

"No. I need to be alone. I need to process all of this."

"I'm not so sure that's a good idea."

Isabelle loved her sister. It would be good to spend time with her again. Just not right now, not when she was so raw, when everything hurt so damn much. "I'll be all right. Please, just let me be. I need to sleep. I'm so tired, Angie."

Angie pressed a cool hand to her forehead, then swept it down her cheek. "You're not alone, Izzy. I'm here. We're all here for you. You're never going to be alone."

Isabelle grasped her sister's wrist. "I never told you how sorry I am."

Angie tilted her head. "For what?"

"For Sicily. For what I tried to do to you."

Her sister smiled, tenderness and love reflected in

her eyes. "That wasn't you, Izzy. You have nothing to be sorry for."

The tears started fresh. "You're too forgiving."

Angie bent down and kissed her cheek, then slid a box of tissues in front of her. "And you're not forgiving enough of yourself. Let it go."

Isabelle nodded. "I'll try."

"Ryder and I are going to stay here with you. We'll be in the other room if you need us."

"Okay."

Angie left and closed the door, leaving Isabelle in blissful darkness.

Exhaustion took over and she fell into a hard, dreamless sleep. When she woke, it was still dark.

Something had awakened her. A sound, maybe?

Fear jacked her heartbeat up to a hard pounding. She swung her legs over the side of the bed and stood.

Maybe it was Angie coming back to check on her. But if it was, she'd be in here by now. Isabelle stared at the closed bedroom door for a full minute, waiting. Nothing happened.

Probably just her imagination. She went into the bathroom to splash cold water on her face, then turned off the light. As she walked through the doorway back into the bedroom, her breath caught as she saw a dark shape stepping through the sliding glass door to the bedroom.

Hadn't that been closed and locked when she'd come in here? She couldn't remember. She glanced at the door leading to the living room, to Ryder and Angie, and back at the figure who stood like a sentinel now that he was fully in the room.

She could scream, or she could run. She could do both.

She had to do something, and now.

"Isabelle. Don't scream."

It was a whispered plea.

In Dalton's voice.

CHAPTER TWENTY-ONE

Isabelle reached for the doorway, dizziness weakening her knees.

Dalton? It couldn't be.

But as he moved toward her, she found herself unable to move. She recognized his walk, though. And the closer he came, the more familiar the shadow seemed.

Was she still dreaming? Maybe she wasn't awake at all.

He reached her, and pulled her upright. And oh, God, it was his face. His hands were warm as he snaked them around her waist to drag her against him. His kiss was tender, and oh, so real.

This was no dream. She sobbed against him, unable to control the flood of emotions that burst from her.

At the same moment, the bedroom door burst open. She pulled away just as Ryder came through, his laser aiming right at them.

Isabelle stepped in front of Dalton and held up her hand. "Don't! It's Dalton."

Ryder flipped the wall switch and bathed the room in light.

"Jesus. You're alive?"

Angelique was right on Ryder's heals, weapon in hand.

"I'm alive."

"What the hell's going on?" Ryder asked.

"I have a lot to explain," Dalton said. "But to Isabelle first." Dalton put his arm around her. "I need to talk to her. Alone."

Shaking, her mind awhirl with questions, Isabelle cast a pleading gaze to her sister. "Please."

"Just give us tonight. I'll meet with all of you in the morning."

Ryder nodded. "We'll head up to the house. I'll let them know you're alive. First thing in the morning you can come talk to Michael."

"Thanks," Dalton said.

They walked Ryder and Angelique to the front door, and Dalton turned the lock, then flipped the lights off, taking Isabelle to the sofa.

"I'm sorry about scaring you."

She didn't care about that. She kissed him, unable to believe he was there, alive. But his touch, his taste, it was all him, and she couldn't get enough. Not when she had thought she'd never see him again. Her fingers tangled in the thick silkiness of his hair, then roamed down over the corded strength of his neck, his shoulders, his arms. And the way his mouth moved over hers, devouring it like he hadn't seen her in years, proved he was just as happy to see her. Reluctantly, she pulled away.

"What happened with the Archangel?"

He dragged his hands through his hair. "I don't know. When I disappeared there was nothing but a black void. I thought for sure the Archangel had granted my wish and I was going to be given over to the Sons of Darkness."

"My demon is gone. I don't feel it anymore."

He grinned. "I know. The Archangel suddenly appeared before me and told me our dual wishes for self-sacrifice were so sweet it was like a sugar overdose. Then he gave me a choice."

"What kind of choice?"

"Redemption or humanity."

She pressed her fingers to her lips, too afraid to ask, but too curious not to. "What did you choose?"

"I'm here, aren't I?"

Her stomach fell. "Oh, God, Dalton. You gave up redemption."

"You were willing to trade your life for mine," he reminded her.

She shrugged. "I'm half demon. The Sons of Darkness were after me. What kind of life is that? You were an angel."

"A fallen one."

She laid her palm against his jaw. "An angel, Dalton. I'm nothing compared to that."

"Apparently the Archangel disagreed, because he didn't accept your offer to die. Or mine, either, for that matter. And I chose humanity because I wanted to be with you, because I love you. What good would redemption be if I'm miserable? I'd just screw it up again and end up damned."

Tears filled her eyes. She'd never been weepy before, but lately she'd been such an emotional basket case. "I love you. I can't believe you did this for me. And the demon blood in me is . . ."

"It's gone, Isabelle. You won't have to fight the demon side of yourself any longer. The Sons of Darkness will have no use for you."

She felt as if a giant weight had lifted off her. For someone who had thought so little of herself for so long, she suddenly felt like she might actually deserve this happiness after all.

"So you're human?"

His brows lifted and he smiled. "Totally."

She warmed at the thought and leaned against him. "I really like the sound of that. I can't begin to tell you how I fell apart when you disappeared. It was like a part of me died."

He sobered at her words. "I'm sorry. I know. I felt the same way. It hurt to leave you. And then I suddenly appeared back at the circle in the woods with the Archangel, and he explained things to me and gave me my choice. I figured you'd end up back here, and I really wanted some time alone with you first before explaining things to the rest of them."

"As soon as you disappeared, this is where I wanted to be."

"We're attached, Isabelle. Physically as well as spiritually. You'll never be able to go far from me without me knowing where you are, without me calling to you without saying a word."

She welled up with so much emotion she couldn't speak. She leaned closer to him, still too raw to believe he was really there, that he wasn't going to be ripped away from her at any moment.

He tipped her chin up with his finger and placed his mouth on hers, and everything was right in her world again. One kiss, and he placed his stamp on her, that utterly sweet and possessive mark that said she belonged to him. The way he kissed her was amazing and powerful, so tender and yet so demanding at the same time, crushing her against him in such a definite way that told her in no uncertain terms that she was his and always would be. She had never felt loved like that before—this was what had been missing from her life, what she had craved and what she would never do without again. This feeling of being whole because she was being held and kissed by someone who truly loved her, truly knew her, and accepted her for who she was.

She kissed him back, accepting the man he was now, loving him because he was strong, because he was willing to give up his life for hers. And because she knew that asked right now or fifty years from now, she would still be willing to lay down her life for him.

The power of love was an amazing thing. It strengthened all her weaknesses, and provided her the ability to give strength to others. She never knew this kind of ability existed before she met Dalton. She had so much to thank him for.

"I need to make love to you, Isabelle. I don't want to waste a minute of time with you."

She smiled up at him, content to look at his beautiful face every day for the rest of her life. "I'm fine with waiting to explain to the others why you're still alive."

He pulled her to stand, took one step back, and began unbuttoning her dress. She was amazed that she could still feel butterflies in her stomach as his knuckles brushed against her breast, as if each moment was like the very first time he touched her. She watched as he slowly, painstakingly, undid each button, keeping his gaze riveted on her face as he did, knowing it was driving them both crazy to wait. When he drew the material apart and reached inside with his hands to surround her waist, her stomach jumped at the contact.

Dalton smiled. "I love the feel of your skin against my hand, how rough I am and how soft you are."

She took his hands and lifted them to her breasts. "I like you rough."

He took the piercings between his fingers and tugged on them. Isabelle tilted her head back, letting the sensations tingle through her nerve endings before looking up at him again. "I love when you do that."

He smiled. "I know." He arched her over one arm, then took a nipple into his mouth, taking the silver ring in his teeth and torturing her further, before sucking her nipple with a long, deep draw that made her whimper and reach for him. She dragged her nails down his arm, hard, and he rewarded her by biting lightly on her nipple.

Maybe they both just needed to feel alive, to know that this was real, but their touch, their tasting of each other was fierce, not gentle. It seemed to be what they both wanted, what they each needed.

Dalton straightened her and stripped her dress off, following the fabric with his mouth, his teeth, licking her ribs, biting her hip, scratching his fingers down her legs and then holding her while she stepped out of the dress. Then he shouldered her legs apart and buried his face at her sex, sliding his tongue between her throbbing lips and tantalizing her with every stroke, every light suck, mastering her body the way he'd mastered her heart.

She shuddered against him, shocked at how quickly he could bring her to the edge of orgasm, but she couldn't—didn't want to hold back—she was too filled with joy, with pent-up passion for this man she loved so much. They'd been given a second chance and she was ready to burst with desire.

He dug his fingers into her buttocks, demanding what only she could give him, and she did, crying out, tilting her hips toward him and giving him everything as she came. He licked her gently over and over again while she trembled against the wash of madness. Then he raised up, stripped off his clothes and drew her down with him to the sofa, taking her mouth in a deep kiss.

Isabelle was lost in the heat of his body, the rasp of his legs against hers as he positioned himself underneath her, then drove inside her with a harsh thrust. She welcomed him with a cry of delight, bracing her palms on his chest and lifting off him, only to crash down against him, impaling her sex on his shaft. Now it was her time to claim him, to show him that he belonged to her in the way that her body gripped his, forming to him, accommodating him, welcoming him with a surge of wetness and heat that belonged to Dalton alone.

"Yes," he murmured against her neck as her breasts brushed his chest. "Damn, yes."

She lifted her butt and then ground against him in a

slow undulation of utter pleasure, feeling him twitch and tremble inside her. She held him tight to her, squeezing her legs together, possessing him completely.

Then he stilled, and she lifted her head, their faces so close they exchanged panting breath. She watched his eyes darken as he pushed inside her, hard and relentless. His smile was wicked, his eyes nothing but passion now. She gripped his shoulders and rode him, watched him, felt him lose it, and went with him, tears filling her eyes as she climaxed, rocking against him while his arms flew around her and held her so tight she couldn't breathe. She fell against his chest and let the beauty of this moment wash over her, knowing that it would always be like this, grateful that they had been given the chance to love each other for as long as they could.

Later, they showered together and Dalton made love to her again, this time gently, washing her first and then taking her up against the wall of the shower. Easy, slow, watching each other the entire time. It was painfully tender and her heart swelled with so much emotion she felt like she'd burst with it.

Then he turned the shower off, dried her gently and carried her to bed.

She smiled as he snuggled up behind her and pulled the sheet over them both.

It would be like this every day. And for the first time in a long time, she fell instantly asleep, no longer plagued by the demons of her dreams, no longer worried by the ticking clock. They had all the time in the world now.

———

"What is it going to take to win against the Realm of Light? Must we always be made to look like fools?"

Aron slammed his fist down on the stone table to make his point.

Tase stood and nodded, trying to keep his own anger in check. It wouldn't do at all for the Master to see him lose control. "I hadn't expected the Archangel to intervene. That's not according to the rules, if you ask me." The Master didn't interfere. Though Tase complaining about it would do no good. What was done was done. He had lost both Dalton and Isabelle. Now it was time to regroup and move on.

"So what are we going to do about it?"

Tase's flames shot out toward Aron, but he quickly reined them in. "Do? We're going to do nothing. In our grand plan, Isabelle and Dalton were soldiers. Just like the others we're recruiting. We have more important things to do, to focus on."

"The humans."

Tase nodded at Kal. "They are more important. Our minions."

"That goes very well."

"Yes, it does." Tase was happy at the progress. So was the Master. "Do not concern yourselves with small losses." Tase smiled.

Losing Dalton was no small loss, Tase.

The Sons of Darkness cowered before the appearance of the Dark Master. Tase, as leader, stepped forward and bowed his head.

"Of course it wasn't, my Lord. I meant no disrespect."

Your mission was to bring both Dalton and Isabelle to us. You failed.

"Momentarily. I can bring them yet."

You failed. They are lost to us. I do not tolerate failure.

Tase sensed his brothers taking a step back, then another, distancing themselves from him.

It would appear we need a new leader.

Tase swallowed. "Master, if I could—"

You could not, Tase. No one leads who does not succeed. Be gone.

Tase steeled himself for what was to come, but one could never be prepared for obliteration. It came with fury, with violence, with pain that could not be measured. Death would be easier than this torment, this hell that he would have to endure for eternity. He screamed as he was eviscerated, burned in flames hotter than even he could stand, and yet would continue to live, to suffer forever.

Kal had wished and hoped for this moment when he could take over. But now, cowering under the dark visage of the Master, even he feared, knowing Tase's fate in the dark pit.

The Master looked down on his remaining Sons.

I need a volunteer to take over as leader. Who believes he can do better than he who came before?

This was Kal's moment to shine or to die.

He took a step forward.

"I'll reign as leader, my Master."

See that you do a better job than your predecessor. We have yet to win in this battle.

Kal nodded and the Master disappeared.

Kal turned to his brothers, who bowed their heads in respect for their new leader.

"Now that I'm in charge, a few things will change. Some of our new ideas have worked; many haven't. The Realm of Light and the side of good has won too many battles. The Master, as you know, is very displeased."

He moved to the front of the table where Tase and those who came before him had sat. This time, it was Kal who took his rightful place as head of the Sons of Darkness.

"It is time for a new start. New ideas, new plans for the future. We will win next time, my brothers. This, I promise you."

A new day had begun.

The next morning was a mix of chaos and utter happiness. Isabelle and Dalton walked through the back door of Georgie's house hand in hand. Nearly everyone was crowded in the kitchen drinking coffee, and when they saw Dalton, there was joy and many hugs were exchanged.

Isabelle was elated. So was everyone else, from a rejoicing Georgie all the way to a smiling Michael, who couldn't believe everything had worked out so well. Though he wasn't quite as convinced that all would be well with the Sons of Darkness. Once the shock wore off and Dalton explained what the Archangel had done, the hunters reconvened at the table and drank coffee together.

"I doubt the Sons of Darkness will take the loss of both of you quite so easily," Michael said.

"You think there'll be repercussions?" Derek asked.

"They're not good losers," Dalton said. "I think there probably will be."

Michael nodded. "I don't expect we'll see anything right away, but it's in our best interests—and in the best interest of Georgie and her family's safety—to pack up and get out of here as soon as possible."

"Agreed," Dalton said. "What about my position with the Realm?"

"All things considered," Michael said, "the Realm needs good hunters. Providing you want to still fight with us, I'll clear you with the Realm. I'll explain everything, and I think they'll understand your motivations. Besides, everything worked out at the end."

Mandy laid her head on Dalton's shoulder and offered up a tentative smile. "Everything's going to be fine."

Dalton hugged her close, then turned his gaze back to Michael. "I'd appreciate that. I would like to continue to fight, though Isabelle is with me now, and she and I haven't really talked about—"

Isabelle laid her hand over his. "This is what you do, what you love to do," she said. "Besides, my sister is in this now. You both are my family. Where else would I want to be?"

Angelique sat on Isabelle's other side and grasped her

hand. "It would be nice for us all to be a family, for us to stay together. I'm glad you're with us."

"Me, too," Isabelle said. She squeezed Dalton's hand and gazed up at him with eyes so filled with love he couldn't believe he'd been given this chance. "I am where you are."

He sucked in a breath, still feeling like he'd really lucked out. "Okay, then. We're in. So now what?"

"Now we head back to Florida and pick up where we left off there," Michael answered.

"With the demons who walk in daylight," Dalton said.

"Yes. The Realm is very concerned about this. We're going to have to figure out how many are out there, how the Sons of Darkness are recruiting them, and start picking them out of the crowds before they begin to outnumber us. The Realm is already trying to figure out if there have been any other similar demon attacks in other parts of the world. We have a lot of work to do."

Dalton nodded. "We'll go pack and meet you outside within the hour."

They dispersed, and Dalton and Isabelle remained with Georgie. Isabelle enveloped Georgie in a hug.

"Thank you," Isabelle said.

"You have nothing to thank me for, *chère*. You and Dalton did this on your own."

"Oh, I think you had a lot to do with bringing this about."

Georgie's dark eyes twinkled with mystery, as always. "I'm just the medium through which mystical things occur."

Dalton laughed, swooped her up in a hug and kissed her cheek. "Thank you, my sister."

"Don't wait so long to visit next time," she said, laughing, a blush staining her cheeks.

"We won't."

At the cabin they packed up their things and changed clothes, readying to leave. Isabelle stood at the window and looked out over the backyard. Dalton came up behind her.

"What?"

"I kind of like this place. I found peace here."

He smiled. "We'll come back sometime."

She turned. "When? On your vacation? Do you get vacations? What will life be like with the Realm, Dalton?"

He shrugged. "We can take time away when we need to. I don't really know how couples do it. We'll have to make our own way."

"I've always loved travel and adventure."

She said the words, but she seemed wistful.

"Are you sure this is what you want, Isabelle? Because if it's not, I'll give it up."

She tilted her head, studied him. "You'd do that, wouldn't you?"

"Of course."

She was silent for a few minutes, then said, "Do you remember when we first met in Italy? When we were both pretending to be someone we weren't?"

"Yes."

"We both said we loved adventure. Neither of us was lying when we said that."

"No, I guess we weren't."

She wrapped her arms around him, reaching up to press her lips to his. "This is your life now, Dalton. It's a new page. You get to create it. And you don't get to live forever anymore. What do *you* want to do?"

He owed it to her to be honest with her, and he knew exactly where he wanted to be. "I want to hunt and kill demons."

Her lips curled. "Then we'll do that. Together."

"I love you, Isabelle."

"And I love you, too, my angel."

"Then let's go join the demon hunters and kick some ass. This war with the demons never ends. And we'll fight it until it does."

About the Author

JACI BURTON grew up in Missouri, spent thirteen years in California, and now lives in Oklahoma with her husband and more dogs than she can keep track of. In her spare time she cruises on the back of her husband's Harley, where she enjoys the wind on her face while plotting her next book.

You can read more about Jaci at her website, www.jaciburton.com.

She is also the author of *The Darkest Touch, Hunting the Demon,* and *Surviving Demon Island,* all available from Dell Books.